ACCLAIM FOR
Deadly Secret of the Lusitania

"A fascinating historical novel with a still-controversial subject: The mysterious circumstances surrounding the sinking of the passenger liner *Lusitania,* an event that helped propel America into the First World War. This is an intriguing, highly satisfying adventure in reading."

—Edward Hower, author of *The New Life Hotel* and *A Garden of Demons*

"A thinking person's mystery. Using the suspicious circumstances surrounding the sinking of RMS *Lusitania,* Light has created an intriguing tapestry, skillfully weaving disparate threads together into his narrative. All the characters come alive on the pages of this well-researched historical novel."

—William Hjortsberg, author of *Falling Angel, Nevermore,* and *Jubilee Hitchhiker, The Life and Times of Richard Brautigan*

"What an amazing novel! This invented yarn may be closer to the truth than the accounts that have been told, believed, and recorded by historians as factual. Here's another marvelous example of the way that truth and fiction are interdependent, each giving rise to the other."

—Metta Spencer, publisher, *Peace Magazine,* Toronto

"A highly readable dramatization of a very important event in American history. The characters, though fictional, could perfectly well have been real as they so well represent the times and events leading up to and following the last voyage of the *Lusitania.* In many ways there is more truth than fiction here."

—F. Gregg Bemis Jr., owner of the *Lusitania*

Deadly Secret of the Lusitania

Ivan Light

To Karen
best wishes
Ivan Light

LOST
COAST
PRESS

DEADLY SECRET OF THE LUSITANIA

Lost Coast Press
155 Cypress Street
Fort Bragg, California 95437
(707) 964-9520
Fax: 707-964-7531
www.cypresshouse.com

Cover and book design by Michael Brechner / Cypress House

Front Cover Painting by Thomas Marie Madawaska Hemy, *Lest We Forget – The Sinking of the Lusitania*; courtesy Brecknock Museum & Art Gallery, Wales.

This is a work of fiction. All of the characters and events are fictional. Resemblance to persons living or dead is coincidental. The historical background is accurate, and the issue of war-crime culpability was something Americans vigorously debated at the time.

PUBLISHER'S CATALOGING-IN-PUBLICATION

Light, Ivan Hubert.

Deadly secret of the Lusitania / Ivan Light. -- Fort Bragg, California : Lost Coast Press, [2015]

pages ; cm.

ISBN: 978-1-935448-37-2

Summary: In 1915, a German U-Boat sank the British passenger liner Lusitania. Many Americans, including women and children, were among the 1,200 dead, so the crime caused a storm of protest in America, and helped plunge the U.S. into World War I. In this gripping novel, an insurance investigator and his fiancée help a murdered longshoreman's widow who's been unjustly denied her husband's life insurance. Finding themselves in possession of documents detailing the Lusitania's secret cargo, the couple are targeted by German and British spies, Irish republicans, a rogue socialist, and the newly- formed FBI, all wanting to use the suppressed material for their own purposes.--Publisher.

1. Lusitania (Steamship)--Fiction. 2. World War, 1914-1918-- Naval operations--Fiction. 3. Shipping--Government policy--Great Britain--History--20th century--Fiction. 4. Neutrality--United States --Fiction. 5. United States--Politics and government-- 1913- 1921-- Fiction. 6. World War, 1914-1918--United States--Fiction. 7. Historical fiction. 8. Suspense fiction. I. Title.

PS3612.I34455 D43 2015 2015932381

813/.6--dc23 1504

Printed in the USA

2 4 6 8 9 7 5 3 1

In Memory
Elliott W. Hough
US Army, 1917–1918

CONTENTS

ILLUSTRATIONS

Take Up the Sword of Justice.
Published by the Parliamentary Recruiting Committee, 1915
(Library of Congress)

PREFACE

A German submarine sank the *Lusitania,* a civilian passenger liner, on May 7, 1915, off the southern coast of Ireland. The sinking claimed the lives of 1,195 passenger and crewmembers. That act of monstrous inhumanity set in motion events that drew the United States into the First World War two years later. The British blamed the crime on the German government's policy of unrestricted submarine warfare. President Wilson agreed with them. The Germans, however, insisted that the *Lusitania* was secretly carrying military explosives that rendered the ship a legitimate military target. When detonated by a torpedo, these munitions had exploded, instantly sinking the ship. If so, the British had callously used civilians as human shields to protect an ammunition carrier traveling into a submarine-infested war zone. The controversy was especially important in the U.S. because if the British shared responsibility for the horrifying crime, the argument in favor of entering the war on the Allied side would have become vastly less persuasive. If the American public perceived the *Lusitania* as a joint British/German war crime rather than solely a German crime, the arguments in favor of continued American neutrality might have prevailed, and the United States might not have entered the First World War at all.

ACKNOWLEDGMENTS

My ABUNDANT THANKS are due to many helpers, but I wish particularly to thank Marina Belozerskaya, Edna Bonacich, Philip Bonacich, Andrew Caddes, Marcyn Del Clements, Stan Fischler, Greg Marshall, Michael Kirk, Barbara Lal, Matthew Light, Nathaniel Light, Martha Lipscomb, Laura Marcoux, Elsa von Scheven, Ivan Stern, John Tauranac, Jess Taylor, Stefan Timmermans, and Joan Zicarelli. The author bears exclusive responsibility for errors of fact, exposition, or interpretation.

Deadly Secret
of the
Lusitania

PROLOGUE

As he stumbled toward the exit gate, Joe Albi tripped over a coiled rope, dropped a crate, and fell to one knee. It hurt and he swore. Hearing the thud, crash, and oath, the night watchman left his shack, directed searchlights at the noise, and leveled his shotgun. Two furious Dobermans lunged against their chain.

"Hold it! Where the hell do you think you're taking that stuff?" the watchman shouted. "The stuff" was the forty-pound crates Frankie Buono and Joe Albi carried under each brawny arm. Frankie recognized the watchman's voice, and decided a prompt change of mood was in order.

"Don't shoot, Mike. We're taking our underwear home to wash," Frankie sang out.

"Then you'll be the only Eye-talians in Manhattan with clean backsides," Michael retorted with good humor, then lowered his shotgun and silenced the Dobermans. The gun still cradled in his right elbow, with his left hand he beckoned the stevedores to enter the illuminated zone in front of the exit. "Oh, dearie me, I thought somebody was robbing the Lucy," joked Michael. He meant the RMS *Lusitania,* the biggest and fastest ocean liner afloat, now loading at this pier and scheduled to depart for Liverpool on May 1, just three days away. The searchlights, barbed wire, watchman, and guard dogs controlled egress from the dockside staging area that serviced the four-smokestack steamship that loomed out of the night fog, occasional lights aboard twinkling on and off. In the moonless night, the ship's massive outline was silhouetted against the illuminated New Jersey shore on the other side of the Hudson River.

Stepping under the tungsten lights, Joe and Frank let the watchman take a good look at them. Certain now that the watchman was Michael O'Connell, Joe Albi put down his crates and motioned Frankie to do the same. Joe shook his head in pity. "Mike, your eyesight is terrible, and you aim that scattergun at your friends. Paul worries that your wife ain't taking care of you." Joe was not interested in Michael's marriage or his vision. His remark was code. Paul Kelly, president of the longshoreman's union, organized cargo theft on the lower Manhattan docks. It was a money-making sideline for a labor racketeer. When Paul wondered whether someone's wife was "taking care" of him, the questioners were really asking whether the man was securely on the take and ready to turn a blind eye to a theft in progress.

Michael's wife was doing her job. "Nothing to worry about," he assured Frankie and Joe. "My wife takes wonderful care of me."

"It's a miracle," quipped Frankie, who could not control his mouth, "since you got a one-inch dick."

"Your mother couldn't get enough of it, sonny," rejoined O'Connell, and the coarse raillery relaxed everyone. The three men had established a congenial atmosphere in which to complete their business. Frankie and Joe understood that Michael had stock taking to complete. Furrowing his brow with mock worry, Michael explained that his wife slept fitfully, and wondered whether Frankie and Joe carried anything that "might disturb her repose?" Taking the cue, Frankie and Joe displayed their crates' address labels to the watchman, who jotted the contents into a notebook he extracted from a rear pocket. That done, Michael hitched up his pants, leaned the shotgun against the wire fence, unlocked and swung open the security gate, and bade the stevedores a good night.

After the gate clanked shut behind them, Frank and Joe loaded the crates onto a hand trolley and then trundled together into the Eleventh Avenue gloom. They took turns pushing the heavy trolley. The labels on the crates read, BULK CHEESE FROM HUNTER, WALTON AND CO. Heading downtown, they estimated that 160 pounds of bulk cheese had a street value of twenty-four dollars, of which Paul Kelly would take half. That would leave them each with six dollars—fourteen hours' wages for stevedores. Although no big score, this heist was worth an evening's effort. Their mood was ebullient.

Twenty minutes later, the two stevedores turned east on Barrow Street and stopped in front of number 36, a five-story tenement near Seventh Avenue. Although it was already eleven o'clock, the late April night was pleasant, and neighborhood men sat on the stoops in shirt-sleeves, drinking coffee, smoking, cursing, joking, and discussing politics. Sometimes, before delivering his opinion, an elder cleared his sinuses with a snort, then spat for emphasis. This offended no ladies because the wives of Barrow Street were all inside the tiny apartments, ironing or playing cards. The lounging men said hello or *buona sera* to Frank and Joe who pushed their load into a basement entrance, and then, having flicked on the 40-watt globe in the furnace room, cracked open the first crate with a crowbar. To their surprise, the crate contained brown canvas bags bearing the insignia of the DuPont Chemical Company in Maryland. The bags read, MILITARY CORDITE: FLAMMABLE EXPLOSIVE. HANDLE WITH EXTREME CARE. DANGER OF DEATH.

Frank and Joe looked at each other in confusion. "What the hell is this?" asked Frankie. He could not read, but he could see these bags did not contain cheese.

"It's cordite," Joe explained. Wordlessly, they opened the other three crates, and found the same brown canvas bags inside them. The bags all contained brown cordite rods, and each crate's interior waybill repeated the warning message. Apparently the explosives had been mislabeled as cheese.

Having loaded tons of cordite onto merchant ships in the previous six months, the stevedores knew it was war materiel bound for the Western Front. But what was cordite worth on the streets of Manhattan? They guessed that its street value must exceed that of cheese, in which case they had had a lucky night. They decided to ask around the next day in case someone knew how much money cordite might fetch on the street. Feeling confident and pleased with their night's work, Joe and Frank locked their stash behind the coal chute and inside the wire cage in which they routinely stored stolen goods prior to fencing them.

CHAPTER 1

THE LOOPHOLE SCROUNGER

BECAUSE OF MOMENTARY inattention to an outdoor cooking fire, a kerosene lantern had exploded, igniting firewood stacked under the LaFarges' porch. The volunteer fire brigade arrived too late to save the bungalow, which burnt to the ground, a total loss. Fortunately for Helen and Walter LaFarge, their home was insured for full replacement value. In their mid-fifties, too advanced in years to start saving for old age, the couple had filed a claim for $14,000 with the Metropolitan Life and Casualty Insurance Company. They had expected prompt compensation. To their confusion and chagrin, however, Metropolitan repeatedly delayed payment, alleging "complications."

Finally, fourteen weeks having passed, Walter LaFarge demanded a claims conference, threatening litigation, and received in reply an apologetic letter from Trevor Howells, whom Metropolitan Life had assigned to their case. His inquiry now completed, Trevor Howells had written to request that Helen and Walter LaFarge visit his office in the Flatiron Building, as the results were too complex to communicate by mail.

Walter LaFarge now glanced apprehensively at the young man who would shortly explain the company's decision. Noticing the man's anxiety, Trevor Howells rose and politely offered a seat to Helen, who took it, affecting a serenity she did not feel. Relieved by the agent's good manners, Walter seated himself next to his wife, and, placing his straw boater in his lap and his feet flat on the floor, demanded that Metropolitan

Life "pay our claim now" as he and his wife were "tired of waiting." He held his chin high, belligerently screwed up his lower lip, and looked down at Trevor Howells past his stylish vandyke beard. He was bluffing. Walter and Helen LaFarge were broke. After living for weeks in hotel rooms and eating in restaurants, they had exhausted their cash, and faced homelessness unless the company promptly paid their claim.

After apologizing again for the delay, Trevor Howells withdrew a twenty-inch scale map of East Orange, New Jersey, from a portfolio. He propped it, facing the customers, on his desk, then stood in front with a pointer. Here was their house, indicated by H, and here was the fire station, indicated by FS. Using a ruler, Howells showed that the distance between H and FS was 1.5 inches, which translated into 1.5 miles on the map's scale. Then, extracting their insurance contract from a drawer, Trevor Howells referred them to paragraph 8B, in which the insured warranted that their domicile was "no more than one mile" from the nearest fire station. Now calling their attention to section 15A of the contract, Howells invited Mr. LaFarge to read it aloud. Walter LaFarge put on spectacles to read the tiny print. "Any misrepresentation of warranted facts by the insured voids this contract." That meant, Howells explained sadly, that the Metropolitan Life and Casualty Company "could not pay any benefit" for their fire damage.

"Do you mean Metropolitan Life won't pay anything?" gasped Walter LaFarge "Because we were half a mile too distant from the fire station?"

"I know it's a shock, but yes, that is what I mean," sighed Trevor, spreading his hands in helplessness. Helen LaFarge sagged in her chair, her face white. She had momentary difficulty breathing. Walter LaFarge glared at the younger man, possibly hoping to intimidate him.

"We paid eight years of premiums for that policy, and now you tell us it's worthless. If we had known that, we would not have paid a single premium."

"I sympathize, Mr. LaFarge, but section 15B assigns to 'the party of the first part,' that is to you, full responsibility for the accuracy of all representations of fact. Read it for yourself. Metropolitan Life bears no responsibility for your failure to correct the distance clause. You did have eight years in which to do so."

"This is an outrage," persisted Walter LaFarge, his face flushed with indignation and dismay. "We did not realize that a half mile could void our contract. You advertised that Metropolitan was supremely trustworthy. Why didn't you warn us?"

"The contract warned you that Metropolitan relied on the accuracy of your warranties," said Howells.

Walter LaFarge regrouped. "Because of this trivial error in small print your company never protected our house against fire at any time in those eight years, am I right?" Trevor blandly agreed. Walter LaFarge thereupon completed his thought. "In that case, Metropolitan Life should at least return all our premiums, which purchased nothing of value in the entire eight years."

"The company considers that you failed to correct the contract and so bear full responsibility for the consequences."

"You thieves will see my attorney in court." LaFarge thumped his fist on Trevor's desk and glared.

"That is entirely up to you, Mr. LaFarge, but unless your attorney can prove that your residence is no more than one mile from the fire station, he cannot help you. I advise you to examine your other options. I hate to communicate bad news, and I truly regret your misfortune." Trevor Howells smiled blandly, nodded gently, sat back, waited several seconds, and then glanced discretely at the in-box on his desk. It was overflowing with cases. Ignoring him, the LaFarges conferred in whispers. Still smiling, Trevor conspicuously consulted his engraved gold pocket watch. The engraving read, METROPOLITAN LIFE HONORS TREVOR HOWELLS, AUG. 15, 1913. He hoped the LaFarges would take the hint and leave. Instead, quite to Trevor's discomfort, Helen LaFarge began to beg.

"We thought our house was fully insured so we prepaid the entire mortgage. All our money was in that house. The fire consumed our life savings as well as our home. We have no money and nowhere to live. Please, Mr. Howells. Possibly Metropolitan could offer some compensation even if less than full replacement?"

"Believe me, Mrs. LaFarge, I deeply regret your loss, and were it up to me I would return your premiums like that." Trevor snapped his fingers, then waved his hands again in helpless acquiescence to the fates. "But these are company policies, and my obligation is to communicate them."

At this point, her elbow resting on Trevor's desk, Helen LaFarge exclaimed, "Oh, God, no," produced a pink handkerchief, and blubbered into it. Enraged, Walter LaFarge bolted out of his chair, placed one hand on his wife's shoulder, and shook his free fist in Trevor's face.

"You won't get away with this," he blustered. Then he took his wife's arm and gently led her, still crying, to the door. Walter turned back from the door, and, shaking his index finger in the air, promised Trevor Howells that Metropolitan Life would "rue the day" that they cheated Walter LaFarge, adding gratuitously, "you goddamn son of a bitch."

Still smiling, Trevor Howells wished Walter LaFarge a good afternoon. When finally the door slammed behind the LaFarges, and he heard their retreating footsteps descend the corridor, Trevor sat back, breathed deeply, unhooked his telephone, and dialed his boss, Winthrop J. Tolson, owner and president of Metropolitan Life and Casualty.

"I denied the LaFarge claim on warranty fraud. The man threatened litigation in his letter, but he lost all his money in the fire. He cannot sue." A baritone voice on the other end congratulated him, then hung up. Setting his receiver into its cradle, Trevor felt sorrow and pity mingled with shame. As an insurance investigator, Trevor had two major responsibilities. One was to expose crooks who tried to swindle the company. He relished that detective work, and was good at it. On one sensational occasion, he had found alive and well in Burlington an octogenarian whose forty-year-old "widow" had cashed a $25,000 death benefit exactly one week earlier. Husband and wife went to prison, and the company recovered $21,000. Trevor got the engraved watch for that one.

Unfortunately, his other major responsibility was unpleasant at best, disgusting at worst, and more common than the first. He called it loophole scrounging. Whenever the company received a valid claim, the actuaries passed it to Trevor who then sought legal grounds that would permit Metropolitan Life to deny or reduce the benefit. He often succeeded. An insurance contract's small print afforded many opportunities to deny claims, and Metropolitan's ingeniously framed policies were full of legal traps. Trevor once counted sixteen, not including the small-print paragraphs. Winthrop Tolson kept track of Trevor Howells's productivity, rewarding with annual bonuses every denial of a qualified claim. In calendar 1914, Trevor had denied $150,000 in benefits against his base salary of $1,500, and his bonus was $1,000. Bonus and salary together represented a substantial income, and, additionally, hobnobbing with attorneys as he did, Trevor hoped for promotion into Metro's legal department. His financial outlook was bright, and he was preparing to marry on the strength of it.

Nonetheless, despite his high pay and prospects, he detested loophole scrounging. It was not just the tears, rage, and insults to which claims denials routinely subjected him, unpleasant as those were. It was not even the occasional death threats, which required him to keep a Colt revolver in his desk. It was the shameful knowledge. Precisely because he fully understood every devious clause in the insurance contracts, Trevor understood that Metropolitan Life had planned to cheat customers from the very beginning. When Trevor finally met them, the customers had fallen into legal traps that clever attorneys had set for them years earlier, and now they struggled liked bewildered animals in the hunter's net. Metropolitan Life harvested the financial bounty of their ruined lives and crushed hopes. A stupid man could fail to understand the legal traps. A callous man could ignore them. Trevor Howells was neither.

He was, however, practical. Growing up poor, Trevor had learned early that in life you ate or were eaten. It was a law of nature. He philosophically reflected that Metropolitan Life would feast on the unwary until they learned how to protect themselves. His denials of benefit educated the unwary, so, viewed in long-run perspective, as he liked to view it, loophole scrounging reduced the world's supply of suckers. Trevor was making the world a better place one unwary customer at a time. When troubled by a conscience-activating denial, such as the LaFarge case, he found that revisiting that philosophical thought enabled him to scrounge again.

Trevor's day was not over. In thirty minutes he faced another denial conference. He selected the Joseph Albi dossier from his pile, examined it, and then put it down with relief. The widow was trying to collect a $20,000 death benefit from her husband's life insurance policy. Denying her huge claim would be unpleasant but clean as a whistle. Coroners had declared the stevedore's death a suicide, and Metropolitan Life had neither sought nor purchased their verdict.

Francine Albi arrived slightly earlier than expected, which freed Trevor to take more time with her if he chose. Mrs. Albi wore a widow's black dress, heavily flounced, and a wide black hat with a black veil, but from the neck up she resembled a fashion model because of her regular features and hairstyle. In her mid-thirties, wasp-waisted and buxom, Francine Albi moved with grace, poise, and, Trevor noticed, determination. Taking the chair he proffered, she resituated it so that the summer sunshine did not strike her eyes. From her shaded spot, she coolly appraised Trevor. Then, leaning forward, her elbows on Trevor's desk, the widow opened their conference with a denial of her own.

"My husband did not commit suicide."

Trevor swiveled his oak chair, picked up the late Joseph Albi's insurance policy, and leafed through it again. The whole-life policy was payable to Francine Albi, the decedent's wife. It had been purchased on January 14, 1915, some seven months earlier.

"Mrs. Albi, the contract is valid, the payments are up-to-date, and you are the beneficiary along with your four children, but the decedent's suicide is a problem. Your husband died only five months after taking out this policy. Is that correct?"

"Right. He died on June fifteenth, and the coroner's verdict came out July thirtieth."

"Mrs. Albi, your husband's employer, the Cunard Shipping Line, appealed the initial judgment of accidental death. You gave testimony during their appeal, right?

"I did, yes."

"The coroner ruled Mr. Albi's death a suicide. The safety stanchions on A-deck were in place around the cargo hold into which your husband fell. It was night but the *Alneria*'s deck was illuminated. That suggests that your husband climbed over the stanchions and leaped to his death. Sadly for you, this verdict relieved the Cunard Line of financial responsibility for his death at work. You will see no compensation from them. But the verdict also invalidated your husband's life insurance. This policy does not pay any benefit in cases of suicide. No life insurance does. Please see paragraph 6C. I am so *very* sorry." Smiling gently, his index finger on section 6C, Trevor handed the policy back to the widow, expecting by this gesture to end the interview and thus avoid a distressing scene.

"But what if the coroner was wrong?" Francine Albi persisted.

Trevor sighed. Looking squarely at the handsome young widow, he removed his green eyeshade and steel-rimmed eyeglasses and spread his hands, hoping to express helplessness and sympathy. "When a decedent owned his policy for less than two years, the company must suspect that, when he purchased it, he intended suicide."

"But, there was witnesses," Francine Albi said.

"Did the coroner hear those witnesses?"

"They didn't pay no mind."

"Mind or no mind, the coroner decides the cause of death. Metropolitan Life did *not* initiate that appeal, the Cunard Shipping Line did. The coroner makes the legal decision. Metropolitan Life accepts that decision, then pays or does not pay depending upon it." He paused. "And Metropolitan Life cannot pay anything in cases of suicide. I wish the rules were different. I know you have children." He nodded, and his eyes showed genuine regret.

Still undeterred, the lady quoted Metro's sales slogan. "The salesman told us that Metropolitan Life is 'the company that cares.'"

Did Trevor detect sarcasm? He ignored it and went to the truth. "Yes, Metro Life cares a great deal," he paused for effect, then continued, "*about contracts.*" Trevor paused, awaiting a reply. Mrs. Albi did not answer, but he noticed that her lower lip was beginning to quiver. He proceeded to the next sorrowful lesson. "Did the salesman tell you *what* Metropolitan Life cares about?" Trevor saw no reason now to hide the truth.

"Can I at least have back the premiums my husband paid? I'm broke. My kids have nothing to eat."

"Unfortunately, no. Metropolitan Life considers that your husband's premiums paid for five months of risk. He got everything he paid for. You'd best consider your other options."

These callous words were the bottom line. Francine Albi sat stunned, gazing vacantly out the window onto the Broadway traffic below. "My other options," she muttered. "Like begging?"

Affecting deafness, Trevor did not respond, and Mrs. Albi looked away, pensive. Not wishing to hurry a lady in mourning, Trevor waited a respectful minute before signaling again the end of this painful interview. He directed his gaze at the dossiers stacked in his in-box, and readjusted his sleeve garters as if preparing to attack the pile. He consulted his pocket watch. Usually, their shoulders slumped by now, the losers shuffled out of his office. To his surprise, the undaunted lady returned to the same rejected point.

"Two witnesses heard men's voices on A-deck. They heard Joe talking to somebody just before he fell. If men was up there, talking to Joe, then they might of pushed him into the cargo hold."

"The coroner rejected that theory." Trevor's voice was slightly louder now, and its tone sharper.

"The coroner didn't know everything. I was afraid to tell them . . . . " Her voice trailed off as she again gazed out the window, then turned abruptly back to Trevor and continued, "Do coroners ever change their verdicts?"

"Rarely. However, if an appellant brings new evidence, coroners can change a verdict. In the case of Joseph Albi, the coroner already changed the verdict on the motion of the Cunard Line."

"They could change it again?"

"Yes, but—"

She interrupted him. "You would know how to change a coroner's verdict?" Francine gazed intently at Trevor, her dark eyes signaling an improper proposal.

"It's my business to know, but Metropolitan Life does not appeal cases closed to its satisfaction. The company is satisfied with the coroner's verdict. If that verdict is to be changed, you must change it without help from Metropolitan Life." He thought that slammed the final door, but Francine Albi was searching his face preparatory to her next move. She feared and mistrusted men with green eyeshades who sat behind desks, wore a taper haircut, and pulled out gold watches, but this man was good-looking, thirty years of age, his face long and thin, with a high forehead, wide-bridged pointed nose, large greenish eyes, and drooping sand-colored sideburns. Moreover, he seemed sympathetic, genuinely regretful, and open to suggestion. She decided to chance it.

"They say coroners respect their friends." She was not alluding to the power of friendship. Trevor explained that bribery of coroners had been common earlier when Julius Harberger ran the bureau. However, Mayor Mitchell was reforming it. Francine interrupted him.

"Would two thousand dollars change your mind?" Silence.

"I don't follow you," replied Trevor, feigning incomprehension. It was best to let clients openly propose an improper option rather than to understand their innuendo and later be declared to have put crooked words into their honest mouths.

Francine Albi leaned forward in her seat, gazing intently into his green eyes, and whispered her proposal. "If the coroner changes his mind, I get twenty thousand dollars from the insurance," she glanced at the closed door, "and you get two thousand from me."

Trevor sat back in his swivel chair and reflected a moment, twisting his pencil. He suddenly became conscious of being alone with a beautiful, determined, and aggressive woman. The feeling confused him. It did not belong in the office. Stalling for time, he put his green eyeshade and his steel-rimmed reading glasses back on. Metro Life would lose money if Francine Albi had to be paid.

"Mrs. Albi, the company prohibits this arrangement."

"They don't have to find out." *Good point,* thought Trevor, wondering how she knew. But instead of responding, he picked up a heavy law book and thumbed through it, hoping to give the impression of research. He was not reading the book. Freelance was not illegal. He had done it twice before, and Winthrop J. Tolson had not found out. Tolson probably would not find out in this case either, and cheating Metro for a customer instead of cheating the customer for Metro would afford Trevor a secret satisfaction. What was more, he mused, $2,000 balanced the risk. If this deal worked out, he would net ten months' extra pay. Trevor Howells had learned early in life to take money seriously, but, working in the insurance industry, he had also learned to assess odds before assuming risk.

"Mrs. Albi, thanks to the crusading Dr. Norris, a New York coroner is now more likely to be a medical doctor than a crooked politician."

"Then I have a chance," she shot back. "Crooked politicians are just what I need."

He had not thought of it that way! "Yes, a slim chance," agreed Trevor, privately astonished that this young widow's street wisdom overcame grief, gender, and legality. Uselessly shuffling more papers on his desk to give the impression of bureaucratic activity, Trevor took another two minutes to reflect. The chances of success were slim, the downside penalties severe. A firm no made business sense. Unfortunately, the woman's good looks had already distracted him. Additionally, Trevor could not avoid reflecting on her plight. It was annoying, but he could not. This customer was a recent widow, thirty-four years old, the sole support of four children, and was broke. Her children were hungry, she deserved help, and she was quite pretty as well in a dark-haired Mediterranean way. Despite the widow's weeds, her brown eyes flashed a worldly intelligence above her full rosy cheeks as she proposed a kickback. Trevor looked up from his law book and, after adjusting his eyeshade and glasses, which he had donned to look inflexible, he addressed the worst case rather than reject her proposal out of hand as he ought to have done.

"What if the verdict doesn't change?"

"Then you get nothing. But, Mr. Howells, if you offer new evidence, maybe the coroner would change it."

"And what would this new evidence prove?" Trevor sat back, skeptical, hands clasped across his middle, inviting illumination but expecting only wishful thinking, which he would have to cruelly demolish, leaving the widow in tears. Her words stunned him.

"It would show that some people had a motive to kill Joe because he was blackmailing them."

Trevor lurched forward in his chair. "Blackmail! You should have told the coroners! Whom did he blackmail?"

"I don't know for sure." Francine Albi thought that the Cunard Shipping Line and the Royal Navy were obvious suspects, but the Socialist Party and Paul Kelly were also possibilities. "Any of them could of killed him."

"You cannot be serious," Trevor snorted. "You expect the Manhattan County coroner to believe that your husband was blackmailing the Royal Navy, the Cunard Line, Paul Kelly's gang, and even the Socialist Party? You've left out only Santa." Trevor rolled his eyes.

Rejecting the imputation of folly, Francine Albi insisted that all of what she had said was true. Trevor pointed out that claiming to know the truth would not change a coroner's verdict. Widow or no widow, he would not waste time on fairy tales.

CHAPTER 2

EXPLODING CHEESE

AT THE NEXT MORNING's shapeup, the walking boss assigned Joe Albi and Frankie Buono to the deck gang that loaded crates of cheese stacked on the dock into cargo nets. A steam crane hefted the filled nets onto the *Lusitania*'s top deck, and stevedore gangs on that deck controlled their descent into the liner's cargo holds. The stevedores had loaded fifty tons of cheese the day before, and expected to load as many again today. When Joe asked the dock foreman whether the *Lusitania*'s cargo included any explosives, the man said no. Explosives could not travel on passenger liners. Then looking quizzically at Joe, he expressed surprise that Joe had not understood that. Covering up, Joe explained that he had "just wondered."

By quitting time, Frankie and Joe had quietly asked several friends whether they had loaded any cordite into the *Lusitania* that day or the day previous. No one had. Several remarked that it would be illegal to load explosive onto a passenger ship. Neither Joe nor Frankie explained that when they had opened four crates of stolen cheese the night before, the crates contained military cordite. But they wondered in private whether the hundred tons of cheese they had loaded might all be cordite.

They asked about the street value of the explosive. No one knew. The stolen crates' interior waybills declared that the value of each crate was $500. At that price, Frankie and Joe had $2,000 worth of cordite to sell, a huge sum, but neither could be sure that Paul Kelly's gang would fence a military explosive at all. Who would buy it? And what would be the price? As usual, Frankie wanted his end, but he left the negotiation to Joe, whom he regarded as the more capable businessman, and Joe turned for advice to his most trusted counselor.

Francine Albi stood at a greasy gas stove and range wearing a gray smock with pockets, but she had her dark hair in a Gibson coiffure, and from the neck up she looked like a fashion model. Francine had attended public elementary school number 41. She spoke English better than she did the Neapolitan dialect, and she dressed in the American style. She had book knowledge that Joe, her husband of ten years, had not acquired in Naples, and, in Joe's opinion, Francine had uncommon business sense "for a woman." Joe tapped her brain whenever he faced a challenging business decision. Idly twirling his stevedore hook, which in his skilled hand circled faster than a cop's baton, Joe signaled a wish to have a "business discussion."

"What now?" Francine asked, swiveling toward Joe. Her black eyes soared aloft as she turned, and her soul was resigned to another sordid confession.

"You remember the cheese I was planning to bring from the *Lusitania*?"

"I remember the cheese you was planning to *steal*," Francine rejoined.

Joe shook his head and waved his hands in denial, his face shining disingenuous innocence, then continued, "Frankie and I broke open four crates yesterday. They contained cordite explosive, not cheese. The bags said DANGER. They might be worth two thousand bucks, but we don't know whether Kelly's organization will fence it. Now, what I wonder—"

Interrupting Joe, Francine ignored the question he was about to pose. "Explosives?" she gasped. Francine knew where Joe stored stolen goods prior to fencing them, and she leaped to the right conclusion. "Where are they now?" Her lips parted in terror, Francine turned her attention from the bubbling saucepan on her gas range and looked over at Joe, the wooden spoon still in her hand.

"In the cellar."

"In *our* cellar? Are you crazy?" Joe acknowledged that the cordite was indeed in the cellar of their Barrow Street tenement, the home of six working families like their own. His response enraged and frightened Francine.

"Get it out of here tonight!" That was not the response Joe had expected. Francine routinely expressed indignation when he discussed a planned theft. A planned theft could go wrong, but a successful theft was another matter. What was done was irretrievably done, and Francine needed extra money to feed their kids, so she sighed, made marketing recommendations, and calculated her cut. But this time, Francine's dark hair fell over her right eye, and her bosom heaved with exasperation. "You have four kids sleeping in the front room, and this whole building could explode. Holy mother of God!"

"Aw, Francine, no one goes down there during the summer." Joe knew his rejoinder was bluster, but he needed to salvage his foresight, a character trait in which he took huge pride.

Unmollified, Francine raged on. "They can trace stolen explosives." And, she continued, if *they* did, he would be imprisoned, and then what would become of her and the children? That appeal normally enabled Francine to control Joe's riskiest projects, but this time she had questioned the safety of Joe's backup plan. *They* would never catch *him*. How many watchmen owed their holiday turkeys to his generosity? Didn't he and Frankie Buono have Paul Kelly's full protection? Weren't the precinct police and judges all in Kelly's pocket? Those points reintroduced and duly appreciated, Joe beat an honorable retreat on the storage issue.

"But you're right—the bags are dangerous. I'll move them to Fifteenth Street right now." Rising from the scarred wooden table, rescued two years earlier from the curb in front of his house, Joe descended the four narrow flights of ill-lit, creaking stairs, pushed open the basement door, and extracted from a steel mesh cage, used in winter for coal storage, four forty-pound sacks of cordite. These he loaded onto a wheelbarrow, covered them with a tarpaulin, and then slowly pushed the whole load uptown along Seventh Avenue, occasionally taking time to rest.

His destination was a derelict building near Fifteenth Street and Eighth Avenue. Although abandoned and dark, the building's massive front door boasted brass locks that defied amateur thieves. Understanding that Paul Kelly protected this building, professional thieves would not trespass. Fire inspectors knew that too, so they gave the building a pass without bothering to go inside, receiving their thank-you gifts at Christmas. Only Kelly associates knew about a square crud-encrusted basement window that was always left open. After crawling through the narrow window, Joe opened the front door from the inside, brought the wheelbarrow into the building, resecured the front door, and stowed the bags under the tarp. Then he exited via the secret window. He deemed it a good solution. His stash was safe, and could be fenced later.

The next day, Joe hailed Paul Kelly's point man, Slate, who helped at blind John's newsstand on the Seventh Avenue subway island. Slate wore a news vendor's multi-pocket smock that proclaimed, I READ THE TRIBUNE. He read only the racing page. Slate counted the cash for the blind man, but his real business was taking bets, delivering payoffs to winners, and connecting thieves to Paul Kelly's organization. Slate knew Paul Kelly in person, and channeled Paul's decisions back to the working level. He was also Joe's friend.

"Morning, Slate. I got merchandise."

"Hi, Joe. What you got?"

"A hundred and sixty pounds of cordite in forty-pound bags."

"What the hell is cordite?

"It's a war explosive the British use."

"Where is it?"

"Fifteenth Street, under a brown tarp."

"If we can sell it, the usual." This meant that Paul Kelly would take 60 percent of whatever a commodity fetched on the street. But his service included delivery to the customer. If no buyer could be found, Joe would get nothing, and Kelly would not return the merchandise. When a customer had paid, and Joe's end came due, Slate would wrap Joe's money in a newspaper and hand it to him. Affiliates never accused

Paul Kelly of dishonesty, but keeping receipts was advisable. Mistakes did happen.

The gang's pickup was scheduled for May 1, the very day that the passenger liner RMS *Lusitania* sailed for Liverpool from the Cunard Line's Pier 54. On the morning before the pickup, Joe ripped off one identifying tag from each of the four interior bags. The tags declared that the contents were cordite explosives manufactured by the DuPont Chemical Company. The tags and waybills showed matching serial numbers, and could support his claim should anyone question how much merchandise he had actually delivered to Paul Kelly. Joe also tore off and retained the shipping labels that addressed the external crates to a box office in Liverpool. It proved a momentous decision, one to which Joe gave little thought at the time because his mind had moved on. He had already identified his next venture, rerouting a case of premium Scotch whiskey from the hold of a White Star merchantman to his tenement's basement locker, and thence to his many friends on the police force and watchman staff.

But the unexpected happened. A week later, on May 8, 1915, the *New York Tribune* carried the banner headline 900 DIE AS LUSITANIA GOES TO BOTTOM. A German submarine had torpedoed the world's fastest ocean liner, darling of the Cunard Shipping Line, sinking it in eighteen minutes. Twelve hundred civilian passengers drowned in the Irish Sea, about one hundred of them Americans. President Woodrow Wilson furiously blamed the Germans for an illegal and barbaric attack on civilians. He demanded an apology, reparations, and assurances against a repeat. Everyone was talking about the Germans' latest war crime. Normally inattentive to world politics, ordinary people expressed indignation at Germany's callous indifference to human life. The German ambassador, however, claimed that the passenger liner had been carrying war materiel, and was therefore a legitimate military target for the submarine. Knowing that the ship was a target for U-boats, the German consulate had for that very reason warned passengers against sailing on the *Lusitania*. The ambassador also claimed that the U-20's torpedo had ignited secret explosives aboard the ship, causing the second, larger explosion that sank the huge ship so quickly.

Francine took an unusual interest in this news story. It was not just that Joe had helped to load the doomed passenger liner; it was not even that her childhood friend, George Zorelli, had been stoking in the engine room when the ship went down, and had probably gone down with it. It was the unique knowledge she and Joe shared. The British Admiralty insisted that the *Lusitania* had carried no explosives, and the Port of New York's collector, Dudley Malone, concurred, a judgment that President Wilson accepted. Yet Joe and Francine knew that President Wilson was in error and so was the Admiralty, and, what was more, Joe had labels and waybills that proved it. The *Lusitania* had carried tons of cordite explosive disguised as cheese. Francine suspected that this knowledge was dangerous.

"I wish you hadn't stolen that explosive," Francine remarked as they walked to the Saint Anthony of Padua Catholic Church on Sunday morning. The four children trailed along the sidewalk after them.

"I thought it was cheese."

"Stealing cheese is a mortal sin," she declared, then, making a wry face, added, "And now you're involved in this war crime."

"Why am I involved?" Joe asked.

As if he doesn't know, Francine thought, but realizing she would have to press the point, she completed her thought. "The British say there were no explosives on board. That's a wicked lie, but the public don't know, and you do."

"So what?" Sensing Joe's determined incomprehension, and herself determined to be understood, Francine filled in the missing details. "Maybe the cordite exploded and sank the ship." When Joe did not reply, and looked evasively away, Francine continued. "If they're lying about the munitions, the British probably don't want the truth to come out." Then Francine turned to adjust Maria's dress and tie her shoes. "Anthony, stand up straight, and take your hands out of your pockets."

These activities provided a momentary interlude during which Joe regrouped his thoughts. "Why should I have trouble?" he asked again. It was another defensive invitation for Francine to elaborate, and turning back to him, she did so.

"You know that the crates contained guncotton."

"Maybe they ordered cheese, and the guncotton was a mistake they didn't want. In that case, they're not lying." His preposterous speculation was off Francine's point, and she would not leave her point.

"Joe, if they find out that you know about the guncotton—"

Joe did not let her finish. "Only Frankie and I know what was in those crates."

"No, Joe. Slate knows, and so does Paul Kelly and whoever they told."

"Nobody asks where stuff comes from."

Skeptical, Francine asked whether in this exceptional case someone might not ask. Waving a calloused hand, Joe assured her again that no one would. Somewhat reassured, Francine did not reply, but this trivial reassurance did not relieve the underlying anxiety that kept her clenching and unclenching her teeth and biting her lip at night. She fretted about Joe's assumption of risk after illegal risk, and each time he announced a new one she worried aloud in his presence that this time his luck might run out. However, since he had purchased life insurance, and seemed to have protected himself in this case, she did not want to provoke a quarrel on a church Sunday, so she did not pursue the point.

Sensing Francine's acquiescence, Joe put her through their matrimonial catechism: He was underpaid at work. She agreed. The shipping companies cheated the stevedores. Agreed. That was a sin before God. Agreed. Without scratch they would never get the new icebox and Victrola she wanted. Agreed. He stole only from thieving companies, and stealing back one's own was not really stealing. "Agreed," Francine replied, and then continued, "But what about Tony Azarello? He got promoted to walking boss and earned fifteen dollars a week."

"Azarello has influence."

"But Joe, you've been working the docks for twelve years, and you're still shaping up. Your back won't last much longer. You need a desk job.

Like that Murphy."

"Pat Murphy works for the politicians." Tammany Hall passed out patronage jobs to Irish supporters at election time. A Tammany job was not one Italians could get. Joe's larger point was, Francine understood, that Italians were up against a rigged system. If extra money was needed, and it was, there was no realistic alternative to Joe's illegal business. And Father Coro would bless the dollar that Francine would place in the collection plate at eleven o'clock. Francine rejoined that God would know and care. Joe assured her that God would understand. Nonetheless, later that day, having made his confession, Joe did say five Our Fathers and three Hail Marys in penance. Walking home, Joe explained that his penance placated the deity, but he left open in his own mind the intriguing possibility of financially profiting from the sin.

On a late spring morning, Slate folded up Joe's newspaper the way he did when it contained kickback money. "Present for you, Joe," he quipped, handing it over.

"Thanks, buddy," was all Joe said as he popped the newspaper under his left arm and turned to stride away. Evidently, Kelly's organization had found a buyer. He wondered how much money he would find inside the newspaper.

"Paul wants to know where you got the merchandise." That was all Slate called at Joe's departing back, but his words were icicles.

"Tomorrow," Joe called over his shoulder, and then hurried away, turning the corner onto Waverly Place. He stopped in a doorway. Inside Slate's package Joe found $200, six weeks' pay for both him and Frankie. But in that delicious moment, Joe recalled Francine's warning. She had been right—Paul Kelly *did* want to know where Joe got the guncotton. In many years of fencing Joe's loot, Paul had never before asked such a question. Of course, Paul understood that all Joe's merchandise was stolen from ships in the harbor. Now, for some reason, Paul asked which ship, and what Paul Kelly wanted to know, a prudent man told him. So the next morning, picking up his newspaper, Joe said one word to Slate: "*Lusitania.*" Slate nodded.

Two days later, as Joe Albi hurried past the newsstand, not intending to buy a newspaper, Slate tapped his shoulder. "The customer wants more. It's two hundred dollars a crate now."

"Damn, I got no more."

"The customer's desperate. He might come to you. Paul says that you should not deal with him if he does. Let Paul deal with him. You're D 'n D if he comes to you, understood?

"Paul can count on me." The next evening, in the Barrow Street tenement's basement, Joe and Frankie divided a case of Scotch whiskey they had just purloined from a White Star merchantman. Of the twenty-four bottles in the case, four went to the pier watchmen, four to the police precinct house, and ten to Paul Kelly. The remaining six would later spread Christmas cheer throughout the neighborhood. Relaxing in the afterglow, Joe mused about the cordite he had sold and for which Frankie had taken his end. "A hundred bucks for one night's work. We hit the jackpot."

But Frankie tightened his lips and lowered his voice to a whisper. "Why don't Paul get rid of the customers instead of passing them to you and then asking you for D 'n D?" Joe did not know, and Frankie could find no reason anyone would want to talk to Joe Albi except to complain about his smelly socks. Frankie's insulting jest brought up Joe's fists in a friendly *gioco di mani,* but he returned to the original question.

"If the customer has influence, Paul might have to pass him through, but he's telling me in private to clam up."

Frankie again dismissed the possibility. "Paul knows you got nothing to sell."

Joe tossed his head, hawked, spat, and then, after adjusting his button cap, disagreed. "Paul's wrong. I got no guncotton, no, but I figure the customers are English, and I got something the English want—my silence."

"Yeah, I'd pay for that too," joked Frankie.

"Wise guy. I know the *Inglesi* loaded guncotton onto the *Lusitania,* disguised it as cheese, and then lied. What if I told the world? Let them give me a grand, then I forget it all."

Frankie looked up in shock. "*Pazzo,* do you think you can blackmail England?" He gave Joe's right cheek a friendly slap. "*You* wise up."

"Why throw away a chance? If they don't pay, I lost nothing."

"Paul said 'no sale, deaf 'n dumb.' Are you planning to hold out his share?" Frankie raised his eyebrows and twirled his wrist expressively. This common gesture introduced any dark topic. "I won't cross Paul," he said. "Count me out."

"Paul don't have to know," Joe replied.

"If you go to the newspapers, Paul will find out."

"*Stupido,* you think I'd go to the papers? If the English won't pay, I forget everything. But the English don't know I'm bluffing, so they pay."

"What if the English whack you out?" It did not take Frankie long to find the worst case.

After a thoughtful pause, Joe replied. "Why should they? For a grand they get all the documents. It's peanuts to them."

"Yeah, but you annoyed them."

"You worry too much. I'm rounding third base and the ball's still bouncing around left field. I can get home in time. But, Frankie, even if they throw me out at the plate, I bought twenty thousand worth of life insurance in January. Now I'm worth more to Francine dead than alive."

Shocked at Joe's fatalism, Frankie rejoined, "Your family wants you alive."

Agreeing, Joe backtracked. "Maybe you're right. It's too risky." They both nodded, and turned back to the crate of whiskey.

The customer came promptly. Two days later, walking out the front door of his brownstone, whistling a cheerful tune, Joe turned right toward Seventh Avenue. A tall blonde man, lean and fit, with a small handlebar moustache and an ascot cap, was sitting on the next stoop. His houndstooth jacket was not from the thrift shop. He got up when Joe came out the door.

"Would you be Mr. Joseph Albi?" he asked in a singsong English accent.

"Who wants to know?"

"My name is George V. Rex. Paul Kelly sent me about some merchandise." So it really was the English, Joe thought triumphantly. He had prepared a business plan for this contingency, but he needed to be careful. Stalling for time, he asked whom Mr. Rex represented, and learned that "interested parties" had sent him. Still stalling, Joe asked what kind of merchandise was in question.

"Cheese," replied Rex. Still playing for time, Joe asked whether Paul Kelly had told the gentleman that he, Joe Albi, was in the cheese business. Unamused, the Englishman went briskly to the point. "Look here, my good man, I bought the cheese you stole from the *Lusitania.* And now I want to buy all you have—no questions asked."

"What did Paul Kelly tell you regarding the current availability of fine cheese?"

"Paul Kelly said you supplied him." There was no use delaying any further. Joe told Rex that he had no more cheese to sell because his supplier was underwater. Expressing no appreciation of this witticism, the Englishman frowned and inquired again whether Joe really had none at all left. Assured again that Joe indeed had none at all, the Englishman stepped back, reflected, then looked away, apparently preparing to depart. Joe realized it was now time to spring his offer.

"However, I do have something else that will interest you."

"And what might that be?" asked George Rex. Looking left and right, then straight at Rex, Joe lowered his voice.

"The cheese was cordite flavor. This flavor explodes." Joe smiled at his joke, but the Englishman had no sense of humor. "There was many tons of this exploding cheese onboard the *Lusitania.* All that melted cheese went to the bottom. What a waste! Melted cheese is great with anchovies and tomatoes." Another failed effort at improving the business climate. Rex still did not smile back. His eyes narrowing, he said nothing, waiting for Joe to reach the point. After a pregnant pause, Joe exposed his offer.

"Maybe all this cheese exploded in the *Lusitania*'s cargo hold." Rex wondered what might be the import of this hypothetical possibility. Lifting his chin and looking squarely at Rex, Joe explained. "Maybe the *Lusitania* carried explosives. Maybe the English allowed those passengers to travel into a submarine zone aboard an ocean liner loaded with explosives, and then they lied about it."

"I don't see what this conjecture has to do with you," Rex hissed.

"No? Well, let me explain," Joe continued, giddily aware that his dangerous trap was now irretrievably sprung. "I know that crates labeled CHEESE contained cordite. To prove it, I have interior waybills. I have shipping labels addressed to Liverpool. I have a true copy of the ship's loading manifest, and I prepared a sworn affidavit that tells everything I know. All that information could become public—or I could forget it."

"Cargo theft is illegal," said Rex drily. "You could go to jail." Joe was ready for that parry.

"I could go to jail, but England could lose the war. Take your pick. Look, Mister Rex, for a grand I forget everything." A flutter of uncertainty crossed Rex's expressionless face. Joe guessed that the Englishman might not understand American. "That's a thousand dollars. It buys you all the documents and my silence. It's a hell of a bargain. Think about it." Joe tipped his cap, then strode away toward Seventh Avenue as if he held all the high cards, and Rex called him back, requesting the name of the shipper on the interior waybills. Joe mentioned the DuPont Chemical Company.

"We have a bargain, Mr. Albi," said George V. Rex.

CHAPTER 3

TAKE UP THE SWORD OF JUSTICE

IN THE NEXT forty minutes, Trevor Howells learned that the late Joe Albi had agreed to sell his silence to "the Englishman" for $1,000. George V. Rex would not reveal the names of his sponsors, but warned Joe that they were "influential" and would not tolerate "opportunism." To protect his own life, Joe prepared and notarized dual copies of an affidavit. Francine had copied out a three-page handwritten document that Joe Albi later had notarized at Ferretti's travel agency on Carmine Street. His friend and co-thief, Frank Buono, served as witness. The affidavits told the whole story of how Joe had stolen four crates marked BULK CHEESE from the *Lusitania* just before she sailed, and had then found guncotton in the crates. The affidavits listed the serial numbers of the crates the explosives had been found in, the serial numbers on the waybills, and the post office box in Liverpool to which the crates of cheese were traveling.

"Mrs. Albi, just because a man has an English accent, you cannot assume that he works for the British government."

"Joe thought so. Later he learned different. No, please, it makes sense. Listen..." Mrs. Albi resumed her narrative. "A couple days after Joe agreed to sell the affidavit and the shipping labels to the Englishman, he got a better offer."

"He did?" gasped Trevor.

"A man from the Socialist Party offered Joe five thousand dollars for the affidavits, the ship's manifest, and the shipping labels."

"Whoa! That's a great deal of money. Why?"

"The socialist said the Englishman worked for the Cunard Line, and Cunard wanted to protect itself against lawsuits by the *Lusitania*'s survivors and the relatives of them who drowned."

"Hmm, that's plausible," Trevor commented, his professional interest showing. "A verdict of "unlawful cargo" would void the ship's insurance. Did Lloyd's insure her?" Francine Albi shrugged. Of course she did not know. She asked if he wanted to hear more, her expression indicating irritation at the interruption and uncertainty about Trevor's continued interest.

"The socialist said Cunard knowingly transported civilians into a war zone on a ship loaded with explosives," Francine continued. "If that became known, Cunard would have to pay the survivors and the relatives of all the dead. The damages would be huge." She gestured with her hands spread wide apart to indicate the vastness of the damages Cunard would confront. Trevor calculated mentally that Cunard's total bill would be the replacement cost of the lost liner and its cargo, as well as reparations to the passengers and their heirs. Obviously, the Cunard Line could not pay such a gigantic claim.

"I understand your point, Mrs. Albi" Trevor interjected. "You suspect that Cunard's agent pushed your husband into the hold of the *Alneria* in order to silence him and thus protect Cunard from liability."

"Well, they didn't want to pay..." Francine said, and then added bitterly, "... any more than *your stinking company*. But Mr. Howells, maybe the socialist murdered Joe to prevent the Cunard Line from buying the documents." Francine sat back, smoothed her floor-length skirt, crossed her ankles, and adjusted her big floppy hat. She had told her tale. Now it was up to Trevor.

The case was exceptional as was the determined widow. Trevor stroked his chin in amazement at both, then took stock. "Mrs. Albi, what you say rings true, but I have to ask questions. It might be unpleasant, but

I must ask."

"Sure, ask. No one else cares."

Trevor attacked two obvious inconsistencies in Francine's story. The first concerned the Socialist Party. "Mrs. Albi, why did the Socialists want to buy Joe's documents? Did your husband discuss that with you?"

"He did. The socialist, name of Ben Williams, said that if the American public learned the truth about the *Lusitania*'s real cargo, then war-minded politicians like Mr. Roosevelt would lose their... their—"

"Their credibility? Their main argument?" Trevor completed the widow's sentence to her evident relief.

"All that. The socialists want to tell the world what was really onboard the *Lusitania.*"

Trevor looked up at the ceiling, mused, and then returned his gaze to Mrs. Albi, who regarded him with a cobra's intensity. "Why would the socialists murder your husband when they proposed to expose his story to the public?" Francine blinked, hesitated, then guessed that maybe the socialists could not raise the $5,000 and were afraid that Joe would sell his silence to the Englishman.

"You don't kill a man to make him talk," Trevor scoffed.

Francine came right back. "But the murderers took his affidavit. Maybe they plan to publish it." This case was trickier than Trevor had anticipated. He moved on.

"Mrs. Albi, what about Paul Kelly? As president of the Longshoreman's Association, he would not want exposure of his clandestine operation."

"What operation?" Francine asked.

"His unlawful sale of stolen goods."

"I didn't mention that either." A pause, then she continued, "But I did warn Joe." This acknowledgment introduced the intermediary role of Paul Kelly's criminal associates in fencing Joe's stolen explosives. "A guy named Slate" had warned Joe to operate strictly through the gang when dealing with the Englishman, but Joe ignored the warning in order to prevent Kelly from taking the lion's share of the blackmail money. "It was dangerous to cheat Paul."

"Your husband took many dangerous risks."

"As he got older, he took more and more. He worried about retirement," Francine replied simply. "But, Mr. Howells, the shipping companies always cheat the stevedores, so everyone steals. It's the only way stevedores make ends meet. My Joe, he was a good man, a good father, a church member... and now they won't even bury him." Mrs. Albi sniffled. Was she going to cry?

"I know something about waterfront pilferage," Trevor continued drily, without acknowledging her emotional upset. Because of organized thieving, which Pinkerton detectives reduced but could not prevent, companies would not insure marine cargoes above 90 percent of assessed value. Shippers had to accept the risk of up to 10 percent inventory shrinkage. The average loss was 1 percent in three days' loading. "I realize that your husband was not the only one who pilfered. Your point puts his character in focus." Francine brightened at the reassuring words, ignoring Trevor's implicit irony. "But it opens the door to another party with some motive to murder your husband—Paul Kelly's waterfront gang."

"That's what I just told you," scoffed the lady. When opening an investigation, Trevor had found that thinking aloud would often reveal new evidence. Francine Albi finally succumbed to despair as the roster of her late husband's many enemies came inexorably to light. She laid her head on Trevor's desk and wailed. Her big hat flopped onto the floor, and her abundant black hair came partially loose from her pompadour, flowing over her shoulders like a shawl. She looked up with tear-filled brown eyes. "Mr. Howells, I have four kids to feed, and no scratch. Only job I can get is hat maker. The priest wouldn't even bury Joe in consecrated ground. The kids cry. I caught them begging meals from the neighbors. What am I going to do?" She pounded her fist on his desktop in a gesture of frustration and futility.

This scene was exactly what Trevor had hoped to avoid, and now that the lady's open despair confronted him, he felt sorrow and pity for Francine Albi and her children. That was exactly what he had feared. Sorrow and pity had no place in an insurance investigator's steel heart. Unfortunately, remembering his own mother's financial struggles, Trevor sympathized with widows, a sympathy accentuated by Francine's heaving and ample bosom, youthful complexion, and luxuriant black hair. He had learned from experience the danger of allowing sympathy to deflect him from tough business decisions, but this time he could not compel himself to take the stern action the situation required. Weakening, and hating himself for it, Trevor removed his eyeshade and put his eyeglasses on the desk. Arising from his swivel chair, he laid a light hand on Francine's heaving shoulder. "Mrs. Albi, I will look into this matter. If I don't succeed, you owe me nothing. If I succeed, and the verdict is reversed, I'll take only one thousand dollars, not two."

Francine Albi looked up from the desktop, her tearful eyes showing relief and gratitude. She grasped Trevor's hand in both of her own and kissed it. "Only one thousand?" Trevor nodded. One thousand was sufficient compensation, he thought, for the slight effort her job would require. "Oh, thank you, Mr. Howells. You are a good and kind man." She accepted a handkerchief that Trevor proffered, daubed her eyes with it, and then returned it. She managed a weak smile that displayed a row of startlingly white teeth. Then, to Trevor's surprise, she abruptly stopped crying, opened her wide purse, and extracted two sheaves of paper. The first was her late husband's handwritten, sworn, and notarized affidavit. The second was four shipping labels and four interior waybills that declared that the contents of the crate were cordite explosive. The words FLAMMABLE EXPLOSIVE were in big letters. These had been on the inner container. The labels identified the DuPont Chemical Company as the sender. She also handed over four shipping labels that addressed "bulk cheese" to a post office box in Liverpool, England. These had been on the external crate. She said that Trevor would need these documents to make his case before the coroner.

Returning to Brooklyn that evening aboard the brand-new, electric-powered subway train, whose hellish shrieks and flickering lights banished dreams and illusions, Trevor reflected upon his pledge. His heart had spoken, and his head now regretted its words. His decision had been emotional, and it put his job at risk. He resolved to tell Mrs. Albi that he had changed his mind. He told himself that "no" was the only sensible choice. Then, staring straight ahead as the train rattled over the Brooklyn Bridge, he rethought his offer in a more favorable light. Sure, her looks had swayed his judgment, and, sure, he had yielded to sympathy, but there were facts in her favor too. Afraid to plead her deceased husband guilty of burglary and blackmail, the widow had not previously mentioned the explosives or the blackmail attempt, so there was indeed new evidence, which supplied valid grounds for reopening the coroner's inquiry. Trevor would not have to prove who killed Joseph Albi. It would be enough to show that many people had a motive. The suicide of a blackmailer had to raise suspicions of murder.

There was, Trevor estimated, about one chance in twenty that the new evidence would induce the coroner to change the verdict; and if the evidence was too weak, handing over one hundred dollars for a coroner's "favorite charity" might strengthen it. In that case, Trevor projected, the grateful lady would turn over to him a $1,000 reward, and he would go on his chivalrous way $900 richer. The effort required would be four or five hours. The possible reward was five months' pay. Admittedly, the odds were weak; nonetheless, Trevor decided that the lady's case was sufficiently plausible and lucrative to warrant taking it up quite apart from the rectitude of so doing, which, after all, mattered too.

That was not how Trevor put it to his fiancée, Lotte Maria Schlegel, with whom he spent that night at her flat on Schermerhorn Street in Brooklyn. "Lotte, I agreed to appeal this case because the widow supports four children. Was I stupid? I could still cancel." Knowing Lotte's kind heart, Trevor hoped she would praise his generosity, a quality in which she normally found him deficient, but quite to his annoyance, after pecking his cheek she criticized his stinginess again.

"No, don't cancel. Trevor, it's not *stupid* to help needy people. Why do you always say that? Was she pretty?" How irritating! Lotte had guessed that a pretty face might affect his business judgment just as it actually had, but her comment reopened a fault line in their romance. What Lotte Schlegel called "lack of compassion" Trevor called "practical wisdom," to which, he gently observed from time to time, Lotte's twenty years of life had not fully introduced her. Lotte would then declare that twenty years was old enough to recognize greed and selfishness; but she did not intended to annoy him about that long-standing difference of opinion on this occasion. Seeing Trevor's face fall, and sensing the quarrel she had unintentionally summoned from a dark cave of memory, Lotte backed up. "You're risking your job to help this lady." Then, batting her eyelashes, added, "That takes courage."

"What else could I do?" Still uncertain in his own mind, Trevor encouraged Lotte more fully to support his decision, but, although a romantic idealist and only twenty years old, Lotte Schlegel was no dope. Adoring Trevor's thoughtfulness, self-possession, good manners, wide knowledge, chiseled face, ambition, and wit, Lotte thought him almost a dreamboat. The trouble was his job. Lotte disliked the Metropolitan Life Insurance Company, and especially its owner. She hated loophole scrounging. When Trevor discussed a day's denials, almost seeming to boast, she reluctantly wondered whether he was the right man for her, so when Trevor intimated that he had taken Francine Albi's case out of human kindness, Lotte wanted to believe him, but, knowing her man, wondered how important money had been. She could be blunt. Young, blonde, and pretty, with plenty of eligible men available on an instant's flirtation, Lotte would not settle for less than her ideal man. She was almost but not quite sure that Trevor Howells was that man.

"Well, you might have taken her case for nothing instead of asking for a thousand dollars." The rejoinder irritated Trevor again. He struck back.

"Why should I do it for nothing when Mrs. Albi has money?

"But Trevor, she's broke."

Trevor closed in, expecting to overwhelm Lotte with actuarial science.

"No, Lotte, she has twenty thousand dollars in the event I obtain a favorable verdict. And I reckon the chance of that is five percent. Five percent of twenty thousand dollars is $1000. That's what I am charging."

"That's preposterous."

"No, it's like buying a lottery ticket. If a hundred tickets have been sold, and the prize is one hundred dollars, then the value of each ticket is one dollar." As Lotte looked puzzled, Trevor continued. "Think of it this way: I would buy that lottery ticket for eighty cents because it's worth a dollar. In fact, I would buy all one hundred tickets for eighty dollars, and then I'd be certain to win the one-hundred-dollar prize. Mrs. Albi's lottery ticket is worth one thousand dollars because I reckon she has a five percent chance of winning the $20,000 prize."

"So that's why she has money?" Trevor confirmed Lotte's surmise. Still dubious, however, Lotte was now uncomfortably aware that Trevor was seeing the case from the viewpoint of an insurance actuary. "Oh, that's all right then. It's reasonable to collect a recovery fee, but, Trevor, it's not charitable. It would be *charitable* to do it for nothing. The chivalrous knight saves the lady in distress for nothing. He doesn't ask for a tip."

"That knight lived rent-free in King Arthur's castle. I pay for two apartments." Trevor shook his head in scorn. "Honestly, Lotte, you are clever, beautiful, kind, and generous, and I love you for it, but we live in the twentieth century."

She sulked, pouted, looked beautiful, but did not answer. Then Trevor added in self-justification, "Lotte, I put my job at risk for this widow and her kids. She offered two thousand and I took it for one. Isn't that enough charity? Doggone it, isn't that enough?"

Now Lotte took alarm. "Enough? More than enough. Golly, you did more good than you realize." She kissed his cheek in appreciation. "Tell me you love me," she whispered. He did. It cleared the air.

"I wanted your approval, Lotte," Trevor acknowledged. In fact, he wanted it so badly that he decided to squeeze out the last dollop, so he continued, "But, what more have I done? I thought this decision through very carefully."

"The widow's story would embarrass Roosevelt if it got out," Lotte said.

Her observation made Trevor uneasy. He had voted for Theodore Roosevelt in 1912 because Roosevelt had made a reforming governor, but Lotte did not share all of Trevor's political views. She supported votes for women, and had applauded when Alice Paul's supporters chained themselves to the White House fence and were dragged to jail in unladylike postures. Trevor thought that women voters would complicate family life. He argued that families were stronger if wives left politics to their husbands, that if women voted, husbands and wives might disagree about the tariff, then quarrel and divorce. This argument could not change Lotte's mind, even though that very scenario played out constantly in their romance and was threatening to do so again at this very instant. Trevor did not want this discussion to turn political.

"I would not have accepted the widow's commission just to embarrass Roosevelt. He laughed cynically. "I'm being honest. Let's not discuss foreign policy, tootsie."

"Yes, Trevvy, but you oppose joining the war in Europe, and Roosevelt will drag us into it."

Too late—the political cat was out of the bag. Trevor would have to respond. "Roosevelt says war is inevitable. We need to be prepared."

"Berlin thinks that Roosevelt means to drag us into the European war. A diplomat told uncle Oskar." Lotte's uncle, Oskar Schlegel, was a man of importance in the St. Louis German community where he frequently met visiting diplomats and learned from them what insiders were saying in Berlin. He passed his information and his opinions along to his favorite niece.

"Tell your uncle that Woodrow Wilson is president, not Roosevelt."

"Berlin mistrusts Wilson too," Lotte protested.

Trevor ignored her comment and completed his own thought. "Were it not for the plight of the widow and those fatherless children, I would not have taken the Albi case. I'd never have accepted that risk, no matter the war in Europe, Teddy Roosevelt's saber rattling, or a thousand bucks.

If I lose the appeal, I'll have risked my job for nothing. Is that terribly uncharitable? Give me some credit, won't you?"

"What a grouchy old bear you are," Lotte said, plopping herself into his lap, and his walls came a-tumbling down.

CHAPTER 4

SEEKING THE TOOTH FAIRY

Two and a half weeks later, Trevor Howells sat as petitioner in front of a coroner's desk located in the Criminal Courts Building off Franklin Street. On the other side of that desk was Dr. Gérard Gelb, a deputy coroner of Manhattan County. A pallid man with bushy white hair and tiny shriveled eyes entombed behind thick glasses, Gelb spoke with a trace of a French accent. He wore a doctor's white coat. He had soft, white hands with extravagantly long fingers that knew how to dismember a corpse. "So, Mr. Howells, you are here on behalf of the Metropolitan Life Insurance Company?" Gelb coughed, awaiting a reply.

"No, Doctor, I am here to rectify an injustice."

"And what was that?"

"The suicide verdict that the coroner's office registered after its inquiry into the death of Joseph Albi."

"It's unusual to have an insurance investigator contest a verdict of suicide."

"I represent the widow, not Metropolitan Life."

Dr. Gelb leaned forward in his chair and placed both hands palm down on his desk. He puffed out his lower lip, and gazed intently at Trevor. Resentment flared in his eyes. "I hope you are not suggesting an impropriety."

This was a dangerous start. The ghoulish doctor evidently smelled an imputation of corruption in his notoriously corrupt bureau. Trevor rushed to brush aside that suspicion. "No, not at all, Doctor. The hearing's result was entirely justified, but there is new evidence. The decedent's wife withheld this evidence because it incriminates her husband, and she feared that his crime would invalidate his life insurance. Now that she understands that it does not, she asks to reopen the case by submitting the new evidence."

"Umm. I see." Gelb sat back, relieved. He fiddled with his pencil and stroked his thin chin. "It's a pity she was not represented by counsel or she would have known better. But what is this new evidence?" At this query, Trevor withdrew twin sheaves of paper from his black leather briefcase. He laid them parallel on the desk in front of Dr. Gelb.

"These documents explain that, six weeks prior to his death, the decedent, a stevedore, obtained secret information as a result of the burglary of a ship in New York Harbor. This ship was the ill-fated *Lusitania.*" The name appeared to shock Dr. Gelb. "Yes, sir, that very ship. The burglar and decedent, Joseph Albi, sold the stolen merchandise, which was one hundred sixty pounds of cordite explosive. However, the secret information he had acquired proved more valuable than the stolen explosive. This information incriminated others, and the decedent attempted to blackmail them."

"The *Lusitania*... a blackmailer. Well, this is getting enormously interesting." Dr. Gelb twisted his pencil in both hands, raised his eyebrows, and blinked his tiny eyes before dryly resuming. "The thieving stevedore was also a blackmailer... and?"

"The decedent's enemies had a motive to kill him."

"And what was the motive?"

"To silence a blackmailer."

"The blackmailing decedent had an enemy?" Dr. Gelb tilted his head to one side as if to deprecate the value of such evidence, an intent that was also clear in his nasal voice. "Who was this enemy?"

"*Enemies,* Doctor. Among them was the Cunard Steamship Line, which appealed the original verdict of accidental death. The risk here is murder declared a suicide on the motion of the murderer."

Shaking his head, Dr. Gelb waved a pale hand, signaling impatience. "Just a minute, Mr. Howells. The Cunard Line obviously did not wish financial responsibility for the accidental death of an employee. We knew that when we reopened the case at their behest. This is not new evidence. What's more, that financial interest does not make Cunard either an enemy of the employee or capable of murder."

"I agree, sir. This evidence does not prove Cunard murdered Albi. Nonetheless, Cunard had a motive to do so."

"Motive is insufficient. You must also show capability, intent, and, if possible, performance."

"I realize that, Doctor. This unusual case is about more than insurance. You need to hear the whole story. Albi's information was of vast political importance. It bears on what was really in the *Lusitania*'s cargo hold. This wasn't a routine burglary, and it was not about a larcenous husband. War and peace were at stake. Whole nations were affected. A murder is quite plausible under these circumstances."

"And these so-called enemies of the decedent, were they capable of murder, or did they include only his wife and the parson?" Dr. Gelb smiled at his little joke.

Trevor smiled back, acknowledging the quip and the legal point it conveyed. "Yes, the suspects were capable of murder."

"Well, let us get to the bottom of this. Exactly who was the homicidal *enemy?*" Dr. Gelb's chin rested on his hand, and his elbow on the table.

"Again, *enemies,* Doctor." Trevor mentioned the interest of the Socialist Party in the decedent's documentary evidence, but averred that he did not think the Socialist Party belonged on the enemies list. Both the British Admiralty and the Cunard Line, however, had a motive for wishing to suppress eyewitness testimony regarding munitions secretly onboard the doomed ocean liner. Paul Kelly's gang was also suspect. In the aftermath of the *Lusitania* disaster, they would not want an investigation of waterfront pilferage. It was unnecessary, in Trevor's cheerful estimation, to ascertain which enemy had murdered Albi. Rather, establishing that Albi was a blackmailer who had many enemies hugely strengthened the possibility of foul play; and this possibility alone would justify a coroner's verdict of "probable homicide" or at least "cause of death unknown" rather than suicide. Either verdict would then require referral to the police, reopening the case. Either verdict would permit Mrs. Albi to receive the life insurance payment for her husband, as well as the right to have her husband's remains interred in consecrated ground. "That's my case," Trevor concluded with a sheepish grin.

Fingertips together, Dr. Gelb studied the ceiling fan, then his black shoes, and finally conceded that the enmity of Paul Kelly's gang might have represented a threat to the decedent's life, given the gang's reputation for mayhem, but he did not think the police would regard either the Cunard Line or the British government in the same manner. Why not accuse the pope?" he inquired with a sardonic smile. "The Catholic Church refused to bury the man; maybe the pontiff ordered the murder. You're fishing, Mr. Howells. And why did you exclude the Socialist Party?"

Trevor smiled benignly, still hopeful that he could find a heart of gold in Dr. Gelb. "The socialists' interest in Albi did not imply murder. If I wanted a fishing expedition, I would have included them."

Satisfied, Dr. Gelb took a new direction. "What proof is there in these documents or anywhere else that the decedent had blackmailed any of these agents?" Gelb's question required Trevor to explain the confidential information Joe Albi had inadvertently obtained in the course of what was supposed to have been a petty theft. Trevor showed Dr. Gelb the shipping labels, interior and exterior. He read aloud portions of Albi's three-page notarized affidavit. If the *Lusitania* carried military explosives, as Albi alleged, then Cunard's management violated US law when it knowingly permitted civilians to sail into a war zone on a military vessel belonging to a belligerent power.

Dr. Gelb objected. "The *Lusitania* was a passenger liner."

"A passenger liner in peacetime, yes, but under British law a military vessel in time of war."

"Oh, is that so? I shall confirm the detail, although I am not sure it matters. But please continue." Sitting back, Dr. Gelb folded his hands in front of him.

"Doctor, if the Cunard Line shipped explosives aboard the *Lusitania,* it would invalidate the ship's insurance. Cunard would be liable for damages to the survivors as well as to the families of the drowned. These damages alone would bankrupt the company, but they would also get no compensation for the lost ship."

Dr. Gelb smiled without commitment, licensing Trevor to continue. "Winston Churchill, boss of the Royal Navy, declared to the world that the *Lusitania* carried no explosives. Would he want to be proven a liar?"

Dr. Gelb shrugged, and then wobbled his head in mild disagreement. "President Wilson agrees with Churchill."

"Yes, President Wilson has accepted the British view."

Dr. Gelb interrupted his explanation. "And you accept the German view?"

"Not exactly. I am merely pointing out that Albi's documents and his eyewitness testimony support it. If the ship really carried munitions—"

Gelb interrupted him again. "If this secret testimony came to public attention, the Germans would very much enjoy it," mused Dr. Gelb. "Isn't that correct?"

"Yes, Doctor, they undoubtedly would, and that confers on supporters of Britain a motive to silence the decedent." Trevor then called Dr. Gelb's attention to the ship's manifest that Joe Albi had clipped from *The New York Times.* The document showed 217,000 pounds of cheese in the ship's cargo hold. Albi claimed to have stolen 160 pounds of cheese, and it was plausible that the remaining cheese had also been cordite explosive. Possibly tons of guncotton exploded when the torpedo struck. The resulting huge explosion would explain why the giant liner sank in only eighteen minutes.

"All right. It's a complex and troubling story," Dr. Gelb conceded when Trevor had finished, "and now I agree that Mr. Albi's testimony regarding the stolen cheese might pose a problem for various parties. The decedent may also have been a blackmailer. Murder is always a possibility when blackmailers die. I take it this summarizes your case." Then eyes glittering, Dr. Gelb waved a bony finger in the air and returned to an earlier point. "I mentioned the pope in jest, but in all candor, I do not see why you have not added President Wilson to your list of Albi's enemies. Wouldn't Wilson's truthfulness also be impugned by the evidence Albi discovered?"

"Quite possibly," replied Trevor, uncertain where Gelb's expedition was heading, and reluctant to add another enemy to his list. "But I do not believe the president capable of murder." It was a judgment he would later recall in disbelief, but the patriotic sentiment sounded right at the time.

Ignoring it, Dr. Gelb returned to the appeal. "But, ahem, you have shown that the decedent did not lack for enemies. Adding another is immaterial. I get the point. So, now, please explain what is in these documents you presented?"

"These documents contain Joseph Albi's notarized affidavit, which tells his story in his own words, plus shipping labels that he detached from the four crates he stole from the *Lusitania.* The widow is also available to testify regarding what her husband told her."

Dr. Gelb grimaced. "There is no more evidence?"

"That copy of the ship's manifest, which Albi clipped from the newspaper."

"Then this here on my desk is all the evidence you are submitting, plus the willingness of the widow to testify?" Trevor nodded agreement. "Although the evidence is slender, the enormity of the issues requires me to take the case under advisement." Dr. Gelb evidently expected a display of gratitude at his forbearance. Trevor bowed his head in humble acknowledgment of the doctor's generosity. "I shall review the evidence and discuss the case with Howard Deliver. We will summon you within two weeks on this matter. Can we reach you by telephone?"

"I prefer that you send a postcard to my home address, because my office telephone is for company use. Thank you for listening, Doctor." Trevor began to close his briefcase.

Dr. Gelb turned to him, a somewhat pained expression on his pallid face. "May I ask, Mr. Howells, are you pro-German?"

Trevor snorted. "No, Doctor, I am of Welsh descent, but my political sympathies are immaterial. The only question is whether there are grounds for supposing that Joseph Albi may have been a victim of foul play."

"Quite right. I am sorry I asked, but the political climate is so heated now. Others would ask if I did not." Dr. Gelb placed the documents in a filing cabinet. He nodded a curt goodbye. Trevor picked up his straw hat and left. Including transportation time, and waiting, his entire presentation to Gelb had only taken two hours. He felt hopeful.

Two weeks later a postcard was delivered to Trevor's residence mailbox. It contained a hand-written message, "Please call for appointment," and an office telephone number for Dr. Gelb.

When Trevor reentered Dr. Gelb's office a week later, right on time for the appointment, he was introduced to Howard Deliver, the deputy chief coroner. Deliver was a florid man, broad in the beam, whose red-veined nose suggested a drinker. It was hard to imagine him carving cadavers, a task that suited Dr. Gelb's thin fingers. Trevor had met the deputy before on company business, and knew that Deliver owed his job to the Tammany Hall political machine. Although medically incompetent, Mr. Deliver could overrule Dr. Gelb, and was rumored to do so when bribed. Possibly Francine Albi had found the crooked politician she needed!

"We recalled you," Dr. Gelb explained, "because we have questions about your motion. The documents you submitted indicate that Joseph Albi, having stolen cheese from the *Lusitania,* found munitions in the crates and then created an affidavit to the fact. Albi was a burglar. Why would a criminal prepare a certified confession of his crime?"

"Doctor, that bears on Albi's decision to blackmail a buyer who represented the Cunard Steamship Line."

"What is the name of this buyer?"

"George V. Rex."

Howard Deliver's mouth dropped open. "George V. Rex? Excuse me, but isn't that King George the Fifth of England?" he scoffed. Deliver looked in exaggerated dismay at Dr. Gelb, who quietly appreciated the jest in a Gothic way.

"It may not be the man's true name," Trevor conceded, embarrassed that he had not detected the fraud.

"And we thought that King George resided in Buckingham Palace," sneered Deliver.

Ignoring the mockery, Trevor proceeded deadpan. "I have been unable to locate this man. I have no idea of his true name much less his address." Actually, Trevor had made no attempt to locate the buyer. This was not, after all, to be a full-scale investigation, but he wanted to give the impression of thoroughness.

"Is this Englishman still alive?"

"I do not know."

"Did he ever exist?"

"I am assured that he did."

"Let me summarize: You cannot find him; you don't know his name or address; and you don't know whether he exists or whether he ever existed. In that case," Deliver continued merrily, his girth and bulbous nose shaking in synchronicity, "what is the difference between George V. Rex and the tooth fairy? You certainly cannot inquire into his motive, and neither can you prove that he made any offer of money to Albi, nor can you subpoena him for cross-examination. For all you know George Rex is a Buddhist monk who wouldn't hurt a fly. And we find no proof in any document of yours that the decedent felt his life was in danger. He did not say so in his affidavit, and neither did he mention the mysterious Englishman."

"Mrs. Albi claims that her husband wrote the affidavit because he feared for his life, and hoped a second copy of his affidavit, the document you have, would protect it. But no, the document does not so state. It doesn't mention Rex either."

"If we declared someone a victim of foul play just because he may have had enemies, well, would anyone in New York City fail to meet that liberal standard?" Deliver guffawed at his own joke, and looked at Gelb for approval. Tiny eyes glinting, Gelb joined his merriment. Ha-has passed around the table as Trevor too joined the cynical chorus, hoping to improve the dreadful rapport he sensed in the room. "We need to see threatening letters or hear witnesses who heard threats, and you offer none."

"Albi told his wife of his fears."

Dr. Gelb folded his hands and smiled wanly. "A widow has a financial motive to find threats that antedate her husband's suicide, possibly even inventing a mysterious Englishman, and no one can validate her memory." Gelb handed back the documents that Trevor had earlier given him, signaling the end to this interview. Leaving the documents on the desk in front of him, Trevor played his last card.

"The evidence before you includes mailing labels that Albi stripped from the crates he opened. The labels identify the contents as cordite, produced by the DuPont Company in Maryland, and addressed to a mailbox in Liverpool. How would a stevedore get these labels?"

"You are not serious," snapped Dr. Gelb. "A dishonest stevedore has many opportunities to strip labels from crates. Who's to say these labels were found on crates in the hold of the *Lusitania?* You would need to prove that, Mr. Howells, and you cannot." Trevor was preparing to object that he might well prove it. Without letting Trevor reply, however, Deliver jumped into the discussion.

"Look here, Howells, we could not admit this evidence even in a routine case, but this case makes sensational claims about concealed munitions on the *Lusitania.* This is a politically explosive situation." Turning to Gelb, Deliver added, with a grin, "No pun intended."

"Very apt, nonetheless," intoned Gelb, thin lips extended in what passed for his smile.

Then Deliver returned to the attack. "Why would someone appeal this case on such flimsy grounds?" He paused as if awaiting a reply, but the question had been rhetorical, and he continued without an answer. "Your obvious intention is to raise doubt regarding the *Lusitania's* cargo and to excuse the German submarine that performed this inhumane and nefarious act."

"I agree that the act was inhumane and nefarious."

"You should know as well," Dr. Gelb interjected hotly, "that my sisters in Belgium have forwarded accounts of German atrocities. They deport workers to factories in Germany, shoot civilians and nurses, rape nuns, and spit babies on bayonets. The village of Louvain was razed to the ground. It's outrageous, barbaric, and unworthy of a civilized country."

"So you see," said Deliver, recovering direction of the conversation, "were we to admit your so-called evidence, which is inadequate on its face, we would also be suspected of pro-German sympathies. These may be *your* sympathies, and you are welcome to them, however contemptible we find them, but you will not receive a forum here to promote pro-German politics." Deliver glared at Trevor. Gelb sneered triumphantly. Checkmate. Further argument was hopeless. Trevor thanked the coroners, packed the documents into his briefcase, and politely took his leave. The mission had failed.

The next morning, Trevor mailed a letter to Francine Albi's Barrow Street residence. He informed her that he had made two attempts to persuade the coroners to reopen the case of her late husband but had completely failed. The coroners had read and rejected her documents, which he would return by mail. The coroners flatly refused to reconsider their verdict. If Mrs. Albi wished to proceed, she required an attorney. He recommended the firm of Howe and Hummel, frequent litigators before the coroner. Even if Howe and Hummel took the case, their fees would consume any insurance benefit she would obtain in the unlikely event of success. In Trevor's regretful estimation, the coroners were correct: Francine Albi's evidence would not support a judgment of possible homicide, and the political climate rendered it impossible even to suggest that the *Lusitania* had carried explosives. He regretfully washed his hands of her case, and wished her and her four fatherless children good luck.

When, a few days later, Francine Albi called him on the office telephone, tearfully begging him to try again, he politely declined. She insisted that her story was true. He replied that truth mattered little in wartime. The widow increased her offer. "Mr. Howells, I'll pay you ten thousand dollars for a changed verdict."

"Mrs. Albi, given the political climate, I cannot obtain a new verdict for you at any price. It's impossible. If you insist on an appeal, you will need attorneys." Privately, however, Trevor thought that he had risked two afternoons on this quixotic mission and that was as much time as he could invest in a futile case. Lotte had reluctantly accepted this sad conclusion. He was off the hook there. *It's a cruel world,* Trevor mused. *Too bad about her kids.* He had done what he could. His hands and conscience were clean, and his head clear of sentimental rubbish. Looking down at his desktop he saw new cases awaiting investigation, and Metropolitan Life was completely satisfied with the verdict in the Albi case. "Mrs. Albi, I will continue, of course, to be alert to any new leads that might enable you to reopen the case, but—"

Francine Albi had hung up in tears.

Trevor thought that was the end of the case, but it was not. Two hours later, still vaguely upset by the telephone conversation with Francine, he heard an unexpected knock on his office door. In walked a beefy man in a sweat-stained flannel shirt, bib overalls, a bushy beard, and dusty leather brogans. The man wore a battered wide-brimmed felt hat. It looked Western. Was this yokel lost? Apologizing for not having made an appointment, the visitor introduced himself as Ben Williams, representing the Socialist Party of America. The Socialist Party understood that Trevor Howells had documents that had once belonged to the late Joseph Albi.

"That's correct," Trevor replied. "And so?"

"We'd very much like to acquire those documents," said Williams. "We can pay."

CHAPTER 5

A PAWN'S LIFE

"PLEASE HAVE A SEAT, Mr. Williams." Trevor motioned to an oak armchair in front of his desk. Williams sat, stretched his legs, extracted a cigarette paper from a wrapper, pulled a pouch of tobacco from his overalls, pinched tobacco along the open paper, rolled it with his left hand, then sealed it with his tongue. He ignited the cigarette with a wooden match struck on the sole of his boot, then expertly flipped the smoking matchstick into the wastebasket. The whole ceremony took thirty entertaining seconds. Williams took a big drag from his cigarette, exhaled, and politely offered to make a smoke for Trevor.

"I'm much too stingy to smoke. But you are free to do so."

The big man had not asked permission. Instead, he glanced around the room and frowned. "I prefer to chew, but you can't always find a spittoon in New York. I see you don't have one." Trevor pushed an ashtray in his direction. When they shook hands, Trevor noted the man's strong, callused grip, but the visitor's penetrating gaze, informed speech, and serious demeanor suggested a workingman of keen intelligence.

"Can we get down to business, Mr. Williams? I have a busy day. You are requesting access to documents that belonged to Joseph Albi, and you represent the Socialist Party? Do I understand that correctly?"

"You do" came the laconic reply.

"Joseph Albi is dead, a suicide. You were aware of that?"

"Yes, we are." Trevor noted his use of *we.* "But it wasn't suicide."

"How can you possibly know that?"

"Mr. Howells, you're an insurance investigator. Don't you know things that other people don't? An Englishman killed him. He works for the Cunard Steamship Line."

"Mrs. Albi called this man George V. Rex."

"A fake name."

"Obviously. What is his real name?"

"We don't know. They call him 'the Captain' or 'Captain P.'"

"A naval officer, then?"

"I reckon."

"All right, you don't know his real name, Mr. Williams, but perhaps you know his address?"

"Nope, and he don't know mine. I sleep better that way." Williams grinned.

Slightly puzzled, Trevor skipped to his next question. "You say Albi's death was a homicide. That conclusion disagrees with the coroner's judgment."

"Maybe Cunard fixed them. Anyway, who killed Albi isn't important. I was just flapping my gums about that. I'm here about his documents. We'd very much like to have them."

Trevor nodded acknowledgment, but also decided to find out what else Williams knew, so he casually returned to the original topic. "Possibly Kelly's gang murdered Albi. Did you consider that?"

Williams waved away the objection with a gesture that left a trail of blue smoke. "Doubt it. Paul Kelly wanted money from Albi. Cunard wanted silence."

"Perhaps Kelly was angry because Albi would not share the blackmail money."

Williams shook his shaggy head. "Would Kelly kill Albi before the money was delivered?" Trevor was unconvinced, but proceeded to the next suspect.

"Maybe the British Admiralty?" Trevor offered this suggestion thinking it implausible, but Williams chuckled in response and enthusiastically resumed.

"The British want to conceal the *Lusitania*'s cargo, that's true, but the Captain was the only person who'd talked to Albi, and the Captain works for Cunard."

"Cunard is a British company."

"Registry didn't matter. If Cunard packed illegal explosives into the *Lusitania,* their insurance wouldn't pay. The lawsuits would bankrupt the company."

Impressed with these deductions, but intentionally deadpan, Trevor decided to explore what more the Socialist Party knew. "Maybe you do not really want these documents. What do you think they contain?"

Williams paused, looked away briefly, and then, taking a long drag on his cigarette, thoughtfully spit a tobacco shred into limbo, and replied, "Right smart question for you to ask. Albi found military explosives in crates labeled 'cheese'. He'd stolen these crates from the *Lusitania.* There are shipping labels too. Is all that correct?"

"Yes, so far."

"Well, that's what we want to tell the American people. The *Lusitania* contained secret explosives, all disguised as cheese, all addressed to Great Britain. That's what exploded and sank the ship. Period. It's the simple truth, but the newspapers won't tell it. And we want to keep the USA out of the damned European war. Like they say, 'A rich man's war is a poor man's fight.'"

At this point, Trevor detected a slight discrepancy between Williams's story and what he had learned from Francine Albi. "Uh, Mr. Williams, it's not true that this Captain P was the only one to speak to Joseph Albi." Williams denied it, then rethought himself and acknowledged that of course he had spoken to Albi himself. But he meant that the Captain was the only *other* party who'd spoken to Albi. Trevor inquired what Williams had said to Albi, hoping to learn whether Williams's version agreed with what Francine Albi had told him.

"I offered to buy the affidavit and the shipping labels."

Correct so far, but Trevor decided to confirm another detail. "How much money did you offer?"

"Five thousand." This detail was also correct, and it confirmed the version that Francine Albi had offered, suggesting that Williams had actually talked to Joe Albi, but Trevor asked for another detail, inquiring what Albi had replied, and Williams got that right too. It now occurred to Trevor that the Socialist Party was in a position to do a very great favor for Francine Albi and her children.

"Mr. Williams, the coroner declined to reverse the verdict of suicide. Your testimony could change that. You met Joseph Albi. You know what he found on the *Lusitania.* You even have knowledge of this mysterious Captain. If you testified to the coroners, you might compel them to reverse their verdict. In that case, Albi's widow could collect her husband's life insurance. Your testimony might even attract press attention, enabling your party to get your message out. Why don't you do that?"

Williams flicked the ash from his cigarette, pursed his lips, and then looked directly at Trevor. "Sure, we sympathize with the widow, and, yes, we might get the story out that way." Williams snickered mysteriously. "Unfortunately, I can't testify. You see, I operate undercover. This is how I know about the Captain. I've encountered the skunk before. Employers have secret agents; the Captain is one, and the working class needs counteragents. I'm one. If I testify, my secret identity becomes public, as does the fact that the Socialist Party employs secret agents. Neither of these facts can become public. If alleged, they would be denied."

"But isn't publicizing these facts exactly your purpose?" Trevor protested again that the Albi case offered a superb opportunity to open the truth to the American public while benefiting the widow. It might even win public sympathy for the Socialist Party. "Possibly these advantages would compensate for the loss of your secret identity."

Ben Williams would not budge. "I wouldn't have a Chinaman's chance in court. Truth is more unpopular in wartime than a bastard at the family reunion."

Trevor smiled at the analogy, but urged his case again. "Then tell the police. You claim to know who murdered Albi. I assume you have some evidence. If so, the police will arrest the culprit, and Mrs. Albi will get her insurance money. If you cannot talk to the police, then ask some third party to deliver the proof to them."

"Sorry, that's impossible too," replied Williams, shaking his head side to side. Nothing, he declared with finality, could induce him to testify.

"Is that because you really have no evidence?" Trevor asked, suspicious now that his visitor was shifting the blame away from himself. *Maybe the widow was right. The socialists killed Albi. Maybe this man killed him.*

"I have no evidence that would convince the coroners without my testimony, and I can't testify." Williams smiled, took another drag, and stubbed out his cigarette on his boot. Trevor silently handed him the ashtray, into which he dropped the butt. That road had come to a dead end. Trevor reluctantly abandoned it. *So much for chivalry,* he thought. The widow was out of luck again. *Lotte will understand.*

"All right, Mr. Williams, let's try another direction: you cannot expose yourself in court, but you want Albi's documents. Is that right?"

"Yes. I can't surface, but if we leak the story to the press, backed up with the documents, the whole world will learn the truth about the *Lusitania.* This truth sinks the bosses' war plans instead of their ocean liners." Seeing that Trevor was not smiling, Williams added defensively, "No one's going to mourn the war plans either." The big man shook in silent mirth, savoring his own wit.

Trevor frowned. "So the welfare of Mrs. Albi and her children is of no importance?"

"Mr. Howells, they're important, but we're frying bigger fish. After we blow the story to the press, contributions will flow in, and Mrs. Albi will get some money—maybe more than the insurance would have paid, but preventing a war is more important than helping one family. Don't you agree?" Williams sat back in his chair and folded his arms in a gesture of certitude. He glanced confidently at the ceiling, then back at Trevor, awaiting a reply.

Trevor did not respond to his question. *I tried persuasion,* he thought, wondering what might now be salvaged. "I see your point. Mr. Williams, and I believe you did talk to Albi. You won't give testimony, and you want the documents. Let's talk business, then. I have the documents, and they are still for sale."

Williams nodded, smiled, and uncrossed his arms.

"What's your offer?" Trevor asked.

"Five thousand, same as we offered Albi."

"That's a lot of money."

"Your industry would call it a risk premium. I have a thousand bucks right here for a deposit." Williams pulled greenbacks from his back pocket, counted ten one-hundred-dollar bills, and held out a wad, inviting Trevor to take it. *The stupidest fish takes the bait first,* thought Trevor, who decided to ask some more questions. Much later, he regretted this hesitation.

"And do you mind telling me how the Socialist Party comes by so much money?" Addressed to a plainly attired workingman, this seemed a reasonable question.

"Union dues, pamphlet sales, and uh ... some wealthy donors. Socialism's a cause people care about."

"I must be discrete." Trevor looked away, and then looked back at Williams. Hint taken.

"Your employer never learns. We pay cash on the barrelhead." A cash offer was essential, but Trevor needed a clearer picture of the exact terms under which those socialist union dues would come to his client.

"What if the documents do not appear genuine?"

Williams did not hesitate. "We inspect them on the spot. If real, we pay; if not, we don't. Don't rush to the racetrack before you see the money." Williams chuckled, then, after blowing his nose into a red bandanna, continued, his thick forefinger now stabbing the desktop. "We already know the truth. We just lack proof." He paused, groping for the right formula. "We pay cash and carry, no refunds, no receipts, no questions, nobody the wiser. How's that?" Williams seemed eager to close the deal then and there.

Trevor was not ready, so he raised another issue. "Your terms are satisfactory, but what about this murderous Captain P? You mentioned a risk premium. Albi died while selling him these papers. If I sell you the documents, do I have to worry about the Captain?" This spur-of-the-moment question came as a lightning bolt to Trevor, who had not previously considered possible risk to himself from involvement in the Albi case.

The question did not stun the socialist. In fact, smiling bitterly, Williams seemed to welcome it. He prepared and lit another smoke, exhaled a blue cloud, extruded his lower lip, and responded slowly and in apparent candor. "Smart fellow! You figured it out. Right now, you have the documents. The Captain would kill you to prevent me from getting them. I'm cutting it straight. The Captain does not need the documents; he needs to prevent me getting them. What conclusion do you draw?" Williams cocked his head as if posing a riddle to a clever child.

"I don't like guessing games."

"Me neither, but you need to understand this: Sell me the documents, and the Captain becomes *my* lookout; keep them, and he's all yours."

Trevor froze, and then remarked drily, "Here's what actuaries call an unexpected hazard." His insurance training supplied a vocabulary that concealed his shock and confusion. Although a seasoned investigator accustomed to annoying people and experiencing their resentment, Trevor had never been the target of a professional assassin. He had undertaken this inquiry from a chivalrous concern to protect a widow and her children, a remote possibility of financial gain, a desire to please Lotte, and because he risked only a few hours of his time. Risking his life had not been on the table when he took up the cause of justice for the widow. He inhaled deeply, exhaled, and drummed his fingers on the desktop, but, thanks to his professional training, his facial expression never changed.

"You make a good point, Mr. Williams." *Drum-drum-drum.* "I am a target for Captain P as long as I have the documents. Is that it?" *Drum-drum-drum.* Williams smoked, smiled, and nodded.

"'Fraid so." His icy assent suggested ruthlessness.

"And how about you? Would you kill me just as you killed Albi?" This was a wild accusation, but Trevor wanted to assess the man's reaction. Trevor had persuaded Francine Albi that the socialists had not killed her husband, but now he suspected that he might have been wrong.

"No, I– we did not kill Albi. We wanted him squawking to the newspapers. I don't propose to kill you either. Hell, I could break your neck right now. You couldn't stop me." Williams's glittering eyes hinted momentarily at a talent for mayhem. Then the big man turned on the folksy charm. "I'm offering you serious money, mister. Take it while the taking's good."

Although he'd spoken hypothetically and then retracted, Williams had threatened to break his neck. Trevor couldn't ignore that. Nodding in an acquiescent manner, and without displaying alarm, he gently removed his Colt from a drawer and placed it on the desktop. He realized uneasily that the cause of justice for Francine Albi had just become the sword of justice. His camouflage smile now vanished. Trevor glared defiantly at Williams.

"Wrong, Mr. Williams. You couldn't break my neck, and I don't like threats. But I heard you: As long as I have the documents, I am a target, right?" Unfazed, the big man grinned, nodded, and waved his smoking cigarette in easy assent. "Unfortunately, Mrs. Albi owns the documents. She loaned them to me for the appeal. I need her permission to sell them."

"That's true, but time matters. The Captain could show—"

Trevor interrupted. "I see no reason why she wouldn't sell them now that the coroner has rejected her appeal, so I will get her answer right away. Can you come back to my office the day after tomorrow? If she approves, I will sell you the documents then."

"Take my deposit now." Williams held out the wad of greenbacks.

"No, Mr. Williams. That would obligate me, and Mrs. Albi might decline permission."

Williams sat back, disappointed. "Sure, we can wait, but I advise you to act fast. You have become," Williams guffawed, "a red pawn in the class struggle, and the white queen kills you on the next move. Play chess? Then you know that a pawn's life depends on protection by his friends."

"But a single pawn can win the game!"

"That's why pawns get protection. We should play sometime. I'm always looking for a strong opponent, and you seem a right smart fellow. By the way, how smart do you vote?"

"I voted for Roosevelt in 1912."

"Why the hell did you do that?" Williams's growled in irritation.

"He was an effective police commissioner and governor."

"Poor reasons, if you don't mind my opinion. But, let me ask you, Mr. Howells, now that you know that the *Lusitania* carried munitions, would you vote for Roosevelt again? I hope you say no."

"Why?"

"We're bettin' five thousand dollars that when voters learn what you already know they won't support blustering, war-minded politicians like Roosevelt."

"I don't want the USA to fight Europe's war," Trevor replied, "but for me personally, this project has meant helping a widow obtain justice. Just like the coroners, you inject politics into what should be a simple question of justice. It amazes me that nobody cares about simple justice."

"You can't avoid the politics in a case like this. Wilson versus Roosevelt is Tweedledee versus Tweedledum. Only the socialists oppose the capitalists' war plans. Did you know that?" Trevor indicated that he did not. "Say, what do you know about socialism?"

"What does it matter? I am representing Albi's widow in an insurance case. That's all. Preventing war is not my problem, and neither is peddling socialism. They're your problems."

"True, your politics don't matter as long as you're selling, but that overfed, pompous windbag, Teddy Roosevelt, he'd sell his grandmother to a glue factory rather than sell us this information."

"And what if I declined to sell?" Trevor tried to look curious rather than alarmed.

"Well, we have to get those documents one way or another," said

Williams, leaving the alternative methods unstated. Hearing this candid avowal, Trevor was glad that his revolver was on the table. Chuckling, and indifferent to Trevor's studied non-response, Williams continued, "But there's an amusing irony. Although you know nothing about us, the Socialist Party stands between you and Captain P, don't you see?" Trevor indicated that he did.

"Of course, we hope the Captain does not know you have the documents."

"Why would he?" Another unforeseen hazard threatened Trevor's expectation of life.

"We have friends in city hall. The Captain also has friends there," then grudgingly, "many friends. By the way, in case you meet him, the Captain is tall, about six feet one inches, a hundred and ninety pounds, and blonde. He sports a military moustache, sometimes wears a monocle, right eye, and he favors tailor-made suits from London. He enjoys French food and French wine, and he'll kick you in the balls when you're shaking his hand. They pay him well too. Myself, I eat beans and rice in pork fat, and lucky to get it four days a week. Am I skinning the wrong mules?" His cheerful query unanswered, the big man continued. "Keep a sharp lookout. Pack that Colt all the time. The Captain might offer you money, but he don't pay his bills. Don't be fooled by the upper-class English patter. See you Wednesday, and good luck to you." Williams then donned his weather-beaten hat and departed, waving a cheerful goodbye from the door.

In the reek of the big man's lingering cigarette smoke, Trevor found his heartbeat elevated. Determined to calm down, he methodically checked his revolver's cylinder, then returned the loaded gun to its drawer. Sitting back, he breathed deeply and took stock. The socialists expected to acquire the documents by purchase. But suppose the Captain offered more money! It would be in his client's interest to accept the higher offer, and then tell the socialists to jump in the lake. Williams did not say that the socialists would never kill him. In fact, reflecting on it, Trevor concluded that Williams had implied that, if frustrated, they might. What was more, according to Williams, the Captain had contacts in city hall. If the socialists knew Trevor had the Albi documents, the Captain must have learned too, in which case he would come looking for them. If Trevor sold the documents to the socialists, the Captain might kill him in the belief that he still had them. If he sold them to the Captain, the socialists might kill him in retribution. It was not a simple situation. Trevor regretted the moment of weakness in which he had taken up the cause of justice for Francine Albi.

After ten minutes' concentrated thought, Trevor concluded that the safest course was to return the documents to Francine Albi at once. Prior to meeting Williams, he had intended to return them to her by mail. If he sent them back, wished her luck, and washed his hands of her problems, she would become their possessor. The Captain might stalk her. From the point of view of personal risk reduction, immediately returning the documents to Francine Albi was the safest way out of Trevor's predicament. Business logic said that this was what he should do. *But what a rotten trick to play on a widow with children!* Trevor did not hesitate. *No. I can't do that.* He had imprudently accepted another risk without financial compensation.

The Metropolitan Life Insurance Company occupied the entire sixth floor of the sleekly modern Flatiron Building, a triangular skyscraper wedged between 23rd Street, Broadway, and Fifth Avenue. The prestige address brought business that justified the building's high rent. Leaving his office after closing time, Trevor descended six floors in the wire-cage elevator, thanked the negro operator, and to save bus fare walked south on Broadway toward Barrow Street. It was a thirty-minute stroll on a warm September evening.

Trevor bought a hot knish from a street vendor for five cents, planning to eat it as he walked, but the knish was cold. Trevor complained to the vendor, a tiny man with bushy eyebrows and furtive eyes. The man took back the knish, hefted it in one grubby hand, smelled it, and handed it back, declaring that its temperature was perfect.

"But it's cold" protested Trevor, "and you advertise hot knishes."

This knish is "exactly the right temperature," the vendor insisted. "Any hotter would burn customers' hands." He then offered to sell Trevor two more knishes for another five cents. "No, thanks. I just want my nickel back," said Trevor. Unfortunately, inasmuch as Trevor had already taken a bite, the vendor announced, no refund was possible. "This is outrageous," Trevor fumed. "You're advertising hot knishes, selling cold ones, and you won't refund money you obtain under false pretenses."

Assuming his full height, the diminutive vendor replied that he did not tell Trevor how to run his business, and would be obliged if Trevor would reciprocate the courtesy. Quite annoyed at the man's temerity, Trevor prepared a nasty reply, then, recalling his dialogue with Walter LaFarge, he simply handed the partially consumed knish back to the quarrelsome vendor and walked on through Washington Square Park. Behind him, the vendor resumed chanting, "Hot knishes, hot knishes."

Francine Albi and her four children lived on the top floor of a crowded tenement in Greenwich Village's Little Italy. Low-wattage globes feebly illuminated the narrow corridors. Silverfish and cockroaches patrolled the dark corners. Trevor ascended the creaking stairs, smelling the neighbors' garlic-enhanced dinners on each floor, and listening to their voices, some speaking Italian, some English. He knocked finally on Francine Albi's flimsy door. A child answered, then, when asked for her mother, cried "Mommee," the other three children taking up the call. Their shrill cries brought Francine from the kitchen.

The family slept and ate in one room; the apartment's sink and gas range were in the other. The water closet, shared with neighbors, was in the hall. Vulgar sounds announced a current user. Francine Albi wore a stained apron and carried a large spoon. Her abundant black hair, previously worn up in the Gibson fashion, was now down and disheveled.

Gibson pompadours made no sense for working women. Francine did not act surprised to see Trevor, but it was clear that he had arrived at an inconvenient moment. After working ten hours in a poorly ventilated loft, Francine was now putting dinner on the table for her children. It looked like a meatball soup with noodles.

Trevor excused himself for the unexpected visit, but explained he had urgent business. The hand with the big spoon went to Francine Albi's hip; the other hand to the back of her neck. Leaning against the doorframe, she was listening. "Mrs. Albi, I have your husband's documents, and can return them now if you like. Sorry, I could not make the coroner's appeal a success."

"You tried, thanks."

"But you should know that a buyer showed up after we talked on the telephone." Francine perked up. "He offers five thousand dollars for your husband's documents. They are useless now that the coroner has rejected your appeal. If you authorize it, I will sell the documents for you, taking twenty dollars as my per diem. If you decline, you may have the documents back now."

Turning away from Trevor, Francine Albi ordered Anthony to stop taking Maria's noodles. Then she turned back, eyes pensively narrowed. "Who's the buyer?"

"That socialist, Ben Williams."

"I could sell him the documents same as you," said Francine. Her words stung. She thought Trevor wanted her twenty dollars.

"You could, but Williams believes that your husband's murderer would kill again to keep Joe's story out of the newspapers. If you hold the documents, you might become his target. If I hold them, I am the target, and I assume that risk for my standard per diem."

Francine did not answer, but Trevor read her suspicion. He was not sure she had understood so he continued, "If you wish to sell them yourself, please take the documents now."

"Just leave them on the chair. I'd invite you to dinner, but there's nothing left to eat."

"Thanks, I had a bite." Then, changing the subject, Trevor pointed out, "If you wait for the socialist, hoping to make the sale yourself, Williams might vanish, whereas I expect to sell the documents to him for $5,000 in two days. Why put five thousand at risk to save twenty?"

"Why should he vanish?" Francine asked suspiciously.

"He said, 'take it while the taking's good,' and he's your only customer. Oh, I assume you would not approve a sale to the Englishman. Is that right?" This inquiry had the effect of a blow. Francine reeled back a half step.

"That English mug's still out there?" she hissed. Then, recovering, "He comes here… I kill him."

"He might kill you first, and," Trevor hesitated, "your children."

Astounded at this horrifying threat, Francine sat down, coughed, and then rasped, "No matter. I wouldn't sell dog pee to that guy."

"We don't know for sure that the Englishman did it, but I accept your decision. Now let me handle this sale for you, getting five thousand dollars from the socialists and rejecting any offer the Englishman makes. The transaction should happen the day after tomorrow." A commotion arose at the dinner table. Francine lightly tapped the nearest boy with her spoon.

"Thomas, sit. You're too big to behave like a baby."

Thomas sat. The children scraped their empty bowls with spoons, and then looked up in hope of refills.

"Any more?" the biggest asked.

"Tomorrow's breakfast will be bigger," Francine assured them. "Now clear the table." Then she turned back to Trevor, still standing in the doorway. "You mean the Englishman might offer to buy the documents, then kill me and the kids, and take the affidavit? And the socialist might disappear. That's what you're saying, isn't it?"

"I am afraid so. If you retain the papers, you might sell them, but you would assume two huge risks."

Instead of responding, Francine turned away and issued a decree to her children. "Anthony, make sure the others wash their bowls. You wash the big pot." Then she turned back to Trevor. "So, if I take back the documents, I run two risks? No sale or a buyer who kills me, or both?"

"Yes, that is the risk."

"All right, Mr. Howells, dip your beak. Now, when do I get paid? The food you see on the table is all there is. I'm out of money."

"I don't see any food on the table."

"There *is* none. And the breakfast larder is empty. I lied."

"Mrs. Albi, I can bring the money Thursday, but let's say Friday at six thirty just to give me some latitude. Agreed?"

"Come back Friday. Bring cash. Uh, by the way, could you advance me a fin?" Trevor took $5 out of his wallet. Francine stuffed it into an apron pocket. Then she handed back the documents, remarking, "That's now the only copy of Joe's affidavit."

"Well, I assumed so," said Trevor, but in truth he was taken aback by another loose end. He had not inquired whether there might be a third. That was an oversight.

"I made two copies of Joe's affidavit. One was hidden in the library of the St. Anthony of Padua Church. The other we kept under the Bible on the shelf behind me. When Joe died, the copy under the Bible was missing. I gave you the copy he stored in the church. Probably whoever killed him took the other copy."

"That seems likely." Trevor acknowledged, then continued, "And I suspect that Joseph Albi's murderer took the affidavit without realizing that you held a second copy. However, because I used that copy at the coroner's office, the Captain might come looking for it just as did the socialist." When the children heard the stranger speak their father's name, they hushed, looking worried, as if aware that incomprehensible events of immense moment were taking place.

"Who's the Captain?" Francine asked.

"Didn't I explain? George V. Rex is not the Englishman's real name. His employers call him the Captain. It's a code name."

"Whose code?" Francine asked. Trevor did not know. Francine looked Trevor up and down, suspiciously assessing his sincerity. "I have to take your offer," she grimaced. "I support four children, and, thanks to the 'company that cares' I get no insurance money. Those stinkers owe me twenty grand and now I beg for five bucks! But I have to take it because if something happens to me, these kids are orphans." She shrugged, and her lower lip briefly protruded, but this time she could not cry.

"I understand your bitterness. May I call you Francine?" She gave permission. "But don't blame me. I did more than you know."

"Yeah, what?" Her dubiety offended Trevor. He wanted her to trust and like him.

"I begged Williams to testify. The coroner would have changed the verdict. You would have gotten you the full insurance benefit. Unfortunately, he refused."

"Another selfish pig," Francine fumed. "But that was nice of you to try, Trevor. Are you kids washing the dishes? " A fragmented chorus of "Yes, Mommees" responded from the adjacent room. Francine turned back to Trevor. "I have to rely on Anthony to bring the others to school and back. When I'm working, they play in the street, and the neighbors watch them. If there was a problem, Mrs. Scarpone would call the factory from the corner store. It's out of kindness. I can't pay her." Francine ruefully displayed empty palms.

Surprised at her frankness, Trevor expressed regret that she could not take personal care of her children now. "That's not all," Francine continued. "When Anthony finishes sixth grade, he must go to work. We need the money."

"My mother worked in a factory too. I had to leave school at fifteen for the same reason."

"How old were you when your father died?" asked Francine sympathetically.

"He didn't die. I say he did to avoid the shame. He disappeared. I was twelve. Mother raised my brother and me. To help out, we earned money. I had a newspaper route. My brother delivered for a shoe-repair shop. He owns it now. My mother learned to guard every penny. So did I, and I still do. Once you learn how, you never forget."

"Trevor, your story's interesting. You're a real nice fellow too, but, like you say, I have to think about money. You owe me five grand. Could you advance me another fin?" Trevor extracted another five from his wallet, closed his briefcase, and opened the door to the gloomy, fetid hallway. He had an unhappy thought. *Now Francine says I owe her $5,000.* "You have the documents now. Be careful." Francine brushed his cheek with her right hand and closed her door. Trevor heard it latch.

An hour later, Francine's door opened again, and she emerged, wearing a triangular black kerchief around her head, a shapeless ankle-length black dress, high-button flat shoes, and a black lace shawl around her shoulders. She carried a mesh shopping bag. As she descended the stoop in front of her tenement, lounging youths greeted her by name and moved aside. At the street level, Francine looked both ways as though expecting someone, then turned left on Barrow Street and left again onto Bleecker, Little Italy's main shopping thoroughfare. Although it was now eight o'clock in the evening, and the daylight was fading, Bleecker Street was astir with commerce. Both sides of the street were lined with pushcarts and horse-drawn wagons from which vendors hawked vegetables, meats, fish, bread, pasta, wine, and every other necessity of daily life. Above the street, laundry fluttered from transverse clotheslines. They began at the second story and continued for six stories above, giving the whole street the festive appearance of a flag-bedecked medieval town, but on the street level, children ducked hither and yon among overflowing garbage cans, and, to the unavailing displeasure of their elders, threw horse apples at each other.

Francine stopped at several wagons, and, using Trevor's fin, bought bananas, apples, bread, and black tea for the next morning's breakfast. Then she paused in front of a wine shop, checked the window display, and went inside. She came out with a bottle of pinot grigio in her mesh bag. Then, instead of returning home with her purchases, Francine continued along Bleecker Street, turned left onto Cornelia Street, and stopped in front of number 80, a conventional five-story tenement that displayed the usual tattered laundry hanging from windows, and desolate flowerpots on iron fire escapes. The young men lazing in front of this house did not recognize her, so they flamboyantly kissed their fingers as she climbed the stoop. On the third floor, a solid black door bore the name ALBERT CASTAGNO on a brass plate. Francine knocked. A muscular man clad in a sleeveless undershirt and tight corduroy pants opened the door and greeted her with a kiss. Francine entered his apartment.

CHAPTER 6

THE DECOY

BACK AT HIS DESK the next morning, Trevor extracted Joe Albi's documents from his briefcase, and typed a verbatim copy of the affidavit. He could not entrust this task to the typing pool. At the bottom of his copy, Trevor listed the delivery address and serial numbers that he recorded from the shipping labels. He could not duplicate the notary's seal, but he could, using a pencil eraser and pen nib, faintly impress the embossed seal onto the typed duplicate. Finally, he forged the signature of the notary onto the typed document. Anyone who examined the copy in detail could easily detect the forgery, but the copy would enable the socialists to evaluate the documents without subjecting Trevor to the risk of theft or murder. A decoy might have saved Albi's life, and it took only an hour to complete.

Rising from his desk, Trevor walked down the hall to the offices that housed the company's top management. Two secretaries serviced four vice presidents. One of these secretaries was Lotte Maria Schlegel, who beat out "shave and a haircut, two bits" on her typewriter as Trevor approached. That was his fanfare of trumpets. Secretarial work was usually a man's job in 1915, but Winthrop J. Tolson preferred to employ women as secretaries because he could pay them less than men. To assure decorum and efficiency, Tolson forbade office romances, and monitored female employees to prevent flirtation. His intrusive and irritating policies reminded office wits of the comic emperor in Gilbert and Sullivan's *The Mikado,* so Tolson was universally known on the sixth floor as "the Emperor of Japan," or sometimes "the skinflint emperor."

A blue-eyed blonde woman of medium height and slender build with a dimpled chin, curly hair, and high cheekbones, Lotte Maria Schlegel had grown up in the German community of St. Louis, and spoke German fluently. Her father was a homeopathic physician; her mother, a disgraced aristocrat widely read, had taught her daughter to love literature. Having completed a commercial curriculum in the public high school, Lotte knew English grammar and Pittman shorthand. She could type forty-five words per minute, understood basic accounting, took initiative on the telephone, and was generally good at her job, which she performed for half of what a male secretary would have cost the company. She was value for the money, and Tolson knew it, but Lotte understood that, in addition to doing her job well, she had to manage her attractiveness. Just as Tolson feared, Metro's vice presidents relished the presence of a young and pretty woman seated in front of their door, and several hoped, the opportunity someday presenting, to broaden and deepen their relationship with Miss Schlegel. They suggested an after-hours rendezvous, and Lotte asked after their wives' health.

Keeping her job required Lotte to discourage the vice presidents without offending them. To this end, she wore her hair in a severe bun at work, made sure that her long-sleeved cotton blouse fit loosely over her plain skirt, and strictly avoided jewelry. She had also let it become known, through Catherine Donohue, a coworker, that she had a beau. Lotte never discussed details of this fictional sweetheart, codenamed Andrew, but Andrew kept Lotte "regrettably busy" when hopeful executives suggested a quiet tête-à-tête after business hours. In reality, Trevor Howells was Lotte's fiancé. They had met in the building's elevator sixteen months earlier, and their romance had progressed irresistibly. Lotte and Trevor understood, however, that Andrew deterred amorous bosses, whereas a fiancé within the firm would cost her job, so they had invented Andrew to keep their romance secret.

"Good morning, Miss Schlegel. Do you have a minute?" Shave and a haircut.

"I do."

Trevor now withdrew the Albi documents from his briefcase. They were wrapped in newspaper and tied with brown twine. "Please store this package." The request was not unusual. Within the company safe, Trevor had a cubby in which he stored papers. In theory, only Winthrop J. Tolson, Catherine Donohue, and Lotte Schlegel knew the combination of the safe. In reality, because of his romance with Lotte, Trevor knew it as well, but protocol demanded that he appear not to. Lotte politely accepted the documents, only raising an unobtrusive eyebrow to signal affection.

Later that evening, Trevor stood in Lotte's cramped Brooklyn kitchen watching her prepare *bierrocks,* a German pastry stuffed with onion, cabbage, and chopped beef. Lotte wore a French chef's apron, which hugged her figure, and, glancing up from time to time, she caught Trevor's eye and smiled. Trevor kissed her graceful neck from behind. Lotte had approved his effort to appeal the Albi decision, and was finally persuaded that money had not been the decisive factor in his generous endeavor. That mattered, because money-grubbing men offended her romantic soul. She also approved Trevor's decision to obtain Francine Albi's permission before selling the documents on her behalf. Trevor was anticipating an easy recital of his latest news.

"I told Mrs. Albi that she could sell the documents herself. I offered her the papers, and, Lottchen, at first she took them back."

"Why didn't you leave then? I hope you weren't angling for a per diem," Lotte said. Trevor smiled. This time he had the correct reply.

"Oh, no. If she took the documents, she risked becoming a target for her husband's murderer. I couldn't allow that."

"No, of course not." Leaving the meat to sizzle, Lotte threw her arms around Trevor's neck and kissed him, and he gratefully resumed his narrative as she hung there, one wary eye on the cast-iron skillet.

"I just explained the risk. She agreed that I should sell the documents to the socialist and give her the cash. I lent her ten bucks. Ahem." He paused, and primped his bow tie. "Our hero saves a widow."

"Oh, Trevor, I love my hero, but isn't there some danger?" Taking Trevor's arm, Lotte sat down, pulling him into the seat next to hers. "Are you a target?"

"Only until the socialists take the documents. Then they have the risk and I have the money, instead of the other way around." Trevor found the insurance joke entertaining. Lotte did not. His admission opened a scary door. Bad enough that Trevor was in danger. Worse, he was in danger *because* Lotte had encouraged him to accept a charitable errand that had ballooned into a dangerous mission. Lotte approved of Trevor because, unlike the vice presidents, he cared about people, even the customers. Lotte encouraged that bold and noble trait because, in order to respect him, she needed him to be generous and bold, but look where her advice had taken him!

"What if the socialist doesn't return? Then you're stuck with the documents, and the ghastly murderer's still on your trail."

"If it were up to me, I'd hold the documents until the Englishman came around, and sell them to him. But the woman won't sell to her husband's murderer."

Lotte's jaw dropped. She was aghast. "You wouldn't sell her husband's documents to the Englishman?"

"No, she forbade it."

"I mean you wouldn't do it, would you, even if she allowed it?"

"Lottchen, if the choices were to sell the documents to the Englishman or to destroy them, what would be in Mrs. Albi's financial interest?" Trevor thought the answer was obvious.

"But the Englishman murdered her husband."

"That's not certain. Anyway, refusing to sell the documents to him wouldn't bring Joseph Albi back or feed his children. Poverty keeps a hard school. I studied in it."

"Trevvy, sometimes you are so callous and stupid." Lotte folded her arms and looked away. She stamped her foot, and then looked back at him, eyes furious. "First of all, Mrs. Albi's right. There's no possible way she could sell those documents to the murderer."

"I already agreed, but—"

"What is more, can't you see that the Englishman wants to cover up the truth for which her husband died?"

"Joseph Albi didn't die for truth. He died for money."

"Trevor, the Cunard Line should pay its bills rather than send assassins to cover their tracks."

"They should, yes but the bills would bankrupt them. Assassins are cheap."

Lotte sulked a moment, then mockingly intoned, "So you shrug your shoulders, you valiant hero, and say, 'this is the real world, let the murderer win'?"

"Lotte, be reasonable."

"Whoever murdered Joe Albi should be punished. That's simple justice. Is justice unreasonable?"

"Justice will arrive on judgment day, Lotte. That's for Jesus to deliver, not me. In the meantime, the Cunard Steamship Line has powerful friends. I have none. Don't fight lions unless you *are* one."

Lotte looked disgusted. "Lions get away with murder because everyone fears them. Doesn't that bother you?"

"You sound like the socialist."

"I do? What did he say?"

"He said that the socialists want to inform the public about the *Lusitania*'s secret cargo."

"Well, they have a point! All this Allied propaganda is dragging America into a war that's none of our business." This was the common opinion among German-Americans in St. Louis, and Lotte fully shared it.

"Lottchen, I agree that our country has no dog in that fight, but preventing war wasn't my goal when I took the widow's case. I can't make it my goal now."

"But Cunard wants to suppress the truth, and that would bring war closer."

"But my client is Francine Albi, not the United States of America. Saving the country from war is neither her business nor mine. We pay Woodrow Wilson to do that for us."

"You have a good heart, Trevor, and it's right to help a widow, but wars matter too. Don't sell the documents to Cunard. Please."

"Doggone it, Lotte, have you been listening? I won't. That's been clear from the beginning. But now *you* pay attention. Refusing to sell reduces my life expectancy." Trevor played a maudlin card to salvage his debating advantage. "If I won't sell him the documents, the Englishman might kill me. You asked me to assume that risk, and I agreed. I agreed! I risk my life and it's not enough? Give me some credit, for Heaven's sake!"

"You're armed?" It had come to this, Lotte realized.

"Yes, I pack the Colt." Trevor patted his coat.

The next morning, worried about the dangerous day ahead, Trevor sat at his desk unable to concentrate on the dossiers that stared up from his in-box. He pulled out an expensive Cuban cigar that Tolson had given him, but then virtuously put it away. Cigars were for victory celebrations. That would come tomorrow. Also, Lotte did not like the odor of tobacco, and he would share her bed that night. While awaiting Williams, he examined his options again, elbows on the desk, hands cradling his head.

Needing to coordinate one more issue with Lotte, Trevor approached her desk, received her typewriter fanfare with gratitude, and again asked if she had a moment. Her neighbor, Catherine Donohue, stopped work. Love is blind. Catherine was not. She knew about Andrew, and witnessed everything that passed between Lotte and Trevor. Feigning indifference to Catherine, but secretly irritated by the need to do so, Trevor asked Lotte to release the Albi file already in the company safe to anyone who requested his "friendship file," which she would find in "the 1-2-3 bin." These code words would authorize her to turn over the documents to anyone who uttered them. Under no other circumstances was she to give those documents to anyone else. If foul play befell Trevor, she should return them to Mrs. Albi and notify the police. Lotte agreed, of course. Trevor considered the procedure foolproof because no one would learn about Lotte, the friendship file, or the 1-2-3 bin without his authorization—and Trevor would authorize only when already holding in his hand $5,000 in cash and lodged in a position of personal safety.

When Williams finally knocked, Trevor felt prepared. "The delivery will be more complex than planned. I have made an exact copy of the affidavit. I added all the information on the shipping labels to it. Your paymaster can decide on the basis of the exact copy whether he wants to buy the originals. If no, the deal dies right there."

"And if we want them?"

"In that case, once back in my office with your money in my safe, I'll hand them over. They are in this building, but they are not in my office, so there's no point in searching it."

Williams looked annoyed. His eyes narrowed and glinted. "Maybe you already sold them to Captain P?"

"No, I have them still."

"But you don't trust us. Hell, I thought you'd come with me, deliver the papers, which we would inspect, and then we'd turn over the cash on the spot. That's what we planned."

"Yes, that's what we planned. That's also what Albi planned, and Albi died. This way, you get the documents once I have the cash and have returned in safety."

"Suppose at the end you've got our money and the documents turn out to be phony, huh?" Williams jutted his jaw.

"Return the documents and I refund your money. Others want to buy them too." This was a bluff because Trevor could not sell the documents to Captain P under any circumstances, but Williams need not know that. Feeling abashed at the change of plan, Trevor added apologetically, "I'm sorry, Mr. Williams, but this is the only way I do business.

However, the documents are authentic, so none of this will happen."

Williams reluctantly agreed, but insisted that Trevor accompany him to the planned rendezvous with his "paymaster." They left the building together, and boarded a motor taxicab in front of the Flatiron building. Williams gave the taxi driver an address on west 15th Street, then sat back and crossed his arms. They traveled together in silence for two minutes as the taxi proceeded west on 23d Street. Finally, Williams requested "a gander at" the copy, avowing that he "might as well" occupy himself that way during the ride. He read through the documents, snorted once or twice, looked nervously out the rear window, and handed the copy back to Trevor.

"It looks authentic."

"How can you tell?"

"Some details match what we already knew. The address on the shipping labels is a post office box in Liverpool. That box belongs to the Royal Navy Weapons Testing Facility. You couldn't have known that." Williams guffawed and slapped Trevor's knee, but Trevor was too shocked to join the funning.

"The Royal Navy was to receive that cheese?"

"Yes. British sailors shoot cheese out of their cannons, and the Germans slice it for lunch."

"They enjoy the smoky flavor, I suppose."

On 19th street, near the corner of Tenth Avenue, a Ford Model T in front of the taxicab stopped abruptly, and the driver exited the vehicle, shrugging his shoulders, palms up in a universal gesture of futility. He put up the car's hood and peered inside. Two men got out of the rear seat, showing irritation, and shouted something at the driver. Forced to wait, the taxi driver craned his head out the window to see what was causing the delay. The Ford remained stalled, blocking the street. Almost immediately, the blocked traffic exploded into raucous complaints. Teamsters yelled and cursed. Motorcars tooted their horns. The Ford's driver looked up from his explorations under the hood and shrugged apologetically in response to the honking and profane shouts. In frustration, the taxi driver honked his horn too, joining his tinny noisemaker to the symphony of urban frustration.

At that moment, the two men who had exited the stalled Ford unexpectedly peered into the rear windows of the Yellow Cab, one on each side of the vehicle. The shorter man was stocky and bareheaded. Punches had flattened his nose, but the black moustache under it was bushy. He wore faded jeans, a blue work shirt, and a brown leather jacket. A gold St. Christopher medallion hung around his neck. He was losing his dark hair, and sweat ran down his cheek. The tall man, quite dapper in a cotton sack jacket, sported an Ascot cap and a small, neatly trimmed handlebar moustache. Both men pointed revolvers at the passengers seated inside the taxi.

The tall one said, "Get out of the car slowly." The taxi driver turned around, eyes bulging. "Yes, you too, lard bucket," snapped the tall man. Then the gunmen opened the rear passenger doors while the taxi driver, not waiting for an additional invitation, opened his door and lurched into the street. "Bugger off, fatso," sneered the tall man. "And leave the motor running."

Although unsure what it "bugger off" meant, the taxi driver understood the speaker's intent. He departed on foot, initially slipping in the mud as he sought traction on the wet street, then, gathering speed, he hustled north on Tenth Avenue, his immense behind swaying with each step.

"Keep your hands in view," said the tall blonde man to Trevor, who had also exited the taxi. Reaching into Trevor's coat, he removed the Colt revolver and laid it on the pavement. His associate removed a weapon from Williams; that done, the man produced a truncheon and delivered a heavy blow to the head of Williams, who collapsed onto the pavement.

"Get back in the taxi now," said the tall man, and with his free hand pushed Trevor toward the open rear door. Trevor reentered the taxi, taking a seat in the rear. The tall man slid in next to him, his gun still drawn. The stalled Ford in front now sped away, freeing the blocked traffic.

The short gunman took the front driver's seat, and, putting the taxi into gear, eased it into motion. "Nothing to see, folks," he shouted out the window to gawking pedestrians. "Undercover police work." He cranked up a side window, and the cab gathered speed. Looking backward, Trevor saw Williams crawl onto the sidewalk, holding his head with one hand and pulling himself forward with the other.

"Mr. Howells, forgive my rude intrusion. My business is urgent. You have some documents that I need," said the tall man, smiling, but still leveling his revolver at Trevor. "I am prepared to buy them." He had a cultured English accent.

"Captain P, I presume?" The tall man ignored this inquiry, but jabbed the gun barrel into Trevor's side.

"I ask the questions. I'll pay one thousand dollars for the documents."

"The socialists offer five."

"Very well, five thousand."

"Show me the money."

"Which of us has a gun?"

"You killed Albi."

"You are in no position to bargain." The gunman again nudged Trevor with his revolver to accent the point. "I need those bloody documents. You are irrelevant." *Does irrelevant mean doomed?* Trevor wondered, so he stalled.

"Where's the money?" Trevor asked again.

"First the bloody documents. I know you have them." Time seemed to stop for Trevor, even though he was desperately aware of the importance of a reply that might save his life.

"I have the affidavit. The shipping labels are in my safe."

"Give me what you have." As Trevor reached into his coat pocket, the gunman's eyes glinted a warning. "Two fingers." As instructed, Trevor retrieved the duplicate affidavit from his coat pocket and placed it on the seat between them. The gunman opened it with one hand, scanned it, and placed it in an exterior pocket of his houndstooth jacket. "Where are the shipping labels?"

Trevor protested that the shipping labels were useless without the supporting affidavit, which the gunman now had. This response did not satisfy the scowling gunman who, holding the revolver in his right hand, punched Trevor in the nose with his left, drawing blood. "Fancy some more?" he asked. He then withdrew an ugly blackjack from his coat. "This isn't like bayoneting babies, is it? Now, where are the bloody labels?"

Trevor's hand went speculatively to his bleeding nose, but he retained his composure. "I don't approve of bayoneting babies. The labels are in a locked safe. They are useless without the affidavit." This retort earned Trevor an open-hand smack in the face. "Who has them?"

"A lady will turn them over to you, if..." The gunman smacked Trevor's left shin with the blackjack. It hurt a lot.

"No ifs. Just spill it all."

"The lady is Priscilla Maginty. She's on the seventh floor of the Flatiron Building. Ask her for "Howells's eighty-six File." It was a trick. Eighty-six would signal Priscilla to call the police.

"Eighty-six me, would you?" He struck Trevor's shin and knee repeatedly with the blackjack. As the blows rained down, Trevor discovered a capacity to ignore pain while thinking carefully. He had told the gunman that the shipping labels were useless without the affidavit. What if the gunman now considered him dispensable? In a moment of enlightenment, Trevor decided that the gunman intended to beat the whereabouts of the shipping labels out of him, and would then kill him unless he could render himself convincingly indispensable.

"Take me back to the Flatiron Building and I will deliver the shipping labels. You cannot get them unless I am present. If I disappear, the keeper will show the newspapers that the *Lusitania* secretly carried explosives addressed to the Royal Navy." Of course, that was not true. Lotte did not know the Royal Navy was the owner of all that cheese, nor had he instructed her to send the documents to any newspapers. Nonetheless, the blows stopped. The gunman considered in silence what to do next. After approximately ten seconds, his indecision apparently resolved, he cocked his revolver.

"Who has the documents?" Answering this question required Trevor to put Lotte in danger. He resolved not to.

"You'll get that information when I am safely back in my office."

"I don't believe you. Last chance," said the hijacker, and, smiling evilly, he pressed the gun barrel against Trevor's left temple.

Lusitania arriving at Pier 54 in Manhattan, 1907.

CHAPTER 7

DOPE, DUPE, OR TRAITOR?

A CHEVROLET TOURING SEDAN passed the taxicab at high speed, and, careening in front, skidded to a halt, blocking the street. The sedan's windows were rolled down, and three heads were silhouetted against the sky. The heads opened fire on the taxicab. Their bullets punched holes in its windshield and shattered the side windows. Shards of glass flew. His handgun already drawn, the Englishman wheeled left, and returned fire. The cabdriver made no attempt to join the gunfight, but struggled to put the taxi into reverse while keeping his head below the dashboard. After very quickly firing six rounds, the kidnapper reloaded, but, as irregular fire from the touring sedan continued, he hunkered down below the window. Bullets hummed through the taxi, tearing apart the rear window screen and ricocheting off interior metal. The Englishman's cap flew off his head.

Taking advantage of the Englishman's preoccupation, Trevor pushed open the right rear door, rolled into the street, and then crawled from gutter to sidewalk, out of the path of the fleeing taxi, which now roared into reverse. Lying prone, he took refuge behind some overflowing trashcans. The reversing taxi stopped, took some more bullets, then squealed into first gear and accelerated in the direction it had come. As it receded down the echoing street, the Englishman fired from the rear window. Seconds later, the smoking, bullet-riddled cab careened onto a side street and disappeared from view. The Chevrolet did not pursue.

An armed man exited the sedan. He had reddish hair and a chubby face. He wore a thin green necktie and gray cotton shirt. "Terrence O'Flaherty at your service. I hope you are not injured?" O'Flaherty helped Trevor to his feet. In the clumsy process, Trevor discovered that his left leg, though intensely painful, was still capable of supporting his weight. O'Flaherty inspected him for wounds, and, finding none, declared that in the last ten minutes he had enjoyed "a year's good luck." Trevor agreed. "You may need this again," said O'Flaherty, handing Trevor his Colt revolver. "We retrieved it from the gutter."

Although dazed and confused, Trevor understood that he had been rescued. In an uncharacteristically impulsive gesture, he flung both arms around O'Flaherty's neck and expressed his gratitude.

"No thanks necessary," declared his rescuer. "An enemy of England is Ireland's friend." Trevor had not considered himself an enemy of England, but under the circumstances, he did not protest. O'Flaherty pointed to Williams who was seated in the sedan. "We fished him out of the gutter too, and his head's no better for this morning's work than yours."

Left knee and shin in agony, blood still trickling from his nose, Trevor hobbled toward the sedan. Seeing his difficulty, O'Flaherty called, "Dennis, bring the motorcar closer." The Chevrolet moved up. Ben Williams opened the rear door and groggily exited. His head wound had left a trail of brown blood down his shaggy hair and denim collar. His jacket was streaked with the mud and manure of Tenth Avenue. Williams transferred the revolver to his left hand, and then shook muddy hands with Trevor. "I told you that you were under our protection. You didn't believe me."

"You saved my life."

"We saved it," he gestured to the Chevrolet. How do you like that Captain P? A mean sonofabitch, ain't he?"

Overhearing this discussion, Terrence O'Flaherty declared that the "English fiends" had given their "snarling dogs" permission to kill whomever they wished, and "Irish patriots" had been compelled to adopt the same wretched standard. Dennis, the driver of the sedan, shouted from inside that violence was the only language the English understood, adding in Gaelic, "*Albion, póg mo thóin!*" to his own and O'Flaherty's immense hilarity.

Taking Trevor's arm, Williams urged him into the sedan. "We will get you to the paymaster, late but alive."

"Oh, damn!" declared Trevor, anticipating the next step. "There's a hitch. The Englishman took my copy. The original affidavit is in the Flatiron building."

Frowning, Williams inquired whether the Captain believed that he had the originals. Trevor supposed that he did, adding that as soon as the Captain examined the document he would discover the forgery. This declaration compelled Trevor to realize that copying the document had almost cost his life. Imagining himself possessed of the original affidavit, the kidnapper believed he had the prize and could now kill Trevor if he pleased, which he evidently did. Trevor did not share this thought with Williams, but guessed the big man had probably figured it out on his own. Williams licked his bloody lips, glanced around the street, and returned his gaze to Trevor.

"We need to verify the license of the notary. I can vouch for the rest of the affidavit. The coincidence of the post office boxes is the key detail. But, do you remember the name of that notary and the date?"

"John Ferretti on Carmine Street. And the date was either June first or June second." Williams thought that, if the name were correct, his comrade had enough information now to authorize payment. The affidavit could not be authentic if the notary did not have a valid license on the issue date, and, if inauthentic, the affidavit was worthless. "Well, we'll know soon enough." Williams motioned Trevor toward the waiting sedan.

At that moment, a clanging bell announced a motorized police wagon. It was turning the corner from Eighth Avenue, two long blocks to the east. "Damn. We can't chat with the bulls," said Williams. "If you stay, they'll look after you instead of pursuing us. I'll contact you. You do trust me now?" Trevor nodded, and realized, in so doing, that, since the hijacking he had become an ally of Williams and his Irish friends. Williams and Terrence O'Flaherty hurriedly entered the Chevrolet, which sped away, leaving Trevor alone in the wet avenue.

"That's the guy!" cried a Brooklyn-accented voice from inside the patrol wagon. The wagon stopped in front of Trevor whose useless revolver dangled from his injured left arm. A bass voice ordered him to drop the weapon, which landed in a puddle for the second time that day. Peeping out the police wagon's window was "lard bucket," the Yellow Cab's driver. Trevor confirmed that he had been a passenger in the hijacked taxi. The police took him aboard, treating him as a crime victim.

The taxi driver's name was Elmer Boganza, although "lard bucket" did more justice to his physique. After the hijacking, Boganza had turned in an alarm from a callbox on a corner, but his alarm had hardly been necessary. The police had received several telephone calls from witnesses. The subsequent gunfight on Tenth Avenue brought yet another call. Declining to pursue the Chevrolet, the patrol wagon's driver declared that police would soon be on alert everywhere in Manhattan. He requested a description of the sedan. Trevor provided it, slightly altering the model and reducing the vehicle's occupancy from three to two. When asked, he could not offer any description of the sedan's passengers and had not noted its license plate, but he provided a close description of the hijackers, especially of the Englishman. Trevor wanted the police to pursue the hijackers, but preferred to have his protectors at liberty, so he adjusted his memory. The policemen telephoned headquarters from a nearby callbox, and then drove Elmer and Trevor to the 34th Street precinct house, a fortress-like three-story building perched atop turf-covered boulders. On the way, Elmer bewailed the loss of his taxicab. Trevor asked about his insurance.

"Metropolitan Life and Casualty," replied Elmer Boganza.

"They're crooks," said Trevor dryly. "Bring a lawyer with you." But Boganza had another demand. Claiming he had rescued Trevor from the hijackers, he requested a reward plus the unpaid fare, which he set at $7, an outrageous sum. Trevor gave him $8. Boganza did not think it enough, and sulked.

Once at the stationhouse, a sympathetic plainclothes detective, George J. Allen, interviewed Trevor, and, still treating him as a crime victim, returned his Colt after verifying that he had a permit to carry it. Allen totted up the felonies this crime had involved. In addition to stealing Boganza's taxicab, the hijackers had kidnapped Trevor, stolen his property at gunpoint, and subjected him to battery. "They could get fifteen years," said detective Allen. After taking his statement, he showed Trevor several "mug books" that contained photographs of known criminals. After two hours, Trevor had found no match to the Englishman or his driver. As he flipped through the photographs, he silently debated what to tell the police. He preferred to send the police after the hijackers while deflecting them from his protectors. In one case, he saw a similarity between a mug shot and the man the others had called Dennis, but did not mention it to the detective.

When, finally, Detective Allen closed the last mug book, two new detectives entered the room, introducing themselves as Andrew Petroso and Casper Franklin. Each wore the squad's standard bowler hat, round-collared white shirt, black leather shoes, black sack jacket, and trim pencil moustache. Trevor explained that the hijackers had interrupted his crosstown journey to a "business meeting." They had knocked down his companion, and then driven away in the taxicab after forcing Trevor to reenter it. Williams, assisted by two Irish gunmen, had subsequently rescued him from the hijackers. No, he did not know the hijackers, and had never seen them before. The detectives asked what the kidnappers wanted. Trevor began to say that he did not know, but then thought better of it.

"They wanted a document they supposed I was carrying."

"Were you carrying it?"

"No, but as a precaution, I was carrying a duplicate, which I surrendered to the tall man at gunpoint. He had hit me, too, as you can see from my nose and left eye. Look, my left leg is bruised and I can hardly stand." Petroso told Trevor that the best remedy for black eyes was raw beefsteak laid athwart the nose, and a cold tea compress for the eye. Bad medical advice, Trevor thought, but intended kindly. He thanked Petroso, but Casper Franklin returned to the crime details without expressing solicitude.

"What was this document?" Anticipating this question, Trevor had decided to provide a truthful answer. This charity errand had proved too hazardous to continue. His arm, shin, and nose ached from the beating. He had narrowly escaped death and his assailants were at large. Trevor wanted to exit the nightmare.

"The documents contained information bearing on the secret cargo of the *Lusitania.* The ship really did carry munitions." That statement awakened the detectives' interest because rumors about the *Lusitania*'s secret cargo of munitions were everywhere but no one had proof. Nonetheless, disregarding the sensational news, the detectives then completed what Trevor considered, from a professional standpoint, a creditable job of taking his statement, which a stenographer recorded. The detectives asked the appropriate questions and expressed little emotion at the answers. They accepted without comment the existence of explosives aboard the doomed *Lusitania.* They asked for the address of Francine Albi and Williams. After ninety minutes, Detective Petroso politely offered Trevor a toilet break.

When Trevor returned, their questions took a hostile tone, implying that he had become a suspect while out of the room. "Where were you headed in that taxicab?" asked Franklin. Trevor remembered West Fifteenth Street, but could not remember the street number. It did not matter, because Elmer Boganza had provided it, and Trevor's testimony confirmed his memory. The detectives seemed to think that this West 15th Street address was of special significance. Trevor asked why.

"This is a German boarding house, frequented by sailors, whores, and roustabouts. Do you know anyone there?" Franklin asked. Trevor did not, and Franklin remarked that this was "as well" because "German spies" were thought to use the boarding house, which was under surveillance.

At this point, Detective Petroso announced that Boganza's bullet-riddled cab had been found abandoned near the Bowery. The detectives expressed interest in the conversation Trevor reported with his Irish rescuers. Franklin declared that the rescuers sounded more like "Irish republicans" than socialists. Petroso countered that they could be both. This observation led to a side conversation about the republican movement. Turning then to Trevor, Franklin asked, "Do you support the Irish Republican Army?"

"I don't even know what it is."

"Did the Englishman make reference to Ireland?"

"No. But he assumed I was pro-German." The detectives requested details. "He remarked that taking his beating was not as much fun as bayoneting babies."

"Are you really pro-German?"

"There's nothing German about me. Well, almost nothing. My fiancée is German-American. But I am neutral in 'thought, word, and deed.'"

Although an exact quotation from President Wilson, his response annoyed detective Franklin. "That German fiancée of yours is a hyphenated American, right?" Trevor nodded agreement. "So where's her loyalty, America or Germany?"

"She's loyal to America but quite sympathetic to Germany."

"Let's see. Your fiancée is '*quite sympathetic to Germany,*' and your socialist friend is also quite sympathetic to Germany, right?"

"He didn't say that. He said that the socialists want to keep the U.S. out of the European war."

"So he's helping the Germans?"

"He did not mention Germans."

"But he'd like to keep the U.S. neutral in the European war. Isn't that enough to interest the Germans?"

"I really don't know what interests the Germans." That debating rejoinder was not quite true, as Trevor knew very well that Lotte, her uncle Oskar, and the Germans in St. Louis desperately wanted to maintain US neutrality in the Great War.

"How else can you explain Irish gunmen helping a socialist against an English hijacker?"

"Explaining that is your job." This answer was reckless, but Trevor briefly lost his temper. The detectives looked at one another, seeming to share a conclusion. After conferring in private, they asked Trevor to wait in an adjoining room while they contacted "a specialist" at the Centre Street station.

"And what about the hijacker? Is he of interest?" Trevor asked this over his shoulder as he exited the interrogation room, but received no answer. Allowed a telephone call, Trevor called Lotte at work. "My appointment was prevented by a traffic accident. I am unhurt, but the police are launching an inquiry. Please make my excuses." Three hours of dreary waiting later, now joined by Detective Richard Fulton of the police department's "Red Squad," the interrogation resumed. The Red Squad was a special unit entirely devoted to tracking socialists and anarchists. A gaunt older man with a stringy white goatee and piercing eyes from which a fierce energy glowed, Detective Fulton reminded Trevor of Uncle Sam. The resemblance proved apt, for, having taken charge of the interrogation, Fulton proved a determined advocate of One Hundred Percent Americanism.

"I am not investigating the hijacking," said Fulton, gesturing to his colleagues. "That's for Petroso and Franklin. I want to identify the socialist. Maybe you can find his picture." Fulton produced a new mug book, and turning quickly to the third page, he pointed to a photograph of Ben Williams.

"Is this the man?"

"I am not sure." Trevor lied, hoping to protect Williams.

"Mr. Boganza said that this man rode with you in his taxicab." Sensing a trap, Trevor backtracked. He asked for another photograph. Detective Fulton flipped the page, and pointed out additional photos of Williams, one full-bearded, and two clean-shaven, with prison numbers. Fearful of further denial, Trevor acknowledged that this man "probably was"

Ben Williams. Detective Fulton snapped the book closed, tugged his chin whiskers, and sat back.

"This man is a Wobbly from Montana. His real name is Carl Houchins."

"What's a Wobbly?" Trevor asked in all innocence. Lotte was astonished to learn later that he had not known, but his genuine ignorance softened Fulton's demeanor. Presumably a radical would have known. Fulton smiled for the first and last time.

"Wobblies are members of the Industrial Workers of the World, the IWW. They ran the Lowell strike and the Patterson strike. Three years ago, this Houchins robbed a bank in Montana on orders of those damned Reds, and then dropped out of sight. We'd heard that he was in Manhattan organizing dockworkers, but from what you say, it appears that he's stirring the political pot for the Germans. There's a shoot-on-sight warrant for Houchins in Montana, and a federal warrant as well."

Trevor said nothing, hoping that lack of interest in a socialist bank robber would reduce suspicion of himself. Silence did not work on Fulton, who explored Trevor's political sympathies. "Why were you collaborating with Houchins?"

Trevor's jaw dropped at the detective's logical leap. "I was selling information, not collaborating."

"Selling *is* collaborating."

Trevor asked whether President Wilson was collaborating with Great Britain by selling them ammunition. The rebuttal irritated his interrogator. "Howells, wise up! Possibly you have information about Carl Houchins that you have not disclosed. You'd be smart to spill it. You were attempting to provide this Wobbly with information, right? Yes or no."

"No." The answer stunned Detective Fulton who, turning now to Detectives Petroso and Franklin, asked them confidently to "tell the suspect what you told me." He learned to his chagrin that Trevor had told them that the Socialist Party was the intended purchaser, not the Wobblies. This annoying clarification caused Detective Fulton to bite his lower lip before he continued.

"So you're a socialist, not a Wobbly?" Trevor then explained that he had voted for Roosevelt, but he now favored neutrality, President Wilson's position, adding unwisely, "if only he meant it." The addendum encouraged Fulton to return to the political attack.

"So President Wilson's not neutral enough for you?"

"Not anymore. I have learned that the British loaded the *Lusitania* with guncotton and then sent civilians into a war zone aboard her. President Wilson should have condemned both sides, not just the Germans. That's why I think his protest was lopsided. Secretary Bryan thought so too. Does that make him a German sympathizer?" Up to this point, Trevor still expected that rational argumentation would sway his interrogator's opinion, but Detective Fulton ignored his shrewd question.

"I suspect that you are secretly pro-German," he said, stroking his chin. His emphasis was on the word German. The tone implied dislike of Germans as well as incredulity that anyone would defend the vermin. Trevor was now tired of political questions. Abandoning conciliation, he responded with irritation.

"No, sir. I am one hundred percent American, so I make a dollar when and where I can." Detective Petroso nodded agreement with this definition of Americanism, but the others visibly disapproved. Unfortunately, it was too late to retract the words. Enlarging his inquiry, Fulton asked what were Trevor's beliefs about socialism. Trevor acknowledged slim knowledge of socialism, vegetarianism, anarchism, syndicalism, Blavatskyism, and pacifism, all of which went together more often than not.

"You know that President Wilson has denied that the *Lusitania* carried munitions?"

"Yes, I know that.

"Then why would you support those who broadcast German propaganda?"

"Detective, you asked about my political opinions so I told you, but that does not mean that my business activities were political. I represent a widow with information to sell. Williams wanted to buy it. When I took this case, I knew no more about the *Lusitania* than anyone else. Now I believe that the ship carried military explosives, and that changes my views. I'm not going to lie about that. By golly, I wish I had never gotten involved in this wretched business, but at the time, all I thought about was fair play for a widow and her children."

"You're paid to represent this widow?"

"I have a recovery fee at stake, yes." Trevor expected that his fee would impress the detective. It did not.

"Doesn't your country's welfare matter, Mr. Howells? And what about the children who died on the *Lusitania?*" On top of the previous inquisition, this badgering pair of fresh questions convinced Trevor that he faced a dedicated antagonist determined to goad him into a confession. Sitting back, Trevor gave the detective a more careful appraisal. Evidently, Fulton suspected that he was in touch with German agents, and now hoped to extract a confession of espionage. Fulton's abusive and determined interrogation reminded Trevor of the hijacker's, and he began to fear the "third degree" administered with rubber hoses in the police station's basement.

"I'm sorry about the children, but my client was wrongly denied a life insurance benefit."

Fulton sighed, and Trevor hoped he saw signs of fatigue in the older man.

"Did you ever hear that birds of a feather hang together?" asked Fulton, quieting down. Yes, Trevor had heard that. "Well, you hang together with dangerous radicals and saboteurs."

'I discussed business with them."

"You took their money."

"I never took any money. You are putting words into my mouth, detective."

Detective Petroso interfered on Trevor's side, pointing out that he might not have understood "who these people really were" when he started to deal with them. Trevor was grateful for the support.

Fulton scowled, then continued. "You say it's all business, but you made no money doing it and you side with Wobblies against the president. Can you explain this coincidence?"

"No, but I'll give it some thought in the future and inform you if anything comes to mind."

Fulton glared at the wisecrack. Petroso tittered until silenced by a dirty look from Fulton. After a moment, his oval face still agitated, Fulton continued his abrasive questioning. Trevor endured another hour of interrogation intended to impugn his patriotism, shame his political naiveté, induce a confession of sympathy with revolutionary socialists, expose his espionage on behalf of Germany, obtain the address of Houchins' hideout, and finally compel blubbering pleas for clemency. None of it worked. Trevor hewed to his story, most of which was the truth.

After holding Trevor eight hours in the police station, the detectives agreed that he would not be charged and was free to go. The detectives cautioned him, however, not to leave New York City or to change residence. "I suppose you realize by now, Mr. Howells," said Detective Fulton, his eyes expressing frustration and suspicion, "that your story, your activities, and the criminals you befriend have national security implications. You're in bed with Reds and German spies."

"Is that so?" Trevor regretted the wisecrack as soon as he launched it. Fulton's oval face renewed a purple tinge, and his eyes bulged behind his pince-nez.

"Yes, it's so, you damn fool! There's a war on in Europe, and that Wobbly is conniving with German spies to keep us neutral. You're helping them. Don't play the comedian. You're a dope, a dupe, or a traitor. Time will tell us which, and we're watching you until it does. Whatever you are, you're over your head, Mr. Howells. I would be very careful. If you see or hear Houchins again, call me right away. Should I learn that you did not, you will see the inside of a jail cell."

CHAPTER 8

THE KNIGHT, DEATH, AND THE DEVIL

BRUISED, LIMPING, MUD-STAINED, and exhausted, Trevor thumped on Lotte's door an hour after leaving the police station. Opening up, Lotte gasped, then pulled him inside. "What happened?" she asked. As Trevor explained his misadventures, Lotte washed his bruised knee and arm and then dressed them with stinging, yellow iodine. Trevor lay down on her bed, and Lotte placed a damp compress on his nose, which she also explored gingerly with a finger and declared unbroken. She cried because a brute had damaged the face she loved and had held a gun to her lover's head. To Trevor's surprise, despite his aches and pain, Lotte's tenderness awakened Trevor's amorous need. As his filthy pants were already on the floor, and they were on the bed anyway, they took advantage of the moment to make love, and, forgetting their fears and his injuries for a little while, they enjoyed its solace.

Later, after a dinner of sausage, cheese, brown bread, beer, and laughter, Lotte dropped her head on Trevor's shoulder and expressed regret for the encouragement she had earlier given to the widow's cause. "I didn't understand the danger."

"Neither did I," Trevor replied, enjoying the pressure of her head on his shoulder. "I thought I was risking a few hours."

"But I asked you to carry your gun. Why didn't you use it?" asked Lotte, reversing her emotional direction and now sitting bolt upright.

Her question implied laxity, possibly cowardice. With effort, Trevor restrained his profound irritation with the question and her abrupt change of mood.

"The Englishman got the drop on us and took our weapons. He had engineered the traffic jam. Williams was watching for trouble and had engaged the Irish fellows to follow us, but even he was taken by surprise."

"Did you grapple with the Englishman?" Lotte asked, reluctant to accept the ignominious defeat of her champion. Her question jolted Trevor again.

"He was holding a revolver to my head!"

"Still, you must be more alert." Lotte declared with annoying finality. She thought that the Englishman's revolver was not a sufficient excuse for Trevor's failure to defeat him. Lax preparation might have caused vulnerability, she reasoned, and she needed to rebuke laxity lest it be repeated. Trevor winced at the reprimand, but recalled that preparation was Lotte's remedy for whatever went wrong. If your pencil point broke, she asked why you didn't have a second one ready. Sensing her inability to express a maudlin sympathy, which at that moment he really wanted, Trevor resisted the temptation to demand it. His prudent silence permitted them to agree that an unforeseen and dangerous situation had emerged.

"And to get out of it, I think you need my help," Lotte declared. Her look proclaimed determination.

"Talking it over with tootsie is help enough." Trevor wanted his tootsie back, but Lotte would not be deflected from duty.

"You need help, Trevvy." Although loving in tone, her insistence threatened his pride.

"Do I lack courage, brains, or what?"

"You lack helpers. This situation is more dangerous than routine insurance investigation." Now she seemed to belittle his occupation. When Trevor looked pained, Lotte sensed his chagrin. Taking his hand, she hastened to mollify him. "Trevor, every knight had a squire. I'm yours." Her brilliant reply resolved their emotional tension. Lotte admired chivalry and often called Trevor her knight. Trevor knew that knights of old did have squires, so it was not an insult to be offered one. Relieved by this recollection, Trevor managed a literary retort. "Some squire you are! Don Quixote's squire advised him not to chase giants." Then he added ruefully, "Of course, the mad fool did it anyway. Maybe that is your point?"

"No. It's different. Your squire says the giants are chasing *you.*" Trevor was glad to lose this literary dispute.

"How do I outrun giants?"

"You can't, but you can outsmart them. You already did so when you copied that document!" Delighted that Lotte gave him some credit for cleverness, even in defeat, Trevor beamed in gratitude, and prepared to tell her that, by concealing her custody of the Albi documents, he had bravely protected her from Captain P. He wished that she knew, but Lotte playfully changed directions before he could launch that story. "Unfortunately, you are such a booby sometimes. I told Tolson that you were uninjured, but you look as if you've gone fifteen rounds with John L. Sullivan. What are you going to tell the emperor tomorrow?"

"I fell out of tootsie's double bed?"

"Are you ready to give your tootsie up for good?" asked Lotte, coquettishly modeling her head with her right hand. "No? Then tell him," she suggested, after sticking out her tongue, "that you lost a bar fight while drunk as a hog, and now you're ready for the temperance pledge." The skinflint encouraged his employees to abstain from alcohol.

"Our youthful hearts with temp'rance burn/Away, away the bowl." Much to Lotte's amusement, Trevor sang the opening bars of a popular temperance hymn. They toasted the emperor with a shared pilsner, and then fell silent, thinking separate thoughts. Her youthful face again solemn, Lotte declared that she was unwilling to sit on the sideline while her man ran dreadful risks that she had encouraged him to assume. Doing that reminded her of the arrogant damsel in Schiller's poem, "The Glove."

"I don't know that poem, Lotte."

"You wouldn't, but German girls learn it. In the poem, a knight rejects his lady because she challenged him to undertake a reckless deed as proof of his love."

Trevor considered that a prudent knight was not Lotte's usual hero, so he played into the rare opening her comment afforded: "Smart knight."

"But your lady wants to share your danger." From the attitude of her determined chin and pursed lips, Trevor inferred that she really did want that. From an actuarial point of view, he thought, recklessly putting two people at risk instead of one made no sense. About to say so, he had a sudden thought: *Isn't love always reckless?* He realized at once that the answer was yes. By sharing his risk, rather than protecting herself, Lotte showed that she loved him. After her rebukes for cowardice and laxity, Trevor needed the reassurance that this thought conveyed. Of course he was also glad to have her help and counsel because he needed them. Still he was glad he had not asked for them.

They agreed that Captain P worked for Cunard. "But why should Irish republicans hate the Cunard Line?" Lotte wondered aloud.

"Well, Cunard is English, and Captain P is 'uppa clawze' English." Trevor mimicked the Captain's accent, which briefly amused Lotte but did not stifle her line of inquiry.

"Irish republicans do not just shoot any English people they happen to meet," she objected.

"Maybe Williams hired Irish thugs from a street gang in Hell's Kitchen. There're plenty of them available."

"Could gangsters have faked the republican banter?" Trevor never answered Lotte's question because she preempted the pause. "Maybe the Irish republicans want to obstruct the English war effort so they help the socialists."

"Or maybe Williams works for the Irish!" Trevor shot back. "Whoever's the boss, the Irish saved my bacon."

"Who's protecting your bacon now?" She put her finger to her pert chin as the thought struck. She was, Trevor realized, a very beautiful young woman.

"Possibly the Irish are outside at this very moment." Energized by the thought, Lotte scurried to the streetside window and peeked past the yellowing pull-down shade. Some pedestrians sauntered down the darkened street, their collarless shirts open to the humid night. A single automobile was parked on Schermerhorn Street. "Oh, there is someone," she exclaimed in alarm. She thought a man was seated in the sedan. They would check again in the morning. When Trevor left the building for work, Lotte would watch from the window, and determine whether the auto was still there and whether anyone was inside.

Next they discussed strategy. Lotte proposed to burn the documents. "If we burned them, no one would know," said Trevor. "We would remain a target."

"What about turning the documents over to that Red Squad detective?"

"The Captain wouldn't know he has them, and I'd wind up in the morgue. And if I hand them back to Francine Albi, I'd resemble a certain risk-averse skinflint." Trevor's sneer brought them together. "Being like Tolson" or "reminds me of Tolson" was a standing reproof in Lotte's vocabulary. Among the many heartless underwriters at Metro Life, Tolson was acclaimed the most unfeeling. According to company legend, Tolson had once denied death benefits to a widow whose sailor husband had been washed overboard in full sight of his shipmates. The sailor's insurance contract required a dead body, and his widow could not produce one. Tales of Tolson's legendary meanness occasioned private mirth when the underwriters got tipsy together after work. But their barroom mirth amounted to a backhand compliment, because the underwriters secretly admired Tolson's meanness and openly admired his money. These actuaries were Trevor's colleagues. He needed their goodwill. Drinking with them after work in a bar, his right foot on the brass rail, his right hand grasping a beer glass, Trevor merrily agreed that Tolson was the meanest boss in the meanest company in the meanest industry, and toasted that distinction with the others, but unlike the others, he did not respect Tolson because of his meanness or his money.

Lotte kept her opinion of Tolson to herself at work. But, she privately detested the man. Whenever Trevor reminded her of Tolson, their romance went on the rocks, but, in this sneer, Trevor rejected Tolson so they shared a laugh. But after the moment's bitter mirth, their conversation had to return to finding a course of action.

"Let's give the documents to Williams. Sooner or later Captain P will learn about the deal," Lotte suggested.

"Let's hope it's sooner rather than later." Trevor held his index finger and thumb to his forehead. "But if the Captain shows up first, I have a decision to make."

"Trevor, I hope you're not implying that you'd do business with that awful man." In truth, the thought had crossed his mind. Lotte guessed it, and continued, "You gave him the documents and he threatened to kill you anyway. There's no trusting him just because you hand over those papers."

"So what are our options?" Trevor asked, then, counting on his fingers, enumerated them: "The cops are too slow. The Captain is untrustworthy. Francine Albi cannot be put at risk. Burning the documents gets no one's attention. Our best course is just waiting for Williams to call, but darn it, Lotte, if it would protect me, I'd sell the documents to the first buyer in line."

"Let's not reopen that issue, Trevor." Lotte warned. "You must run a risk, so run it for the best reason. Don't negotiate with the devil. Defy him. Be my knight errant." Taking Trevor's right arm with one hand, Lotte gestured with the other to her wall copy of Albrecht Dürer's celebrated engraving, *The Knight, Death, and the Devil.* Understanding Lotte's fondness for the image, Trevor had taken time to examine it in the past: A fully armed knight on horseback ignores death and the devil who mock him. Lotte said that the knight must ignore death and the devil or he lacks courage. Trevor rejoined that ignoring the risk of death was stupid, not courageous. Unwilling to reopen that controversy, Trevor paid Lotte a diversionary compliment.

"I wonder if the knight had a beautiful girlfriend. If not, he had less to live for than I do."

"I'm sure he had a beautiful girlfriend," Lotte brightly returned, pleased at the compliment. "He completed his mission, and they lived happily ever after."

"The knight is wondering whether his life insurance is up-to-date."

"If not, he assumes the risk, and does so gladly because that's what knights do."

Trevor and Lotte resolved to wait two days for Williams to initiate contact. If he did not, they would deliver the documents to their second choice, Detective Fulton. They also agreed that, in the event the Captain cornered him before the two days were out, Trevor would decide whether to surrender or resist, and would choose whichever option seemed safer. But Lotte asked that Trevor carry his gun and, if possible, shoot the Captain before the Captain shot him. Lotte Maria Schlegel was no pacifist.

Just as Trevor had reconciled himself to waiting anxiously for Williams to surface, Lotte hit upon a better alternative: "Maybe the socialists know how to contact Williams. Let's ask them for help."

"Williams said they would deny knowledge of him."

"Yes, but he said they know who he is. Maybe they can pass your message to him." That seemed possible. It could not hurt.

The next morning, as Trevor left her apartment building and headed to the Nevins Street subway stop, Lotte peeked out her window. Last night's automobile was still there. Lotte watched as Trevor limped across the street and passed behind the parked vehicle, turning right on the sidewalk. A minute or two later, a man opened the passenger-side rear door, exited the vehicle, and turned right onto the sidewalk, following Trevor. He wore a black bowler hat, black sack jacket, white shirt, and black shoes. Lotte could not see his face. When the man was out of sight, Lotte descended the three flights of stairs to the street and approached the parked car. No one was inside. She committed the license plate to memory and then continued to the subway that would take her to work. Walking to the Nevins Street station, she wondered how she might learn the ownership of this parked vehicle. Trevor would know.

Lotte realized with a start that whoever was stalking Trevor must understand that they lived together on Schermerhorn Street. She could be taken hostage or shot. She shivered. From the stalkers' point of view, Lotte glumly realized, she was already game, and taking Trevor's side had been self-protective, not just righteous. Lotte grew indignant to think that whoever had killed Joseph Albi had also threatened Trevor, and that now she too was a target. Cunard's assassins would stop at nothing—how hateful they were! She trudged on, more determined than ever to identify Trevor's enemy and to defeat that person. Once arrived at work in the Flatiron Building, Lotte left a note in Trevor's office mailbox.

Trevor realized that the black derby hat was tailing him down Schermerhorn Street. Without displaying awareness, he boarded the subway as usual, changed trains at the Brooklyn Bridge, then walked south from 23rd Street and Fourth Avenue to the Flatiron Building. Inside, he boarded an elevator, noting as he did that derby hat had just entered the lobby. Instead of getting off at the sixth floor, Trevor exited the elevator on the second floor, and slipped down the rear fire escape to Broadway. He then proceeded uptown to 20th Street, and, convinced that he was not followed, he doubled back and approached the offices of the Socialist Party from the west.

The party's national headquarters was located on the second floor of a stone building that fronted onto Union Square from 14th Street. Union Square was New York's main location for leftwing rallies, and the square's orators were unofficial instructors in the people's free university. Their street-corner oratory and dialogue flourished there every day and well into the night. A speaker did not require much knowledge to attract a crowd. As Trevor passed, a man in shirt sleeves denounced "imperialism" to a small and restless crowd. Most listeners showed interest only in the spirited exchanges between the speaker and a well-dressed and well-informed heckler. In Union Square a speaker's battle of wits with hecklers was a free sporting event the unemployed could enjoy while awaiting the revolution.

How convenient, Trevor thought. *Socialist speakers can harangue a May Day crowd from their office window.* As he entered the socialist headquarters, Trevor noticed a rough-looking man slouched in a folding chair beside the door. Flicking up his head, the man examined Trevor from underneath his plain cloth cap, and then resumed scrutiny of his scuffed shoes. Trevor thought that this loafer was probably a plainclothes security agent like Williams. The socialist headquarters had two distinct parts. The small office portion occupied the rear of a cavernous loft. Three typists clicked away. In the larger portion at the front, four long racks contained books, pamphlets, buttons, banners, and sheet music for sale. A male receptionist sat behind a wooden barrier with a swinging gate. Perusing the racks in hope of looking like an adherent, Trevor picked up a pamphlet by Eugene Debs entitled "Sound Socialist Tactics." The pamphlet discussed Wobblies, a subject newly of interest to him.

Approaching the counter, pamphlet in hand, Trevor signaled the benign young man that he wanted to make a purchase. "I used to vote Republican," confessed Trevor genially, "but your organizer convinced me that Republicans and Democrats are conniving to involve us in Europe's war. How do we avoid it?"

The young man looked pleased. This was the right question. "Vote Socialist! We cannot rely on Wilson to keep us out of Wall Street's war."

Trevor nodded, intending to indicate agreement and to prepare the ground for the dangerous question he was readying. Sensing a need for elaboration, however, the man continued, "If the Entente loses, Uncle Sam cannot collect the money they owe us. Wilson will go to war to protect Wall Street."

"That's right," said Trevor who, truth to tell, had never encountered or considered this opinion. His feeble agreement did not signal a desire for advanced political discussion, so the disappointed young man asked whether he could do anything else for Trevor. "Have you subscribed to our newspaper, *The Call,* or possibly our magazine, *The Masses?*"

"I buy at the newsstand, but, yes, there is something you can do for me: I'd like to find the Socialist Party organizer who influenced me. His name is Ben Williams. Possibly you can help me contact him?"

The young man looked puzzled. Turning around, he called to a woman typing nearby. "Debbie, do you know a Ben Williams? He's an organizer for the SP." Debbie had not heard of this man either. "Let me ask inside," said the man. "Please wait." The receptionist knocked on the door of a frozen-glass interior office, waited, got a response, and then walked inside. Minutes later he came out, accompanied by a graying, bearded man in a rumpled three-piece suit. He reminded Trevor of Karl Marx, but he was blowing a bulbous nose, which did not fit the German's pompous image.

"You are looking for Ben Williams? *Honk-honk.* So are the police. A Detective Fulton came by. Sorry, I do not know Williams's whereabouts." He chuckled nervously as if his ignorance were funny, then changed the subject. "You are buying that pamphlet? Good choice. My name is Ferdinand Buzaro. What's yours?" They shook hands. Trevor interpreted Buzaro's request for his name to include a statement of his business.

"My name's Trevor Howells. I have confidential information that Ben Williams wants, but I don't know where to find him."

"I did meet Williams once or twice. I recollect a big fellow with a Western hat, powerful hands, yellow teeth, and a vile tobacco habit, but very strong for unions." Trevor explained that Williams was a secret agent for the Socialist Party, but Buzaro replied that the Socialist Party employed no secret agents. "What's more, I have no idea where this fellow is. Anyway Williams is a Wobbly, not a socialist." Trevor asked what was the difference, and got more answer than he had expected.

"It's all explained right there in the pamphlet you're holding. Wobblies believe in direct-action unionism, whereas the SP proposes voter education and electoral politics. That's the nub of it."

"What is direct action?" Trevor was not trying to impress Buzaro with his political education.

Sensing the deficit, Buzaro gladly filled the gap. He had much practice explaining this topic to beginners, and he loved to do it. "Direct action embraces many tactics. Some of these, such as a strike, boycott, or a protest demonstration, the SP endorses. But direct action also includes sit-down strikes, industrial sabotage, working-to-rule, and violent reprisals against employers' thugs and brutal cops. The Wobblies endorse these, and don't believe in voting. We stress voting, including votes for women. Comrade Debs says that if the working class votes for us, we won't need an armed revolution, and if the working class won't vote for us, we don't deserve power. I hope you agree with us? " Buzaro paused, watching for an enthusiastically partisan response.

"Oh, sure, makes sense." Trevor responded, nodding weakly.

His feeble assent did not impress Buzaro, who was at that moment assailed by new doubts. "Say, what are you really? A cop, a fink, a spy, a reporter?"

"None of those. I have important information that Williams wants."

"And what is this important information?" replied Buzaro, baldly skeptical.

"It's about the *Lusitania.* An eyewitness has proof that the ship carried secret munitions."

"An eyewitness has proof? Holy cow!" Buzaro leaned forward, and lowered his voice. "Can you tell me more?" His confidential tone confirmed Lotte's guess. Williams or no Williams, the socialists wanted this information. Trevor realized that here was an alternate way out of their dilemma. Amazed that they had not thought of it earlier, he answered Buzaro's question with a question of his own.

"Suppose you had proof, what would you do with it?"

Buzaro did not hesitate. "Assuming this testimony holds water, which seems unlikely, then we'd bring it to the public's attention in hopes of halting the drift to war."

"That's the right answer. Tell you what: If I can't find Williams, I'll come back with the evidence in two days, and it's yours free! How's that?"

Buzaro's conspiratorial smile turned into a suspicious grimace, and he tilted his head to the right, skeptical again about the identity of the man in front of him. "Sure. Come back later. The pamphlets are fifteen cents each."

Returning to his office on foot, Trevor mulled the wisdom of offering the Albi papers to the Socialist Party that very day without awaiting word from Williams. Since he and Lotte had not discussed this option, he decided to propose it right away. Once back on the sixth floor, he found the note from Lotte in his mailbox. It confirmed that a man in a derby hat and black suit had followed him from Schermerhorn Street. She provided the automobile's license. As an investigator, Trevor often had to call upon a friendly policeman for confidential information, so he turned again to Sergeant Reilly at the Centre Street station house for help in tracking down the license plate. It was illegal for Sergeant Reilly to give this information to a private citizen, but a bottle of whisky enabled the sergeant to see his way around the obstacle.

"Hello, Seamus, how are you?"

"Same old problem. I'm always thirsty."

"Yes, it is a medical problem for which a remedy exists."

"Would that be snake oil, cod liver oil, or castor oil?"

"None of those! I am in a position to provide a pleasant elixir in return for a small favor. There's a license plate, YY207, whose owner I would very much like to know."

"Doctor, your cures are a blessing to mankind, and, having knocked, the portal shall be opened to you in two days."

Sitting back in his oak swivel chair, his feet on the desk, and his straw hat tilted rakishly over his brow, Trevor evaluated the situation.

If Williams failed to return, the Socialist Party would take the Albi documents and publicize them. The Captain would find out right away. It was the perfect solution. Unfortunately, someone was already following him, possibly an assassin. The thought was chilling, but fear would worsen the situation so he rejected it. About the only active role Trevor could undertake now was to clean, oil, and recheck his Colt. That job just begun, his telephone rang.

"Hello, Trevor. It's Big Hat." Excited, Trevor sprang from his chair. The switchboard might be listening, he realized, but there was no escaping this conversation.

"Ben, a fellow in a bowler hat is following me. Your guy?"

"No. But your tail complicates the delivery plan. If the cops are watching you, they could nab me. They may tap your telephone too."

"What the hell?" This was a spontaneous expression of irritation. There seemed no end to hateful invasions of Trevor's privacy.

"But it may not be the cops."

"The Captain?"

"From your description, not in person, but he has helpers. Here's a plan. Leave the Flatiron Building tonight at nine o'clock. Walk to the subway station at Fourth Avenue and 23rd Street. I'll follow your tail. If it's Captain P, we can trap him when he exits the Nevins Street Station and finish the bastard for good. If not, we'll find out who he is. As you exit the subway station, wait for your tail on the street, and watch for my signal from behind. Bring your gun."

The Knight, Death, and the Devil **by Albrecht Dürer.**

CHAPTER 9

THE AMBITIOUS PLAN

At nine o'clock, Trevor left the Flatiron Building and walked east to Fourth Avenue where he boarded a subway train to the Brooklyn Bridge. If someone was following him, he had to admire his shadow's technique. Trevor changed trains at the bridge, and savored the illuminated Manhattan skyline as he crossed the East River. Still he saw no one following. He knew that Williams was tracking his movements, and guessed that Captain P was doing so as well. The danger made him nervous, but fear increased his risk so he rejected it.

Leaving the Brooklyn train at the Nevins Street Station, Trevor saw three women and two men get off at the same stop. One man wore a sack coat and bowler hat, and the other a brown cotton sweater and blue watch cap. He looked like a laborer. Trevor walked to the Flatbush Avenue exit. Arriving at the top of the stairs, he ducked around the corner of the stairwell. From this vantage, he could survey the stairs below. Fifteen seconds later, the bowler hat began to climb the stairs. Trevor could not recall having seen the man before, but the hat was from that morning. Williams loomed immediately into view five paces behind this man, and pointed wordlessly at the bobbing hat ascending the stairs. As the man reached the top of the stairwell, Trevor stepped in front of him. "Excuse me," he said. "Do you know what direction is north?"

The man stopped, looked directly at Trevor, and replied, "Sorry, I don't." He was preparing to brush past Trevor when Williams tapped him on the shoulder from behind. The man turned, and received a squirt of tobacco juice full in his eyes. With a cry of anguish, his hands went to his stinging eyes, and in the man's distress, Williams dropped a garrote loop around his neck, jerked it tight, and, bending over, hoisted the man onto his wide back. As Williams was a large man, the maneuver brought the snagged man's feet off the ground. His bowler hat incredibly still on his head, the strangling man grabbed the rope with both hands, but, owing to the tightness of the line, which carried his full weight, he could not wedge his fingers under it. Asphyxiation began. His mouth opened in a silent scream, his tongue lolled out, and his face turned blue. His legs thrashed the air. The strangling man's anguish made him an easy mark. Trevor reached into his interior coat pockets and retrieved a police special Colt revolver, the same model that he himself used, as well as the man's wallet.

Opening the wallet, Trevor found a badge from the federal government's newly formed Bureau of Investigation. "He's a federal cop," he whispered. Williams cursed, but dropped the man onto the pavement where he lay semiconscious, gasping for breath. Williams cut his garrote line and then, picking up the agent by the collar and seat of the pants, as if he were a sack of potatoes, heaved him halfway down the stairwell. "That's for Patterson," Williams called after him. Finally the bowler hat flew off. The man's head knocked audibly on the iron step, and, after a flaccid bounce, he lay still.

"Time to skeedaddle," declared Williams. Taking Trevor's elbow, Williams directed him around the corner. They hurried north along Flatbush Avenue. As they strode, Williams examined the policeman's wallet and examined the contents. "Damn. Homer Arthur Loman, an agent of the Bureau of Investigation. How am I going to get those documents now? You still have them, right?" Trevor indicated that he did. "The feds will swarm around now. They obviously suspect you. How the heck did that happen?"

"Possibly the Red Squad tipped them off," Trevor stammered.

"Did you meet Fulton?"

"We chatted," Trevor replied archly. "He says you're stirring the pot for the Germans."

"And he don't like my soup, huh? He'd like it more if he'd ever eaten Mulligan stew." Then he turned serious. "Look, Trevor, I'll signal you soon but it won't be easy. You may have to mail the documents and get the money in a paper bag from a garbage can. Our password is *ambitious plan*. Remember it! So long." Waving farewell, Williams veered off into the night taking along with him agent Loman's badge, wallet, and gun. Trevor followed him down Flatbush Avenue.

"You don't work for the Socialist Party. You're a Wobbly."

"I was," and Williams spat out his chaw, then continued, "but Bill Haywood was scared of my new friends so I went independent."

"Your real name is Carl Houchins. You robbed a bank."

"My name don't matter, but it's not Williams. Sometimes a fellow takes risks for a cause. The banks rob the working class every day, and from time to time we reciprocate. I apologize for the white lies, but it wasn't all lies. I do work for *socialism* if not for the Debs bunch. Hey, you take a big chance hanging with me." Head down, hat pulled over his face, Williams hustled down the dark street, quite athletically for a man of his size. Trevor kept pace.

"Who are those mysterious friends of yours?"

"People serious about keeping the U.S. out of Europe's war."

"The Germans?" Trevor asked, dreading confirmation.

"It's better that you don't know. But I work with them, not for them. Hey, the cops will be here soon. We must separate. Go home and wait for my contact. Remember the password." At the corner, Williams gave Trevor a polite shove that impelled him down a side street, and this time, Trevor took a circuitous route back to Lotte's apartment house. The mysterious car was still parked across the street, and a man sat inside.

It was nearly eleven o'clock when Trevor unlocked the door to Lotte's flat. He wanted to sleep, and Lotte had put out his pajamas, but then she insisted on talking through the day's events. It was well that she did.

Sleep had to wait. Lotte thought that federal policemen implied new issues. "Why would American agents want to protect a British company?"

"Williams said they do."

"Trevor, Williams even lied about his name."

"He saved my life. I trust him," wailed Trevor, aware that his trust defied logic.

"You cannot believe anything that man says," Lotte relentlessly persisted. "Oh, I suppose the really opposes the war, but everything else might be lies." Lotte had learned something important from the public library: Lord Mersey's commission in Liverpool had already relieved the Cunard Line of any financial liability for the *Lusitania*. The Mersey Commission pinned the full legal responsibility on Germany's Kaiser Wilhelm II. "The British courts have settled that legal issue. As far as Britain is concerned, *Lusitania* survivors should sue Germany, not Cunard," said Lotte, and then added bitterly, "Of course, it's all Germany's fault."

"Fat lot of good that does the victims," agreed Trevor. "But if Cunard is free of liability, then Captain P can return to England." Then after a pause during which he contemplated his adversary's options, Trevor added, "Of course he knows that."

"Possibly Captain P has already gone back," said Lotte.

It was a plausible hope, but Trevor rejected it in hope of demonstrating his mastery of all options. "So we can relax? That might prove fatal," said Trevor. "Anyway, his work's not really done, because Cunard still has to answer in American courts." Lotte nodded, uncomfortably aware of the risk of premature relaxation. Glumly, Trevor concluded, "We must assume that the wretched Captain is still out there."

Lotte grimaced, but acknowledged the wisdom of his reasoning. Then she leaped nimbly to a conclusion. "Who do these people really work for, Trevor? Suppose the Captain represents the British government, not Cunard. In that case, his job wouldn't end when Cunard was excused from liability." This observation led Lotte into renewed discussion of Trevor's rescuers. "Maybe the Irishmen knew something we don't." Trevor opened his mouth to reply, but Lotte was not finished.

Trevor listened in a state of dopey fatigue mixed with apprehension as Lotte wondered who were these "serious people" who backed Williams. They probably were German spies, just as detective Fulton believed.

"The *Times* claimed that the Germans are paying the IWW," Trevor observed in grudging support. "Maybe there's some truth in it."

"It would make sense, wouldn't it? I mean the IWW and the Germans both want to keep the U.S. out of the war."

"Lotte, that's what I meant. Wobblies don't care who wins the war, but the Germans want the U.S. to stay out so *they* can win."

Ignoring that remark, which belabored what she already understood, Lotte, index finger on her chin, continued, her speculations wiser than her years. "Would the federal government station a detective in front of my apartment to protect a British company?"

"If they thought that I might lead them to Williams, yes, they might."

"They'd be right, wouldn't they? You might lead them to Williams, and then Williams leads them to German spies. That's their jackpot."

Trevor got into the algebra. "If the Captain is a British agent and Williams works for the Germans, then the Captain vs. Williams reduces to England versus Germany. And if the Bureau of Investigation is hunting Williams in hope that he'll lead them to German spies, then it's the U.S. versus Germany. In either case we confront rival teams of spies. And that's just what Fulton said!"

"Confront, heck, we're right in the middle," Lotte rejoined, shaking her golden curls in dismay. Their motion was almost enough to distract Trevor from the sobering discussion.

"And now," Trevor said, "Williams has throttled a federal agent. The Bureau will react. We may see them very soon." This was a prescient conclusion.

The next morning, as Lotte prepared breakfast, thunderous knocks brought Trevor to the door of her flat. In the hallway stood two men in gray fedoras. Showing badges, the men identified themselves as Felix Lightner and Arthur Shovelhalter, agents of the Bureau of Investigation, a federal police agency headquartered in Washington, D.C., and with branch offices in major cities. "Are you Trevor Howells?" they asked. They were assured that he was. "We would very much like to talk to you."

"Am I under arrest?"

"No, we just want to talk to you."

"What if I'm too busy?"

"In that case, we will arrest you on suspicion of espionage and interview you in the police station. You will spend several nights in jail." There was no use resisting. Turning to Lotte, Trevor asked her to ring up the company's attorney and ask him to recommend a lawyer. Lotte tearfully agreed, and blew a kiss as Trevor disappeared down the hallway, sandwiched between the two policemen.

As they walked, Agent Lightner, a middle-aged man, somewhat paunchy, with troubled eyes, a puffy face, and an old-fashioned walrus moustache, asked whether Trevor knew anything about an attack the previous night on one of their agents.

"Uh, no," Trevor replied.

"Well, he saw you at the subway entrance."

"Oh, was that your agent? Yes, last night I intervened to save a fellow attacked by a ruffian. The attacker ran away. I gave pursuit but lost him. Possibly the man attacked was your agent?"

"Apparently so. Thanks for intervening. You may have saved his life. Can you describe the assailant?"

Trevor reflected, then took a plunge: "Yes. He was tall, about six feet one, thin, and blond. He wore an ascot cap and was surprisingly well dressed. I'd estimate his age at forty-two. He also spoke with a British accent. Oh, and he had a small handlebar moustache." Shovelhalter wrote the description in a handheld pad.

"Did the assailant speak to you?"

"He told me to 'bugga oaf,' said Trevor, imitating the British accent to the delight of both agents. "Also, I had seen and talked to this man before when he kidnapped me from a taxicab."

Lightner ignored that reference. "You called the attacker 'a ruffian,' but you also said that he was well dressed and spoke with an English accent. That doesn't sound like a ruffian." Lightner's challenge forced Trevor to cover his fib.

"All right, a criminal, not a ruffian. I judged the man's deed, not his clothing."

"Our agent noticed a burly man, bearded, with a wide-brimmed hat, who spit tobacco juice," said Lightner, no longer interested in the Englishman.

"I saw no such man," said Trevor. "And how could your agent have recognized me unless we'd met before?"

Lightner ignored this question. They had reached the outside stairwell of the apartment house, and Agent Lightner directed Trevor down the steps toward a parked vehicle, which they entered via its rear door. Trevor sat in the middle flanked by the agents. The situation reminded him of the hospitality he had received in Lard Bucket's taxi. The driver turned back to look at Trevor, who was relieved to see it was not Homer Arthur Loman. Lightner indicated that they intended to interview Trevor in the car, and expressed a hope that Trevor would cooperate. It would only take thirty minutes.

In a delayed response to Trevor's prior question, Lightner explained that the Bureau of Investigation had been tracking him for two days because of reports, received from Detective Fulton of the New York Police Department, that Trevor had contact with a wanted felon and Red revolutionary, Carl Houchins. "This man was in contact with German spies." Lightner looked grim. Also, he added, Fulton suspected that Trevor might be a German spy. "I'm telling you this so you know where you stand. We are here for good reason." That said, Lighter added that German spies sought to exploit rumors of secret munitions on board the *Lusitania.* Possibly Trevor knew something about that?

"Agent Lightner, I represent the widow of a stevedore who loaded the *Lusitania.* This stevedore stole crates labeled cheese from the ship before it sailed, but found guncotton in the crates. He left an affidavit to this effect, as well as shipping labels he'd stripped from the crates."

"Why do you represent his widow?"

"Her husband died mysteriously while loading another Cunard ship, and the coroner declared his death a suicide. That judgment invalidated his life insurance. His widow retained me to appeal. She wants to claim her husband's death benefit from the insurers."

"Yes, sure, we heard all this from Fulton. And that's how you came in contact with Williams, right?" Trevor assented. "And Williams offered you money for those documents, but you were hijacked while going to deliver them? Trevor assented again.

"We understand all that. What we don't understand is whether you are an unlucky insurance investigator who blundered into a dangerous situation, a traitor, a goddamned Red, a German spy, or all of these, so I am giving you a chance to explain yourself."

"Fulton asked this same question a dozen times. Excuse me if I show irritation. I am grateful that Wilson kept us out of Europe's war, but knowing what I know now about the *Lusitania,* I think the president failed to apportion the blame equitably. The Germans fired the torpedo, but the British hid munitions onboard the ship, so who was to blame? As far as I can see, both sides are guilty, not just the Germans. Don't you agree?"

"Mr. Howells, our opinions don't matter, but Agent Shovelhalter has recorded your statement." Shovelhalter displayed the pad on which he had scribbled shorthand notes.

After seventy-five minutes of additional questioning in the back seat, Trevor had explained, yet again, his political views, his vote for Roosevelt in 1912 and subsequent regrets, the nature of the Albi documents, the circumstances under which he'd taken the Albi case, his futile appeal to the coroner, his initial contact with Williams, the hijacking of the taxicab, and his rescue by the Irish gunmen. Thanks to Detective Fulton's briefing, which they frequently referenced, the federal agents seemed already well informed about his story. They made it clear that they shared Fulton's hatred of Reds and suspicion of "hyphenated Americans" of German descent.

Fortunately, the preceding evening's attack on the Bureau's agent enabled Trevor to add a new detail to his story. He explained that the man who had attacked the agent had earlier hijacked the Yellow Cab, kidnapped him, and threatened his life. Possibly the Bureau should hunt this Englishman. Agent Lightner told his younger colleague, who appeared to be his subordinate and, by dint of his muscular physique and sloping forehead, his enforcer, to check that description against lists of known felons. But Lightner showed little interest in the hijacker. Instead, he inquired about the whereabouts of the stevedore's documents.

"They are in my company safe in the Flatiron Building," said Trevor, who had resolved to spill this story to the police if necessary, and thus exit the dangerous drama at the earliest opportunity.

"We'd like to view them," said Agent Lightner. Trevor agreed without hesitation, and the unmarked car started from the curb and sped across the Brooklyn Bridge toward Manhattan at 30 miles per hour, well over the speed limit. On the way, Lightner conferred with Shovelhalter regarding the chances for the World Series in 1916. Asked his opinion, Trevor declared himself a Brooklyn Robins fan, in response to which Shovelhalter, who otherwise spoke little, announced that the American League pennant was "in the bag" for the Boston Red Sox, probably the World Series as well, but he conceded that, if lucky, the Robins might win the National League pennant. Lightner concurred, citing batting averages, pitchers, and bases stolen. The Red Sox were clearly superior to the Robins in all these, and would take the series. Why back losers? Little interested in baseball, Trevor expressed an obstinate determination to support Brooklyn despite the ragging he endured from the two Red Sox fans.

Once accompanied into the Flatiron Building by the two federal agents, Trevor requested the Albi documents from Lotte, who recognized his companions as the policemen who had banged on her door that morning. They recognized her too and flashed badges. When Agent Lightner remarked, "We thought we might meet you again, Miss Schlegel," Catherine Donohue stopped work to eavesdrop.

As requested, Lotte opened the company safe, extracted the documents, and handed them to Trevor, who advised her, "Don't worry—this business is finally winding up."

Lotte worried anyway, and Catharine noticed. Thirty minutes later, she told the four switchboard operators that Trevor had arrived with two policemen who recognized Lotte from an earlier encounter. Catherine led a hurried discussion regarding the meaning of this coincidence. Trevor frequently had business with police—that was unsurprising. The consensus was that the police had found Lotte in Trevor's apartment early that morning. Apparently, Lotte had spent the night in Trevor's apartment. In several days, that shocking rumor made its way to Winthrop J. Tolson. There would be consequences.

The Albi documents secured, the federal agents returned to Trevor's office. Agent Lightner scrutinized each document, and passed it to Agent Shovelhalter. Trevor, seated at his desk pretending to work, watched the agents peruse the affidavit, the ship's manifest, and the shipping labels. While they worked, Trevor's telephone rang. It was Sergeant Reilly reporting on the license check. "That license belongs to the federal government's interagency motor pool," he said. "Any government agency can use that car."

"That fits," Trevor said. "Thanks. The doctor will send along your medication." Trevor hung up the receiver, little anticipating how soon and how seriously he would need Reilly's help again. After putting on his eyeshade and reading glasses in hopes of looking businesslike, he made a renewed show of perusing documents from his in-box as the agents read. Fifteen anxious minutes passed without conversation. At last, Agent Lightner, looking up, broke the silence.

"This shipping manifest is only what the newspapers reported. From Fulton's rendition, we thought the stevedore had somehow obtained a copy of the supplementary manifest." Trevor asked what that was. "The supplementary manifest was radioed ashore from the *Lusitania* at sea," explained Lightner. "It's the official manifest. The one you have is unofficial."

"So there is an official manifest?"

"Oh, yes. The port collector passed it along to President Wilson. We thought that the only other copy went down with the ship, but it appeared that this Joe Albi might somehow have gotten one. Now we know that he did not."

"President Wilson knows what was aboard the *Lusitania* when it was torpedoed?"

"He has the official manifest."

"What about the cordite disguised as cheese?"

"What about it?"

"Well, the newspaper manifest shows one hundred ten tons of cheese onboard the ship. Does President Wilson know whether that really was one hundred ten tons of cordite disguised as cheese?" This was a terrifyingly dangerous question to which the whole world wanted a straight answer. War and peace hung on it. Trevor looked intently at Agent Lightner, but received in return only a neutral stare.

"Possibly he knows, possibly not. Probably it was cheese—so what?"

"So why doesn't Wilson publish the supplementary manifest? Then the world could see what the *Lusitania* was carrying. That would clear away the rumors."

The agents guffawed, elbowed each other, and looked at Trevor in amusement. "Does President Wilson explain his decisions to us?" Lightner joked. "How the hell do we know his reasons? Ask the president yourself. You're a voter." That response was so amusing that the federal agents guffawed again as if in mockery of Trevor's naiveté. The momentary humiliation opened an epiphany for Trevor, who understood abruptly that Dr. Gelb had been right: President Wilson should have been added to the list of Joe Albi's enemies. *Did the president order Albi's murder?* The thought was terrifying. Trevor kept still about his suspicion, but having thought it just once, he saw the world differently ever after. In his new political worldview the public stage contained zones of darkness and zones of light, and evil inhabited the darkness. What everyone could see was not the whole truth. To his intense dismay, the agents' inquiry was not over, and Lightner held up the notarized Albi affidavit.

"Did Ferretti have a valid notary's license on the date of the affidavit?"

"Ha-ha. How do I know?" Trevor recklessly echoed Agent Lightner's prior merriment, then, seeing the policeman unamused, continued abjectly, "If not, it's worthless, right?" Declining to answer, Lightner asked Trevor instead what the socialist had proposed to do with these documents.

"He intended to publicize them."

"Did he say anything else about the documents?"

"He said that the Liverpool post office box belongs to the Royal Navy. He said that I could not have known this, but he had friends who knew things."

Lightner passed no judgment on the accuracy of Williams's information. He paused, turned to Art Shovelhalter, and conferred briefly in whispers. Shovelhalter nodded, and Lightner turned again to Trevor. "Your girlfriend is Lotte Maria Schlegel?"

"She's my fiancée."

"She corresponds with one Oskar Schlegel in St. Louis?"

"He's her uncle."

"Your fiancée sent Oskar Schlegel a telegram in which she advised him of the existence of these documents." Lightner rattled the Albi papers in his right hand. "She declared that the documents contained eyewitness testimony to the effect that the *Lusitania* carried military explosives."

"I honestly didn't know that. I mean, sure, I knew about the documents, but not about her telegram."

"Well, it gets worse. Oskar Schlegel passed this information along to one Franz von Rintelen at the German embassy. Von Rintelen passed it along to Berlin, and for all we know, the Kaiser is reading it at this very moment. We suspect that von Rintelen directs a German spy and sabotage network in this country."

"Honestly, Agent Lightner, I had no idea that Lotte had written such a telegram, but she was only forwarding a personal message to her uncle. Please understand that." Trevor was embarrassed to offer this feeble excuse, but he could think of nothing better.

"We understand that your fiancée sent sensitive information to someone who passed it along to a German spymaster. Had that someone not been her uncle, we'd consider Miss Schlegel a German spy. As it is, she's under suspicion—and so are you."

"Lotte's uncle has always been someone to whom she turns for advice." Trevor stammered, but Lightner wanted to hear no more.

"Mr. Howells, you've reached the end of your leash. We are confiscating these documents in the interest of national security. The Bureau appreciates your cooperation, and I request that you bring to my immediate attention any future attempts by Houchins to contact you. Here's my telephone number and mailing address. Call or telegraph me anytime, day or night." Agent Lightner deposited all the Albi documents in the inner pockets of his coat.

"You're just taking them?" Trevor asked, aghast.

"No, we are confiscating them."

"Hold on. The documents belong to my client, who expected me to sell them. She should get compensation."

Agent Lightner turned to his companion. "Hey, Art, he wants compensation for expenses incurred while spying for Germany!"

"How about a cell in the Atlanta penitentiary? It comes with twenty-one free meals a week," suggested Shovelhalter, grinning.

Lightner found his aide's suggestion entertaining, but Trevor objected.

"Spying? Heck, no! I am a patriotic American. Just compensate Mrs. Albi for her property. And what about my fee? It was a thousand dollars for me and four thousand for her. You're taking private property without compensation. And what about a receipt?"

"We do not give receipts in matters of national security."

"If you took bananas, you'd give a receipt and pay compensation."

"Bananas don't sabotage our shipping."

Trevor was dumbfounded and stymied. His eyes narrowed and his pulse spiked. He decided to beg. "Have a heart. When her husband was murdered, Mrs. Albi was left with four children to support. She hoped to gain five thousand dollars from the sale of his documents. You're condemning a grieving family to poverty."

"You're breaking my heart," sneered Arthur Shovelhalter, who daubed his dry eyes with an imaginary handkerchief. His callous gesture angered Trevor, who imprudently decided to bring his legal experience into the debate. "What is your legal authority to confiscate private property?"

"Oh, we have the authority," Lightner stated.

"What exactly is it?" Trevor persisted. In response to this last question, the atmosphere turned even chillier.

Agent Lightner did not answer. Instead, signaling Agent Shovelhalter to wait, he turned back to Trevor with some advice: "Howells, you're not a lawyer. If you want to know our authority, get one. Maybe he can keep you out of prison too. I am telling you again that this is a matter of national security. We suspect that Houchins works for German spies. These are the same German spies whom Oskar Schlegel informed about Albi's documents thanks to your hyphenated girlfriend. That's all *you* need to know. And let me warn you, Howells. I am going easy on you because you saved our agent's life last night. Otherwise I'd have the cuffs on you already. Do not discuss this case with anyone. Tell your sweetheart to shut her trap. There are serious penalties for abetting espionage, and these days the courts hand them out like cotton candy. I have enough evidence now to put you in the federal penitentiary for three years. You can't fight Uncle Sam, Howells. Just forget the Albi affidavit. Shut your goddamn mouth and maybe you can stay out of jail—and your German girlfriend too."

Eugene V. Debs released from
Atlanta federal penitentiary, 1921.

CHAPTER 10

BETRAYAL

As the policemen prepared to leave, taking Albi's documents with them, Agent Lightner paused in the doorway and then turned back. "So you're a patriotic American, are you?" he asked. Trevor reaffirmed his fervent allegiance to the stars and stripes. "In that case," Lightner said, "I see a way for you to serve your country, earn some bucks, and get your girl off the hook. It's a package offer."

"I welcome it. What's in the package?" Trevor sat back, grateful for a second chance.

"Houchins thinks you still have Albi's papers. If he contacts you, arrange to meet him, proposing to sell the documents at the meeting. Then notify me where and when the meeting is to take place, and we can nab him there." Looking newly interested in Trevor, Lightner sat down in the visitor's oak armchair. "Well, are you game?"

"Tell me more."

"Simple. You help us catch Houchins, you get paid, and you and your girlfriend stay out of jail. You don't have to do it, but if you agree, we compensate you like that."

Bargaining was a craft Trevor had learned. "Does your offer include my recovery fee?

"You're not going to sell these documents."

"That's clear now, but I was hoping they'd fetch five thousand."

"Uncle Sam doesn't have to outbid bank robbers," snorted Lightner.

"And you're in no position to bargain," interjected Agent Shovelhalter, who had been silent to this point. "We can jail you right now." To dramatize this unpleasant capability, Shovelhalter leaned over Trevor and wordlessly dangled a set of handcuffs in front of his nose.

"Who's bargaining?" Trevor asked, feigning innocence. When bargaining with a lion, he had learned, the fox presents counteroffers as trembling capitulations. Lions are vain, and can be gullible. "I just stated the financial loss you caused. That suggests a fair compensation value, and, Agent Shovelhalter, if imprisoned I cannot help you nab Williams–uh, Houchins."

With a hard sideways glance at his junior partner, who had talked out of turn, Agent Lightner resumed the dialogue. "Five thousand dollars is too much; I could, however, get you one thousand on my personal say-so. That's the best I can do." Lightner folded his arms like Chief Cochise. He had spoken.

"Ahem, let me restate: You pay me one thousand dollars and you guarantee me, Lotte Schlegel, and her uncle immunity from prosecution in return for helping you entrap Houchins. Is that it?"

"I did not mention the uncle."

"Well, you can throw him in at no cost to the taxpayers."

"We cannot excuse a spy." Lightner, paused, conferred briefly with Shovelhalter in low tones, then resumed. "Oh, all right, we'll add the uncle—unless he's really a spy. We cannot fix that. If you help your country, you clear your name of any suspicion of espionage, but I cannot *guarantee* that you or your girlfriend or her uncle would never be prosecuted. The attorney general has the final authority. However, given your help, prosecution seems unlikely, and, were you prosecuted, I would testify on your behalf. The same goes for your girl and even her uncle, but if the evidence against him is strong, my testimony won't keep him out of prison."

"Good enough, but I can only arrange a meeting if Houchins contacts me," Trevor explained. "I have no way to contact him."

"Understood," said Lightner.

"Will you compensate me even if Houchins never sounds again?" Agent Lightner hesitated, then declined. Trevor would be paid only if he arranged to meet Houchins.

"That seems fair," said Trevor, disappointed but thinking fast, "but would you expect me to be present when you trap Houchins?"

"You're the bait," said Lightner grimly.

"In that case, I depend on your protection. What if you don't come?"

At this, Lightner snorted, then turned to Art Shovelhalter, who also found ridiculous all possibility of official negligence. "Don't worry. We will be there. Nonetheless, you run unavoidable risk. You realize that?" Trevor nodded, glumly acknowledging yet another deadly hazard. "Houchins is desperate. It's unlikely you would be injured, but I cannot guarantee your safety. Understood?"

Trevor nodded once again. "I might not survive."

"Or you might be injured. This offer is not a free lunch. If you want a free lunch, go to Atlanta," chuckled Lightner, looking at Agent Shovelhalter, who enjoyed his own joke, now served up anew as the boss's own.

"What if I decline?"

"If you *decline?*" Lightner paused and scowled. "Well, in that case, I'd conclude that you, your girlfriend, and her uncle are German spies. Wouldn't that make sense to you, Art?"

His narrow brow furrowed, his head jutting forward, agent Arthur Shovelhalter concurred, adding, "And spies belong in prison." Lightner pursed his lips, awaiting Trevor's reply.

"What's on the menu in Atlanta?" asked Trevor, as if intrigued by the prospect of three years of free prison food. The unwise joke earned no smiles. Trevor realized too late that his quip implied that he preferred prison to collaboration. He backtracked hastily: "Agent Lightner, you are not paying me to assume risk; you are paying me to assume risk *if called upon to do so.* There's a difference. If Houchins doesn't contact me, I can't arrange a meeting, but I have volunteered to assume risk in the event he does. That's a contingent risk. You should pay me for agreeing to that." Lightner understood the actuarial distinction, but refused to sweeten his offer.

"Sorry, but you get the package only when you have arranged a meeting with Houchins." Then, out of patience, "Well, are you in?" Trevor signaled reluctant assent, and at Lightner's request, Shovelhalter drew out his steno pad and entered a shorthand record of the bargain.

Noticing that, Trevor decided to seek more compensation. "If I were killed," he asked, "would the government compensate my fiancée?

"Hell, no!"

"What about medical care if I'm injured."

"See a doctor," was Lightner's acid suggestion.

"I put my life and health at uncompensated risk to get your reward."

"Now I'm wondering whether you love Germany more than the red, white, and blue. You wondering too, Art?" Showing a toothy grin, Shovelhalter looked up from his pad. He wondered too.

Undeterred, Trevor pressed ahead. "Soldiers get life insurance and health care in exchange for assuming these risks. You call *them* patriotic. If I assume a risk of death or injury to help you nab Houchins, don't I deserve another thousand dollars on top of the thousand you already promised?" Trevor was amazed and frightened at his own temerity. Bargaining this aggressively, he was pulling and twisting a lion's tail. Having spoken, he wished he had not. To his surprise, however, Agent Lightner conceded the claim.

"I see your point. All right, in lieu of life insurance you get a second thousand dollars *if* we nab him on your tip-off; but see here, I cannot issue a receipt, much less a contract. If challenged in court, I know nothing about this deal, and neither does Art."

"Your credit is good, but let's make sure we agree. I get the one thousand and the security from prosecution if I arrange a meeting with Houchins? And two thousand if you nab him?"

"You play square with us and we will play square with you. But if I even *suspect* that you failed to report his call, or failed to make an appointment, or went to the newspapers, or if Uncle Oskar finds out, or if you fail to show up, then the Bureau will recommend your prosecution for abetting espionage. In that case, you will do time in Atlanta, and so will your girlfriend and her uncle. It's all at my personal discretion." He leaned forward. "My sole discretion. I guarantee it. Understood?"

Trevor did understand. Through no cowardice or incompetence, he had lost the Albi documents to the police. Lotte could not blame him. It was a huge relief, even a blessing. That danger was passing. Of course, the Captain remained a threat; however, once he learned that the federal government now controlled the Albi documents, the Captain had no more reason to hunt Trevor. It was the perfect solution.

Things were not so clear to Lotte, who was outraged at Trevor's duplicity. "Houchins saved your life, and now you betray him—for money? How can you be so vile?" Lotte crossed her arms across her chest and turned away in scorn. Her face was a mask. Although sometimes critical of Trevor, she had never before treated him with scorn. "Vile" was the cruelest adjective she had ever directed his way. In fact, in the past she had often praised him more than he deserved, trying to please. Now she humiliated him for his slimy betrayal of a friend. Trevor felt the more embarrassed because he had his own misgivings as well.

Nonetheless, he put up a defense. "Well, the money benefits Mrs. Albi more than it does me. Also, this deal will save you and me from prison. I said *prison,* Lottchen. Why did you send that message to uncle Oskar? He passed it along to the German embassy, and the Bureau of Investigation intercepted his communication. Your telegram makes it look as though we are spies."

"They know about my telegram?" Now Lotte was shocked. "They cannot just open people's telegrams, can they?"

"Apparently, they can. Federal agents read the telegram because your uncle forwarded it to von something-or-other in the embassy. Lightner said that he'd consider you a spy if Oskar Schlegel were not your uncle."

"I wanted to share my indignation about the *Lusitania.*"

"You must have known that Oskar might pass this information to the embassy."

"Of course, I knew. I even told him to forward the information if he thought it important. But I left the decision to him." Lotte shrugged. "The embassy told Oskar that they already knew."

"Lotte, you should not have sent that telegram without consulting me. It makes me look pro-German."

"What's so awful about being pro-German?" Lotte snapped back. "Don't you like Germans?"

"Lottchen, I adore a beautiful German lady and her whole Teutonic tribe, but she's dragging us both to the penitentiary."

Lotte fumed, but said nothing.

"I explained that Oskar's your favorite uncle," Trevor continued. "It helped. But to them you look like a German sympathizer with links to a German spymaster. You have to admit, that's a dangerous coincidence."

"I *am* a German sympathizer," Lotte declared defiantly, turning to face Trevor and stamping her foot. "Think about it. Why should British propaganda go unanswered day after day, month after month? The British loaded munitions onboard a passenger ship, lied about it, and then sent those civilians into a war zone as human shields. Maybe they even wanted the *Lusitania* destroyed to get a propaganda advantage. I would not be surprised. Bastards! Hypocrites! And then they call the Germans barbarians, and Wilson endorses their lies! And next we march off to war to avenge the *Lusitania!* Just watch what happens next."

"Now, calm down, Lotte, and never declare that you're a German sympathizer. Just ask for fairness in reporting," said Trevor, anxious to prevent her outrage from wrecking their romance and landing them in jail.

Ignoring him, the infuriated Lotte continued. "Wilson is allowing the British to push us into war. Let the people know the facts before we go to war over that ship."

"Lotte, you know that, I know that, the Germans know, the British know, and President Wilson knows, but federal agents have Albi's documents. No one will pay the slightest attention to our claims of British complicity without them."

"Yes, but you overlook—"

"*You* overlook. Police seized the documents. Hell's bells, we can't get them back." Lotte's face of stone melted, and she acknowledged dismally that she could not change the foreign policy of the United States.

"But that does not mean we have to betray Houchins," she added, resuming a resolute and defiant air. "How could you?"

"Lotte, if I play ball we stay out of prison. Then we can get married and start a family." This line should have been the signal for a hug, a sigh, and a kiss, but Lotte was not playing by the old rules now. "You're just like the skinflint! All you care about is money! Where's your integrity? You think that the U.S. should not be entangled in the European war. Thinking that is your right, so why are you hiding your opinion?"

"Lotte, I told the police exactly that."

"At least Houchins fights for his convictions. You betray yours for money!" Lotte's cruel retort shamed Trevor, and threatened to break up their romance and shatter his dream of future happiness with her. Sometimes a woman's rebuke focuses a man's mind, especially when he feels inside that it is warranted. This happened to Trevor, who hated to see reflected in Lotte's eyes a cringing chameleon where recently he had seen her heroic champion. As Lotte's cruel words sank in, Trevor scrambled to find a way out of the dilemma, but he pretended that he had long prepared this option when in fact he had just invented it.

"Lotte, I have a plan, but I wanted your approval. If Houchins contacts me, I will secretly warn him not to show up at the meeting. If he doesn't contact me, there's no problem. What do you think?"

It worked. Taking both his hands in hers, Lotte acknowledged this was a good plan even though by warning Houchins they would risk imprisonment. Trevor assured Lotte that he was willing to assume that risk, and added gamely, "What's more, if we keep Houchins in the game, we sustain a fighter for neutrality. It's a bonus."

"So we can influence foreign policy after all, can't we?" Lotte shot back triumphantly, but still holding Trevor's hands.

"A little, and we should try, but I can't make this decision alone. You'll risk prison?" Given her righteous indignation over his betrayal of Houchins, Lotte could hardly reject Trevor's solution; neither did she want to, and moreover, Lotte hated the demeaning image of Trevor that she had just presented to him and to herself—as well as the probable collapse of her own romantic hopes for their future together. Lotte Schlegel could not love a coward. She knew that truth about her heart, and she had to protest whenever Trevor resembled one. She needed Trevor to defy death and the devil. She had wanted to be this knight's girlfriend, mentor, advisor, and sidekick. Now that her knight was back on his charger, she could assume her own heroic role again. Her romantic ideal fell back in place, so Lotte relented, accepted Trevor's risky plan, brought her champion back into her warm eyes. They tearfully embraced, then sank onto the bed, but even at that sweet moment of reconciliation, she was not entirely persuaded that Trevor would have warned Houchins without her insistence, and she worried about it because, in that case, he was not the right man for her. On his side, Trevor worried too, because he suspected that Lotte's uncle really was a German spy. Neither of them slept well.

At work the next morning, Trevor received a telegram from the Northern States Mutual Insurance Company in Wausau, Wisconsin. Their vice president for personnel, Amos K. Bandy, explained that his company had an "ambitious plan" for expanding its operation in New York State. Having heard about Trevor's stellar performance at Metropolitan Life, Northern States Mutual proposed to hire him as their chief investigator at a substantial increase in salary. Mr. Bandy would be in New York City in two days, and wanted to meet with Trevor in the restaurant of the Chelsea Hotel on West 23rd Street, not far from the Flatiron Building. If Trevor would bring his "résumé and supporting documents" to the dinner, Bandy was confident that they could reach a "mutually advantageous hiring agreement right then and there." Trevor should arrive in the restaurant at 7:00 p.m., but be prepared for a short wait as Bandy would be arriving late that afternoon and could not be sure exactly how long it would take him to reach the hotel.

Houchins's telegram posed a dilemma. Lotte and Trevor had hoped that Houchins would not contact him. Now that he had, Trevor must notify Agent Lightner or face imprisonment, but he and Lotte had agreed to warn Houchins. Trevor assumed that Lightner had read Bandy's telegram and would identify its author as Houchins. But how best to warn the man? If Houchins did not initiate another communication before the meeting, then he might show up at the Chelsea and be arrested on the spot. Trevor felt trapped.

"I could go to the Socialist Party headquarters on my lunch break, carrying our warning for Houchins. Maybe they can get the message to him," Lotte proposed. "If you go, the police might follow you, and you cannot enter Socialist Party headquarters without arousing suspicion."

"Suppose the police follow you, tootsie? Maybe there are police spies in the socialist office."

"Of course, we might both wind up in prison, but we agreed to warn Houchins, didn't we?" Trevor agreed.

"Well, is there a better way?" Lotte asked.

"No, this is the only way. You are a spunky gal, Lottchen. Ask for Mr. Buzaro."

During her lunch break, Lotte walked south and entered the Union Square Hotel via the Broadway doors. Inside the hotel, Lotte walked through the lobby, and immediately exited the hotel onto Fifteenth Street. She undertook this evasion in case someone followed her. She quickly found the right building and mounted the steps to the Socialist Party's national headquarters. Inside, she purchased a pamphlet entitled "Votes for Women: The Time is Now." Then she asked for Mr. Buzaro. After five minutes, the seedy manager emerged from the rear office clutching a dog-eared notebook, his reading glasses low on his nose. He looked surprised and pleased. Attractive young women never asked for him. Lotte reminded Buzaro of Trevor's previous visit in search of Ben Williams, and encountered the expected disavowal. Buzaro still had "no idea where to find Williams," who had never worked for the Socialist Party. "We have nothing to do with Ben Williams," he insisted.

"I understand that you don't know his whereabouts," said Lotte, "but possibly you know people who do. We have an urgent message for him, and we need your help."

Buzaro hesitated, but then decided to take a chance on this earnest young woman. "You know, the man's a fugitive. The police came here looking for him. Still, It's always *possible* that someone out there might know his whereabouts."

"That's right. Please try," Lotte replied.

Buzaro paused, considered, and then changed the subject. "You purchased that pamphlet on women's suffrage?"

"Yes. Women should vote."

"You agree with us—splendid!" said Buzaro, pleased to encounter a pretty young woman militant about the suffrage. Perhaps her progressive opinion, uttered in all candor, relieved his suspicions, for Buzaro returned to the earlier topic.

"I know people in all aspects of the movement. Bill Haywood or Leonard Abbott might pass along your message. Tell me, what does it concern? I forget." He had not forgotten, but wanted to verify her story.

"It concerns a naval disaster you discussed previously with the gentleman who spoke to you about Williams."

"Oh, yes. He said he would return, then did not." Neither Lotte nor Buzaro named the naval disaster in question, but Buzaro was clearly aware of its importance.

"The police are watching him. He sent me."

"Hmm. I see. What's the message?"

"The message is simple," said Lotte. "Ben Williams: Avoid restaurant meeting all costs. Sign it 'Ambitious.'"

Buzaro agreed to ask around, hoping that someone in his

acquaintanceship might know where to find the fugitive. It was not likely, but he would try. Lotte thanked him and turned to leave, but Buzaro called her back. "Miss, we often have interesting lectures right here. In fact, Professor Scott Nearing is speaking tonight about our plutocracy. Why not come back for his lecture at 6:30?"

"Sorry, I am busy."

"Another time then. Subscribe to *The Masses* to stay abreast of our speakers. If you are shy about meeting new people, don't worry—I will introduce you."

"Thanks," Lotte laughed. "But I make friends easily." Her problem was keeping men at bay.

Back at the office, Lotte used a bathroom break in order to confer with Trevor in a hallway. They agreed that going through Buzaro was all they could do for Houchins. If he now contacted Trevor by telephone, Trevor would mention that Buzaro had a plan. As his own telephone might be tapped, Trevor could say no more. If Houchins did not call, they had tried to warn him, and Houchins was aware that federal agents were stalking Trevor. Presumably that was why he had telegraphed a job offer from Wisconsin rather than using the telephone. But they did not forget their arrangement with the Bureau of Investigation. While Lotte was talking to Buzaro, Trevor had called Agent Lightner and duly informed him of the planned rendezvous with Houchins at the Chelsea Hotel in two days.

"We know," said Lightner. "Good that you called." He did not explain how they knew, but Trevor was mightily glad that he had reported the contact. The trap was now set. Trevor would hand over a bogus document in the restaurant, and would take Houchins's money in exchange. If Trevor waved his hat, a signal for danger, the federal agents would swoop down on Houchins then and there. Otherwise, they would follow Houchins back to his base and arrest both him and his German "handlers."

Trevor and Lotte shared a dismal repast that evening. The meat was tough *and* overcooked, and the mashed potatoes had burned. Even the sour-cream topping was spoiled. Lotte could not concentrate on cooking. Their mood was despondent because the odds of getting a warning to Houchins through Buzaro seemed slim, and if that warning were not delivered, Houchins would walk into Lightner's trap. They would earn the Bureau's reward, but the arrest of Houchins would reignite their quarrel. They would blame each other and break up. There was also the gloomy possibility of imprisonment if the Bureau saw through their ploy. As they were glumly stacking dishes in the sink and heating dishwater on the gas range, someone knocked at Lotte's door. They were not expecting company. It was not the police this time. Instead, Francine Albi was there with two men whom she identified as her brother, Albert Castagno, and brother-in-law Filipo Albi.

"I've come about the money you owe me," Francine said.

IWW Rally, Union Square, New York City, 1914.

CHAPTER 11

THE TRAP

HOSPITALITY SEEMED THE BEST OPTION. "Come in, Francine. I had meant to contact you. Excuse the delay. You won't believe what's been happening." Trevor bowed a welcome, sweeping his right hand, palm up, like a Turkish pasha. Francine and her two companions did not budge.

"This is not a social call," said Francine icily. "I want my money."

"Francine, I could not sell the documents."

Francine's shoulders squared. She appraised Trevor. "That don't matter now. Just give them back."

"Uh, Francine, the situation requires explanation. I cannot explain it while you stand in the doorway. Please come in."

Wordlessly relenting, Francine entered the apartment, accompanied by her brother and brother-in-law. Like Joe Albi, his brother, Filipo, was a stevedore. Francine's brother, Albert Castagno, was a meat packer. Although not tall, both men were solid and muscular. Francine glanced at Lotte, whom Trevor introduced as "my fiancée." Lotte smiled sheepishly, pleased finally to meet Francine and impressed by the older woman's poise, but alarmed by the burly men who accompanied her. Albert and Filipo took off their cloth caps, and found seats in the tiny living room. Albert perched on the edge of the two-seater sofa. Lotte brought glasses of water for everyone.

"Have you been in a fight?" Francine asked Trevor.

"Not exactly. I was beat up."

"I'm glad I'm not marrying you." Here Francine cast a pitying look at Lotte. "But you're her problem. I came for my money."

"And we're here to make sure you pay," interjected Albert Castagno, whose mission Trevor had never mistaken.

"I understood that," said Trevor, cautiously acknowledging Albert's threat. "Unfortunately, the option of returning Joe's documents no longer exists. I don't have them. Federal policemen took them yesterday."

"What? You don't have them?" Francine asked, incredulous.

"No, and I cannot get them back— ever. Neither can you. No one can." Albert glowered, rose, and prepared to object, but Francine waved him back to his seat.

"Can you prove that the police have them?" asked Francine, now waving a sputtering Filipo Albi to silence.

"Well, no. The policemen refused to issue a receipt. I asked."

"No money, no documents, no receipt, no proof?" Francine was pulling it together in her head. "You got nothing to show?"

Trevor nodded sheepishly. "Nothing. But I hope—"

"This is bullshit," interrupted Albert Castagno, rising and extracting a fourteen-inch lead pipe from an inside coat pocket. He looked at it calmly, let others look, then, peering down at Trevor, said, "You're trying to cheat Francine. Somebody beat the crap out of you, but we will put you in the cemetery." Adding his silent approval of Albert's proposal, Filipo Albi stood, grabbed Trevor's collar, and jerked him to his feet.

"Don't bullshit us," he spat out.

"It's not bullshit," gurgled Trevor, his windpipe constricted by Filipo's chokehold.

"Release him, you brute," commanded Lotte, determined to show spunk.

"Shut up, sister," growled Filipo, who nonetheless released his grip on Trevor's shirt and pushed him back into his seat. Trevor, shaking his head to recover his wind, stammered an explanation.

"Here's what happened. Federal cops grabbed all the documents. They told me to forget about your husband's documents or Lotte and

I would face prison."

"This is all phony," announced Filipo to no one in particular.

"Wait! I can tell you who has them. His name is Felix Lightner. He's an agent of the Bureau of Investigation in Washington. I can even give you his telephone number. I have his business card."

"Albert, should we t'row him out da winda?" It was a rhetorical question, intended to elicit Trevor's truthfulness, but Albert threw open the window. Filipo again grabbed Trevor's collar with both hands and dragged him toward the window. Lotte screamed.

"You bag of shit," said Albert, and slapped Trevor with his right hand. Trevor saw stars.

"Let me go. I'll get you the documents," he said. Trevor went into the bedroom. He returned with his Colt revolver in his right hand. His left hand covered his stinging cheek.

"Now, Albert, you and Filipo sit down, and let's have a civilized discussion. No one is going out the window tonight." Trevor slammed the window shut. Wordlessly, they all sat. Trevor now presided over the deliberations, glad of the authority the Colt conveyed. "I do not have the documents. There's no receipt, and I cannot produce the money. It looks as if I sold the documents, kept the money, and am now holding out on Francine. I did not do that, but I understand your suspicion."

"You understand nothing, buster. If we leave without the money tonight, we break your legs later in an alley. That rod don't get you off."

Ignoring Albert's threat, Trevor turned to Francine. "You need the money, yes, but what do you want with these documents anyway? They just bring danger."

To Trevor's surprise, Francine had a ready answer. "I want to sell them to Paul Kelly."

"Paul Kelly wants to buy them?" Trevor gasped.

"Yes, a gangster came by last night, asking about them. He offered five thousand bucks. I told him that you had them. I said maybe I could get them back. Then I would sell them. He agreed."

"How do you know this man was Kelly's agent?"

"He said so, and he knew about Joe's connection to Slate. Also he looked *mafioso*—you know, a tough guy."

"Did this man wear a brown leather jacket with a wide collar?"

"Yeah, he did."

"Did he have a flattened nose like a boxer's?"

"Yeah."

"And was his hair short and dark, but balding on top, and he had a bushy moustache?"

"Yeah. You know this guy?"

"I think so. Was he about five foot seven, broad-shoulders, and wearing a gold St. Christopher medal?" Francine thought that sounded correct. "In that case, I recognize him. A man of this description drove the hijacked taxicab when the Englishman tried to kill me. Rex called him Roy."

Rocco was the name the *mafioso* had given Francine, but the physical resemblance enabled Trevor to launch a detailed account of all that had transpired since he acquired Joe Albi's documents. It took thirty minutes to spin the tale, but Francine and her enforcers listened intently, occasionally breaking in with a question. At the end, stroking her chin, Francine drew her conclusion: "Now you think that this Captain works for the British? But you told me before that he worked for Cunard."

"The socialist said so. It made sense then, but not now. Lotte found out that the British courts have excused Cunard from all financial liability for the *Lusitania,* so the socialist's explanation seems unlikely."

"What's financial liability?" asked Filipo.

"Cunard won't have to pay anything to the families of the dead passengers."

"And that's something you can check on in the library," interjected Lotte to no apparent effect. The visitors ignored her opinion, deeming her too young, too female, and too blonde to offer one, and they never visited libraries in any case.

Trevor continued. "I suspect that the Captain's task is to prevent any hint of British co-responsibility for the *Lusitania* from reaching the newspapers. The British want the Germans to bear the whole disgrace."

"And this Captain pushed Joe into the hold of the *Alneria* after robbing the documents off him?" asked Francine.

"The voices the others heard on A-deck might have belonged to the Captain and Roy."

"Roy helped the Englishman kill Joe?" Trevor thought so. "And the sonofabitch came to my door wanting the documents!"

"Worse, Francine, if you actually had them, Roy might have killed you too. I did warn you of that danger, didn't I?"

"Yes, you did," Francine acknowledged. Albert and Filipo took notice of her concession. Trevor looked at Lotte, hoping for approval. She nodded back, recollecting their quarrel over this very point.

"That's why I requested your permission to sell them. I was afraid they'd threaten you. Instead, they pursued me as I told you they might. They beat me up, and would have killed me except for the socialist and his Irish helpers." He rolled up his pants leg. "I have bruises here too." Francine inspected them and then sat back, an angry, puzzled expression on her handsome face.

"You protected Francine?" Filipo looked confused.

"Yes. That's true." Francine's eyes flared. "He did protect me. And the guys who killed Joe beat him up. We're sorry we threatened you. That murderer Rocco is coming back tomorrow to get the papers off me. What should I do?"

"We'll hide in your kitchen. When he comes we whack the bastard out," Albert declared with relish, slapping his palm with the pipe in gleeful anticipation of cracking Roy's skull.

"Then we t'row him out a winda," suggested Filipo, to whom this option invariably appealed. The trouble was, as discussion made apparent, Rocco's fall from Francine's window would bring reprisals from Kelly. Moreover, killing Roy did not punish his English paymaster. A gloomy silence briefly descended on the room. No one knew what to suggest. Sometimes a crisis opens into an opportunity. Trevor saw one now, and determined, without reflection, to seize it. He lay down his firearm, confident that the others were with him.

"I have a plan." The others perked up. "Maybe we can punish Roy and the Englishman for Joe's murder, and also get the insurance money for Francine—and we can do all that without any risk to Francine or her children." That sounded good. Heads nodded. They wanted to hear more.

"Suppose Albert and Filipo are present tomorrow evening when Roy returns. They would keep Francine safe. Then, Francine, you tell Roy that I wouldn't give back the documents because I plan on selling them to the socialist for five thousand dollars, giving you only one thousand. Then, tell Rocco that you know where and when I propose to meet the socialist, and that you'll sell my secret for twenty dollars."

Francine objected that Rocco might not carry that much money, and Trevor recommended that she extend credit. The important task was to convince Rocco that she hated Trevor because he had stolen her husband's documents, proposed to sell them to the socialist, and would give her nothing for them.

"Why would I know your plans?" asked Francine.

Her question took Trevor by surprise, but, thinking fast, he found an awkward answer. "If he asks that, tell him you're consorting with me for money." The women looked at each other in embarrassment. Lotte blushed. "The social evil" was not a topic discussed in mixed company. Sensing their discomfort, Trevor sweetened his discussion. "Only mention that if he asks. The main thing is to pass on the exact information about tomorrow's meeting. We want him to show up at the Chelsea Hotel. Then the police grab him."

"If the cops nail Rocco, won't Kelly come after Francine?" Albert asked. Trevor thought not. After all, Francine was passing along accurate information. He did intend to meet the socialist at the Chelsea Hotel in two days.

"I meet the socialist in the restaurant at seven. Whoever carries my briefcase out of the hotel has Joe's documents. Tell Roy that." Francine repeated back the details of the plan as Albert and Filipo listened. Trevor ended with a pep talk: "We hope that Roy will tell the Captain, and that the two of them will show up at the Chelsea tomorrow night. The federal cops will arrest them both and charge them with Joe's murder." Then, turning to Francine, he concluded, "When they are convicted, Joe will be avenged, and Metro Life will have to pay you the death benefit. This way we even the score for Joe and get all the money. So what do you say?"

Francine's full lips tightened; she took time to reflect before replying. "What if your plan don't work?" It was a shrewd question. She had been disappointed and cheated before. Filipo and Albert sat up, recognizing that Francine's bill-collection team had not yet disbanded.

"Then I will turn over to Francine the thousand dollars I receive from the federal cops for helping them. After that, the murderers might come after me again, but they won't bother Francine," said Trevor, realizing that he still wanted to protect Francine.

Trevor beamed when Francine, Albert, and Filipo approved his plan. Everyone shook hands. Francine kissed him on both cheeks. He was also delighted that Lotte loved it. Her valiant champion was back on his warhorse. It suited Trevor too. Apart from his score to settle with Captain P, a resentment compounded with humiliation, and apart from the justice for Francine Albi, Trevor also welcomed apprehension of the criminals who threatened his life and Lotte's. The danger was, of course, that if Williams attended the appointment, the federal agents would arrest him, but this, Lotte later reminded him, was a contingency they had already reckoned with—it was why they had tried to warn Williams. Baiting a trap for the Captain did not heighten Williams's risk. For the first time since the hijacking, Trevor and Lotte felt as though they were making things happen rather than reacting to threats. They felt hopeful.

Filipo Albi telephoned Trevor from the corner store the following day. Rocco had just come to Francine's apartment, and she had passed along Trevor's plan. The trap had been set. Trevor left the Flatiron Building the next evening at 6:45, carrying his briefcase. The Chelsea Hotel attracted bohemians and artists. Walking toward it, he wondered why a Wisconsin insurance executive would select such a hotel rather than the Plaza for their meeting. Then he recalled that he was not really dealing with an insurance executive, he was dealing with a fugitive Wobbly in disguise. A hotel with an avant-garde clientele probably had several employees in sympathy with the IWW. The Chelsea was a safer choice for Williams than the Plaza. Approaching the hotel, Trevor watched for disguised policemen lurking in doorways, but spotted none. At the request of Agent Lightner, he had left his Colt in the office. What if the federal policemen failed to show up? Although this was a risk he had assumed, he felt incipient panic and resolved to ignore it.

Trevor entered the Chelsea Hotel on the stroke of seven, carrying his briefcase. In the lobby, amid the potted plants, four unescorted ladies lounged on rattan chairs. One brazenly smoked a cigarette. If a man called at the desk for his room key, he could look over the seated ladies while the clerk fetched it. Then he could beckon from the wire-cage elevator and the lady would join him. The seated ladies regarded Trevor with professional interest. As he passed, he tipped his straw hat. When he turned right into the restaurant, instead of left to the hotel desk, the ladies lost interest.

The maitre d'hôtel escorted Trevor to a table in the rear of the restaurant, and wished him "*Bon appétit.*" From this table Trevor could observe the restaurant entrance as well as the bay window. He placed the briefcase conspicuously next to him. It would be visible from the street. Then he looked around, taking stock. The restaurant contained fifteen tables. Only three were occupied. At a distant table, a man and a woman were having an animated discussion. They probably were not his contact. At a nearer table, a solitary young man with long hair sipped an aperitif while reading a script. He wore a three-piece brown suit, cravat, and round collar with gold stickpin. He resembled a theater impresario, but possibly was a policeman in disguise. This young man was probably not his contact. Trevor's instructions had indicated that Amos Bandy would arrive after Trevor was seated.

Carrying a towel over his bent right arm, a waiter approached Trevor's table. He provided "*Monsieur*" a menu. *Anyone here might be a Wobbly, a German spy, an assassin, or a policeman. Even the waiter.* Trevor was acting a part. Anyone else might be acting too. Trevor ordered a glass of Chablis and osso buco well done, reasoning that it would take a long time to prepare the meat.

"Monsieur would perhaps prefer a Burgundy wine with meat?" A mirthless smirk illuminated the waiter's face. Trevor had ordered a white wine with meat! This was an embarrassing faux pas. He hastily changed his order, and the sneering waiter penciled the correction into his pad. *Well, that proves I'm not a British agent and he's really a French waiter.*

After fifteen minutes' suspenseful waiting, the stem glass of Burgundy untouched in front of him, Trevor watched a short, portly man enter the dining room. He was fashionably dressed, wore a white boutonniere, and carried a tall silk hat and a gold-headed cane. Could this be Amos Bandy? The prosperous man sat down at the table next to Trevor's even though other tables were free. That choice implied an intention to communicate, but the man was in no hurry. The mild exertion had rendered him out of breath, and he wiped his brow with the table's linen napkin. Trevor guessed that the man was his contact and would open a conversation; however, the man said nothing, studied the menu, and then addressed his order to the waiter. When his pork chop was served, the portly gentleman dug in with gusto, and, having demolished the chop and accompanying fried potatoes and coleslaw, called for chocolate cake, coffee, and Grand Marnier. He was a sloppy eater: gravy spilled from his plate onto the floor, and the restaurant's calico cat took an interest.

Hoping to initiate a conversation, Trevor said, "Here, kitty, kitty," proffering a morsel. Still, his neighbor ignored him, as did the cat. At last, tired of uncertainty, Trevor leaned forward and addressed a coded inquiry to his neighbor. "Might you have some sort of plan you wish to discuss?" The man paused in mid-slurp, his dram of Grand Marnier poised in midair. He regarded Trevor with disdain, and then swallowed it.

"Yes, I do have a plan," he said. "It's awaiting me in the lobby, and it doesn't include any fairies."

No one else approached Trevor. At nine o'clock, as arranged, Trevor paid the restaurant's exorbitant bill, leaving a generous tip for the waiter, who bowed him into the hotel lobby. Trevor left the dining room carrying his briefcase, which signaled a failed rendezvous with Williams. Grateful for that failure, the fulfillment of his hopes, Trevor silently passed Lotte, who also waited in the lobby, seated near several ladies of the night. Lotte was much younger and more beautiful than her "competitors." Mistaking her profession, two men tried to chat her up while the disgruntled professionals sulked nearby. Intent on claiming Lotte's interest, the bigger man swept the smaller behind him with his right arm, starting a fight. A cigar-chomping house detective intervened, threatening arrests, and the men dispersed. Despite the distractions, Lotte managed to give Trevor the "all-clear" signal. She had seen no sign of Williams or the Captain inside the hotel. Relieved, Trevor walked down the front stairs of the hotel and turned right, his briefcase in his right hand.

About half a block later, Trevor became aware of a tall man catching up to him. "It's a pity," the man said softly, "that your socialist friend did not join you for dinner." In the dim glow of the street lamp, Trevor recognized Captain P.

"A thousand dollars for the briefcase" muttered the Englishman, holding out a thick envelope as he walked along. Trevor took it and glanced inside without breaking stride.

"The socialists offered me five thousand, and after the beating in the taxi it will cost you six."

"Just follow me around the corner," the Captain hissed. "I have more money in the car. Don't run—I know where you and your girlfriend live."

The Englishman sped up and turned right at the corner. Trevor followed ten paces behind, praying that federal agents were tracking him. The Englishman stopped at a parked car and leaned in to speak to the driver, whom Trevor could not identify in the gloom, and the driver handed over an envelope. The Captain turned to face Trevor, and, giving him the second envelope, took in return the briefcase that Trevor extended.

"No tricks this time. Is everything inside?" the Captain asked. Trevor assured him that it was. "Excellent. Otherwise you're a dead man," hissed the Captain, who thereupon hopped into the parked car. Trevor waved his hat in farewell—the prearranged signal that should bring the federal agents.

Just as the Captain was returning a two-finger insult, a motorcar pulled abreast of his vehicle, blocking its exit from the curb. Three men jumped out. One was Felix Lightner. The other two emerged from the shadows. "Hold it," said one. "Police." The two policemen trained guns on the muscular driver and the Englishman.

"Keep your hands in sight and get out of that car," barked Lightner. "Move slowly." Reaching into the Englishman's trench coat, Lightner removed his revolver and wallet. Agent Art Shovelhalter held an electric torch as Lightner read the man's documents.

"You reside in London, but you work for the Cunard Line here?" asked Agent Lightner, looking up. "You are a British subject?"

"Yes, quite right about all that," replied the Englishman.

Agent Lightner asked Shovelhalter to shine the flashlight on the Englishman's face. "Wait—I know you. You're Guy Percival, right?" asked Lightner.

"Your memory is excellent. How are you, Felix?" responded Percival.

"I'm flabbergasted. We expected a bank robber." Then, turning to Trevor, Lightner demanded, "Howells, what the hell is going on?"

"Mr. Lightner, this man murdered Joseph Albi, hijacked a taxicab, held me prisoner in it at gunpoint, and just finished threatening me with the weapon you took away from him. He also assaulted your agent at the subway stop."

Lightner ignored his remark. "Put away your guns, fellows. I know this man. This is very awkward, Guy, but I'm afraid you and your driver must accompany us to headquarters. I will keep your guns until we clear this up."

CHAPTER 12

A REGRETTABLE MISUNDERSTANDING

Agent Lightner instructed Trevor to appear at the Bureau's midtown field office at eleven o'clock the next morning. When Trevor arrived, gloating over his enemy's arrest and basking in Lotte's appreciation of his successful trick, Agent Lightner merrily announced that he had some "offley good news" and some "offley bad news," a pun on the Bureau's New York director, William Offley. Having just read Offley's name on the frosted glass door, Trevor managed an appreciative chuckle. The "offley good news" turned out to be the Bureau's decision to pay Trevor $1,000 despite the failure of Houchins to fall into their trap. Of course, Trevor had promised that money to Francine, but it was nonetheless the only product of his crusade and the success pleased him. The "offley bad news" was no surprise: The Northern States Mutual Insurance Company had no Amos K. Bandy on its payroll. Anyone could have telegraphed that bogus offer of employment. "I'm afraid you won't be getting that big promotion," Lightner quipped.

Trevor gamely acknowledged an "offley big disappointment," then inquired whether Lightner had any important news regarding the suspects. The answer dismayed him. Lightner explained that the Bureau could find no legal grounds for detaining either Guy Percival or Rocco Caprioli for more than another few hours. The Cunard Line had verified that Percival worked as a part-time purchasing agent in their New

York office; however, Cunard had no knowledge of any business that would have required Percival to contact either Joseph Albi or Trevor Howells. On the other hand, Cunard's representative commented, since Percival's employment was only part-time, he engaged in independent business to augment his income. The Cunard Line had no knowledge of any persons whom Percival consulted in connection with his independent business. The Bureau of Investigation was now awaiting a response from the British consulate regarding any knowledge they might have of Guy Percival. Possibly the British police were hunting him, but once that remote possibility was eliminated, the Bureau would release Percival immediately.

"You're releasing him? This is incredible," Trevor sputtered. "I trust your prior acquaintance with him ... May I ask how you came to befriend Percival?"

"We are colleagues, but I assure you that did not influence my decision."

"No, of course not, but I still wonder how you happened to know this man." Trevor tried to sound curious rather than outraged.

"I have met him at conferences on maritime security. He represented the British consulate. We want American goods to reach Great Britain, and they want to receive them, so we share an interest in secure harbors. That's all I can tell you."

"It *would be* maritime security, wouldn't it?" Trevor muttered.

"What exactly does that mean?" asked Lightner, annoyed by the aside.

"It means that this criminal has access to information that I am denied. And he is a noncitizen as well as a murderer."

"A murderer, that's what *you* say. A noncitizen, yes, and detailed by a friendly government to coordinate maritime security with us."

"Did Percival work for the British consulate when you 'coordinated' with him?"

"No, but he worked for Cunard, and he has a military background, so they put him in charge for their side." Trevor asked whether Percival was a British agent. Lightner shrugged. "The British consulate says that he works for the Cunard Shipping Line. Obviously, he's batting for Britain in the war, but if he works for their government, that's of no interest to us."

"Why is Britain friendly and not Germany too? We're neutral in their wretched war."

"Britain is a huge customer, and they pay for what they take home. That makes for warm friendship. Germany doesn't buy anything from us." As for Percival's driver, Lightner continued, the Bureau had identified him as Rocco ("Roy") Caprioli, age forty-five. Caprioli had a long police record, starting at the age of fifteen, and between 1909 and 1911 had served three years in Sing-Sing Prison for burglary. This was his only felony conviction. Caprioli now operated a car-and-driver service with which Guy Percival had contracted for transportation on several occasions, including the previous evening. Percival paid for Caprioli's service, and Caprioli knew nothing of Percival's business acquaintances, including Joseph Albi and Trevor Howells. Lightner conceded that, judging from his police record and known associates, Caprioli was probably affiliated with Paul Kelly's waterfront racketeering. Still, the Bureau had no legal basis for detaining him. "As far as the law knows, Kelly is a labor leader, and Caprioli operates a legal business."

"That is doubly 'offley awful,'" said Trevor, resurrecting Lightner's pun in hope of sweetening the agent's sour disposition. Judging from his face, the agent found no humor left in it. Now Trevor felt desperate. He had been counting on the Bureau to hold, indict, and convict Percival and Caprioli of Albi's murder, armed robbery, grand theft, and kidnapping with bodily harm. Instead they would be released in a few hours.

"What about the briefcase and the money you saw him give me? Why did he give me that money?" Trevor sputtered.

"We asked him that very question," said Lightner who nodded in recognition of the question's pertinence. "Percival says your briefcase contains a work of fiction that you were preparing for publication. It's based on what a stevedore told you about the *Lusitania.* Percival bought the rights from you for two thousand dollars. We did not tell him that you had no story. I assume you're glad of that?"

"Oh, sure, thanks," Trevor gasped, sensing a cryptic reference to the confiscated documents.

Shaking his head in pity, Lightner continued, "Percival bought a briefcase full of your trash paper because of some delusion he has about your intention to publicize Albi's story in a work of fiction. We didn't tell him that he's deluded, but he'll find out when his property is returned." Lighting his pipe, he delivered this message without any disturbance of his poker face.

"This is absurd. I'm an insurance investigator, not a playwright."

"No need to shout, Mr. Howells, I hear you. Look, we don't know whether you offered to sell Percival your literary fiction or not, but he insists you did so on two occasions—once in the taxicab and again in front of the Chelsea Hotel." Trevor denied it. "Mr. Howells, you had Percival's two thousand dollars in your hand when we arrested him. That's money you accepted in payment for whatever you were selling."

"Well, yes, he did offer to buy Albi's documents. I declined. How could I sell him what the Bureau had already confiscated?" Lightner stiffened at the forbidden reference. Trevor noticed, but continued, "And then he pressed that money into my hand, threatening to kill me if I sold him more junk. But I did not agree to sell." This objection registered no effect on the agent's poker face.

Frustrated, Trevor turned to contract law. "Does he have a written contract?"

Lightner hit that one back. "You took his money. He has 'valuable consideration.'"

"Baloney," Trevor snorted. "If it was a business meeting, why did he carry a gun?"

"He said that when he conferred with you in the taxicab, a gang attacked him. His driver confirms this. He feared the gang might return, so he brought a gun, and asked his driver to do the same."

"He wanted to buy Albi's documents. Surely you must realize that."

"I must? Let me remind you that, in return for your patriotic service, the Bureau quashed espionage charges against you, your girlfriend, and her uncle. What's more, you agreed to forget about Joseph Albi's bogus documents. I thought you understood all that and were prepared to enjoy your freedom. Was I mistaken?" Lightner scowled. It was a dangerous moment.

Shaking his head, Trevor waved both hands in front, signaling surrender. "Oh, no, I have not forgotten our bargain, Mr. Lightner." Trevor laughed nervously. "I quite understand what the Bureau wants, and I intend to comply." Trevor sighed. "But without the Albi documents, the murder of Albi, the hijacking, the beating in the taxi, and the interception at the Chelsea Hotel make no sense. This literary nonsense turns the murder and hijacking into a farce… a police farce."

Agent Lightner finally cracked a smile. "Clever, Howells, but it's no farce; it's a civil disagreement over a contract. The Bureau has no interest in any commercial promises you made to Guy Percival. It's a free country. You can sell trash to suckers in it." Then, shrugging his shoulders, he added some advice. "What's more, if you have nothing to sell, that's ideal. Just return Percival's money and explain that it was all a regrettable misunderstanding."

"'A regrettable misunderstanding?'"

"Yup, that's right," said Lightner. Then, apparently losing interest in the conversation, he shuffled some papers on his desk, glanced at his pocket watch, and reignited his pipe.

Trevor understood the cues, but he persisted. "Did you advise Guy Percival that the Bureau had seized Albi's affidavit and shipping labels?"

"We told him that we'd confiscated a stevedore's documents in the interest of national security, a concept he understands better than you. We also explained the bargain we struck with you. In the light of that, it seems to Arthur and me that your confrontation with Percival is over. He has no beef with you now. I very much hope you will return his money and apologize, so you can go your merry way and he can go his."

"Is he owed an apology for roughing me up?" Trevor's angelic smile masked bitter irony.

"'A smile and kind word take one far in life.' Didn't your mother teach you that?" This banal advice shocked Trevor, who thought it a feeble attempt at humor, but rather than offend the agent, who seemed to believe it, he proceeded deadpan.

"Thanks for reminding me, although, from my experience, Captain Percival prefers a gun to a kind word or a smile. But, Agent Lightner, these two men murdered Joseph Albi to get those so-called documents from him. Was that just a regrettable misunderstanding?"

"No, that would be murder, but Percival has an alibi: He had an appointment in Hoboken on the evening Albi died. His business contact there vouches for him and for Caprioli."

Trevor settled back in his chair, dazed. After a brief silence, Lightner continued, "But legally it wouldn't matter to us if they had killed him in front of one hundred witnesses. Murdering Joseph Albi on a Manhattan pier was not a federal offense. New York has jurisdiction."

"And the hijacking?" Trevor asked, dreading what he guessed would follow.

"Hijacking is not a federal crime unless the vehicle crosses state boundaries. The taxi didn't."

The truth was not working, so Trevor lied: "All right, but what about the attack on your agent at Nevins Street?"

"That *was* a federal crime, but Agent Loman could not pick Percival out of a police lineup and does not recall that he was present. Loman described an older and stockier man wearing a wide-brimmed Western hat. That description fits Carl Houchins, who is a federal fugitive."

"Bank robbery is a state crime."

"Yes, but Houchins fled across state lines to avoid prosecution."

"Surely you can refer Percival and Caprioli to the New York police for prosecution?"

"Yes, if we had sufficient cause, but we don't. There's no evidence to back your accusations. We cannot refer people for state prosecution against whom no evidence of wrongdoing exists."

"How can you reach that preposterous conclusion?" Trevor shouted, momentarily losing his composure, a loss he quickly regretted as Agent

Lightner's eyebrows came together in a frown, and Art Shovelhalter rose from his chair. Backing down, Trevor submitted quietly that Percival, as an employee of the Cunard Line, wanted to suppress evidence that incriminated his employer. There was the motive. As to opportunity, "He threatened me twice in hope of snagging the Albi documents—once in the taxicab and once in front of the hotel."

A dark cloud settled over Agent Lightner's dismal face. "The Albi documents? You mean Albi's bogus story. I warned you of the consequences of idle chatter about a stevedore's so-called secret documents. This reckless talk just feeds Germany's rumor mill. If there were any truth to those rumors, Secretary Bryan would have mentioned it when he resigned."

"Maybe Bryan knew more about the *Lusitania* than he told the public."

"Bryan did not dispute Wilson's facts. No one disputes them except the German kaiser and you, Mr. Howells. Maybe in fifty years you could get away with exploiting rumors about secret munitions aboard the *Lusitania,* but the courts will not tolerate unpatriotic speculation today."

"Maybe in a hundred years," growled agent Art Shovelhalter, who rarely spoke or smiled, but on this occasion did both.

"Exactly," continued Lightner, nodding to Shovelhalter, then scowling at Trevor. "I thought you understood."

To every thing there is a season, Trevor thought, hating himself for moral cowardice. A season to express righteous indignation to the police, and a season to eat whatever crap they dish out. And this was the second season, so Trevor replied meekly that he had not intended to imply the validity of claims Joseph Albi had made in writing. "Oh, certainly not," but Guy Percival had believed them accurate and had acted accordingly. That belief had caused Guy Percival to hurl Joseph Albi to his death in the hold of the *Alneria,* and Percival's crime was real even if his belief was unfounded.

"But we cannot prove it, and even if we could, it's not a federal offense. Thanks for coming to headquarters, Mr. Howells. Agent Shovelhalter will see you out. If you hear from Houchins again, notify me at once. We consider that you are still engaged to help us to capture him. Understood?"

"Oh, sure, I'm your pigeon." Hearing that, Shovelhalter rose, grinning, from his chair, and stood over Trevor. The discussion was over.

Now thinking again about personal survival, Trevor changed the subject. "Agent Lightner, Percival threatened my life yesterday. You didn't hear it. I did. You took his revolver. Will you return it to him when you release him?"

"Yes, he gets all his property back. You will get your property back at the same time. That's the two thousand dollars that were in your hand. Just return his money, apologize, and walk away."

"Money or no, once released, he'll be free to stalk me, and he threatened to kill me." Lightner's face did not change at this news. "In view of his threats, I ask that you do me the kindness of explaining when you intend to release Percival and Caprioli, so that I can prepare my personal defense."

"Unless we get unexpected evidence, we will release Percival and Caprioli at nine o' clock tomorrow morning. You have twenty hours, Mr. Howells."

Returned to the Flatiron Building, Trevor hurriedly discussed these disastrous events with Lotte, who first gasped in dismay, then, recovering, reminded Trevor of Detective Fuller. Possibly he would show interest in murder, kidnapping, and armed robbery in the city of New York. "Fuller even asked you to call him in the event Williams surfaced."

Trevor immediately called Fuller, but the detective was away from his desk. It was four o'clock in the afternoon when he returned Trevor's telephone call. The detective was still unfriendly, and when he learned that the Bureau of Investigation had failed to apprehend Houchins, despite a stakeout, he lost interest.

"You say this Englishman kidnapped you and killed somebody in Manhattan, but the Bureau of Investigation says they lack sufficient proof so they can't refer the suspect for prosecution. Lack of proof is lack of proof in New York State too. In a free country the police don't charge a man with crimes just because somebody asks them to. Why should I believe you rather than the Bureau? They say there's no proof, that's good enough for me. By the way, when you heard from Houchins, you should have called me as well as the Bureau. At least you called somebody, so you're off my hook, but I'm still hunting Reds, so call me right away if you see or hear from Houchins again."

After Fuller's brushoff, Trevor realized anew that his situation, and Lotte's, had gone from victorious to dire in just five hours. The socialist and the Irish gunmen had protected him from Percival in the taxicab, and the Bureau had protected him in front of the Chelsea Hotel. Now the police were preparing to release both assassins, and the socialist was on the run. Worse, Percival had promised revenge if the briefcase did not contain the Albi documents. Percival had fallen into Trevor's trap, and presumably understood that he had been set up a second time. *He must be seriously annoyed,* Trevor mused, pleased at his enemy's discomfort, but worried about his revenge.

Trevor nursed one hope. Just as Lightner had proposed, Percival understood that Albi's documents were already in the hands of the Bureau of Investigation. Therefore, Percival understood that their contest was over and he had won, but it was possible that a furious, resourceful, and vengeful Percival might stalk Trevor and Lotte just because he had a grudge and knew how. Lightner had advised Trevor to return Percival's money, apologize, and remind him that the documents now belonged to the federal government. Here was an easy way out, but would it suit Lotte? If this exit looked like cowardice to her, it might cause another quarrel. Doggone it! There was no escaping a conference with Lotte. She had proposed the call to Fulton and would want to know the upshot. Then, suddenly, instead of fretting about Lotte, Trevor had an unexpected insight into his own state of mind. He did not want to apologize to the man who had humiliated, beaten, and threatened him. He could not be strictly rational about it because his own anger had become an emotional fact for him to acknowledge. *I want revenge. But it's so unprofessional.*

Rising from his swivel chair and nervously pacing back and forth, Trevor considered how best to approach Lotte. Their conversations were increasingly difficult in the office. Their business was too frequent, too complex, and too private to discuss at her desk. They could not meet in his office because Lotte was only permitted to enter the offices of the four vice presidents. Moreover, the company's work rules allowed her four trips a day to the bathroom, none of which could exceed five minutes. Otherwise she was required to sit behind her desk from eight in the morning until six 'o clock every evening, with forty-five minutes off for lunch. Although Lotte and Trevor concealed their romance, he knew that their frequent tense consultations in hushed tones had generated gossip; therefore, although he was in his Flatiron office, Trevor dialed Lotte's extension rather than show himself at her desk. Even this conversation had to be coded lest the switchboard women eavesdrop.

"Miss Schlegel, this is Mr. Howells. I am calling about Fulton."

Yes, Mr. Howells."

"He will not intervene. The results will be released tomorrow at nine. I am considering alternatives. Please leave any written suggestions in my mailbox."

"Very good, Mr. Howells. Oh, Mr. Tolson was looking for you, sir, and he was not happy." Her warning was ominous, but facing Tolson had to be tomorrow's problem. Lotte and Trevor would later spar over which of them had first thought of Sergeant Seamus Reilly at the Centre Street police station. Trevor maintained that Reilly was already in his mind when he picked Lotte's message out of his mailbox, reminding him that Sergeant Reilly was local, friendly to Trevor, and, like most Irish-Americans, unfriendly to Great Britain. If the attitude of the police toward Percival depended upon political winds, as it apparently did, Reilly's winds blew in the right direction. Although only a sergeant, with luck he might influence the watch captain to arrest Percival and Caprioli when they left federal custody the next morning. It was just a possibility, but they had no better option.

"This is Sergeant Reilly," said the mellow voice on the headquarters telephone.

"Seamus, it's Trevor. Are you busy tonight? I'd like to take you to Delmonico's."

"Delmonico's? How extravagant! And you eat beans on Christmas Day just to save six bits! Yes, I am free, and much obliged. Whose license is it now, the Grand Pasha of Albania?"

"I'm on the level, and, yes, I do need a serious favor."

"Not a license plate, then?"

"No, something much more important, but first let me ask you a simple question: suppose a British agent committed murder in New York in order to suppress news about Britain's complicity in the *Lusitania* disaster."

"Suppose the dirty bastard did that. Then what?"

"Then he got away with it because of powerful friends in Washington, and he returned safely to London. And then the U.S. intervened in the European war on Britain's side because of it. How would you like that?"

"I wouldn't like it at all," said Sergeant Seamus Reilly.

CHAPTER 13

A SEASON FOR LIES

AT 9:15 THE NEXT MORNING, Percival and Caprioli strolled out of the Bureau of Investigation's midtown headquarters, discharged, at liberty, and bearing a written apology for their detention. Percival carried Trevor's briefcase. It belonged to Percival now, and, Trevor guessed, Percival's revolver was probably inside. To the intense surprise of Percival and Caprioli, Trevor awaited them on the sidewalk outside.

"Hello, it's Mr. Howells. Your little frame-up did not work, did it?" asked Percival, tipping his trademark ascot cap.

"I suppose you know," Trevor replied, resisting a barb, "that the Bureau of Investigation has seized all of Albi's documents?"

"I heard."

"And you know that I am ordered never to mention their existence?"

"I got that message."

"Well, it means that our contest is over. You won. I will return your two thousand dollars. You can go back to London."

Percival sneered. "You apologize, and you'd like to purchase forgiveness?"

"I thought you were a professional. Apologies are for amateurs."

"Amateurs should stay in the Flatiron Building. War is not an insurance claim you pay off. I don't like being set up for arrest, especially by bloody accountants. I warned you."

"You did, but—"

Interrupting, Percival laughed maliciously in Trevor's face. Then, turning to Caprioli, gaily said, "Our puppy wags his tail to avoid a spanking. What do you say, Roy?"

"You're fucking dead," growled Caprioli.

"A splendid summary," enthused Guy Percival, his thin nose curling with sinister disdain. "See you on Schermerhorn Street."

Trevor touched the back of his right hand to his forehead in mock despair, and then straightened up. "I guessed that's what you would say, so I arranged another surprise." He waved his right hand and pointed his left at Percival and Caprioli. Two uniformed policemen came up right away. "Meet Sergeant Seamus Reilly of the New York Police Department. The other's patrolman O'Connor."

"Guy Charles Percival," said Sergeant Reilly, "you are under arrest on suspicion of murder, grand theft, armed robbery, kidnapping, and unlawful possession of a firearm. Hey, where are you going, greaseball?

"I'm bringing my grandmother some potatoes," said Roy.

"Rocco Caprioli, you are also under arrest." Reilly blew a silver whistle and a horse-drawn Black Maria rumbled around the corner. O'Connor threw open the rear door. "Have you ever seen the inside of a paddy wagon in London, Captain Percival?" asked Reilly. "O'Connor will show you ours." Percival had no comment. New York's finest thereupon escorted Percival and Caprioli "downtown" where they were booked, held without bail, and consigned to the Tombs—a dank, foul-smelling jailhouse erected over a swamp.

Events moved swiftly. The immediate requirement was a police lineup in which Elmer Boganza, the taxi's driver and owner, and Trevor were asked to identify the hijackers from a group of eight. Each did so. The arrestees thus successfully fingered, which provided sufficient grounds for arraignment, Sergeant Reilly arranged an interview for Trevor that very afternoon with John O'Dwyer, the assistant district attorney for New York County. A wiry, genial man, clean shaven, with close-cropped light-brown hair and ruddy cheeks, O'Dwyer had acquired the basics of this case from Sergeant Reilly prior to meeting Trevor, whom he nonetheless requested to retell the entire story. It required an hour. O'Dwyer took notes.

At the end, heaving a sigh, O'Dwyer acknowledged that this was the "damndest case" he had encountered in ten years of prosecutions. "You claim that the Bureau seized Albi's documents from you and now won't acknowledge that they did so?"

"Worse. If I say the Albi documents existed, my fiancée and I will be charged with espionage."

"Well, the Bureau wants to keep the truth out of the courtroom. In Ireland we'd call it a cover-up."

"That's what we call it here too."

"You're sure that Percival is an English agent, not just a lunatic?" O'Dwyer raised a quizzical eyebrow. "I don't prosecute lunatics." This detail was apparently important, so Trevor assured him the Captain was of sound mind.

"In that case," O'Dwyer said, "let's talk conviction. You hand me a tough case. We have crimes and criminals, but no motive."

"The motive is suppression of headline-grabbing information about the *Lusitania*."

"Mr. Howells, you say that, and I believe you, but that's because, long before I heard your story, I understood that the English were maneuvering Uncle Sam into their war with Germany. That's the Irish in me, I suppose. But convincing a jury requires proof. And where does your story leave me? I might as well be discussing leprechauns, for I cannot pronounce the words 'Albi documents' in court, and what's more, if summoned, the Bureau won't acknowledge that they seized them. You have no receipts and no eyewitnesses. If I cannot obtain the Bureau's verification, then the documents don't exist, and in that case, what you call suppression of eyewitness testimony drops away as a motive. Help me out if you can." He sat back, arms crossed behind his head, skeptically awaiting enlightenment.

Trevor minimized the difficulty. "Boganza and I testify that Percival and Caprioli perpetrated the hijacking. Isn't that sufficient to convict them of armed robbery, hijacking, and kidnapping? Police records confirm that the assailants we described that day fit the men we picked out of your lineup today. They both carried illegal weapons when arrested. What more do you need?"

"Yes, we can convict them of carrying illegal weapons," O'Dwyer shrugged, "but to convict them of the serious felonies, I need a motive. Or should I tell the jury that Percival and Caprioli did not like your face?" O'Dwyer mugged, opened his eyes wide, and turned his palms face up in a gesture of dubiety. Trevor pondered, but said nothing. O'Dwyer sipped cold breakfast tea from a mug on his desk, licked his lips, and then continued, "And what about the murder? No one saw them. Worse, they have an alibi."

"They have no motive for the hijacking, and they have alibis for the murder," Trevor summarized, his mind spinning unproductively, and then he groaned. He had hoped that saying the words would solve the problem. It did not.

O'Dwyer nodded, still waiting, then broke the protracted silence. "That all boils down to a difficult case for hijacking and kidnapping, and no case at all for murder." Another silence ensued.

"What if you drop the murder charge?" Trevor asked. In years of lawsuits on behalf of Metropolitan Life, he had worked closely with attorneys, and in so doing had acquired an understanding of civil and criminal procedure. He was accustomed to plotting legal strategies. "In that case, you can prosecute them for hijacking the taxicab, for kidnapping, and for unlicensed possession of a firearm."

"There's no chance of conviction on the murder charge. I must drop it."

Trevor and Lotte had anticipated that decision, and had prepared a strategy to deal with it. New York's Sullivan Law barred convicted felons from gun ownership, and prescribed a lengthy prison term for any caught with a weapon. Although Captain Percival would get off with a fine for this offense, Caprioli, as a convicted felon, faced a prison sentence for the same crime. Trevor proposed that the prosecution could induce Caprioli to testify against Percival by offering to drop the weapons charge against him in exchange for his eyewitness testimony. It was a perfect solution to the courtroom dilemma, and O'Dwyer declared it "worth a try." He agreed to bring the plan to the immediate attention of Brian Davies, who was in charge of Caprioli's prosecution. They left it at that.

Two days later Trevor received a telephone message from O'Dwyer. Caprioli had rejected the plea bargain. The case would go to trial. Defense attorneys were requesting bail. O'Dwyer asked Trevor to come downtown for an immediate consultation. The unwelcome news required Trevor to reschedule several denial conferences, but, leaving that task to Lotte, he rushed to O'Dwyer's office. When Trevor entered, the prosecutor was scraping sardines into his garbage can. "I hate fish sandwiches," he explained.

"So do I," Trevor replied, "but I wouldn't waste the fish. Feed them to the ivy plant." Thereupon O'Dwyer scraped his sardines into the flowerpot, buried them with a pewter spoon, and dumped cold tea onto the muddy surface.

"Good suggestion," he said with satisfaction. After admiring the prosecutor's tidy widow garden, Trevor reminded him of the emergency message that had summoned him. He learned that Brian Davies had offered to drop all charges against Caprioli in exchange for his testimony against Captain Percival. By all rational calculation this offer should have worked. Caprioli faced certain conviction on the weapons charge, which would bring up to five years in prison, but, to the utter amazement of both prosecutors, Caprioli twice declined the offer, the second time with profanity, and was returned to his cell.

"I have two possible explanations," said O'Dwyer, philosophically stroking his chin. "One is that the man's not guilty and has a conscience." If Caprioli were not guilty and knew as well that Captain Percival was not guilty, O'Dwyer explained, then to obtain his own freedom Caprioli would be required to falsely denounce an innocent man. No one with a conscience could do that. "But Caprioli is guilty and doesn't have a conscience. That leaves the possibility that Caprioli feels confident of the trial's outcome." If Caprioli expected the jury to exonerate the Captain and to recommend clemency for his own weapons violation, then he would escape prison without having to testify against Percival. This alternative seemed quite plausible to O'Dwyer, but, he declared, "The uncertainty is damned annoying, because I have to ask myself again whether we have charged two innocent men with serious crimes."

"But," said Trevor, "you know they committed the kidnapping because you have my testimony as well as Boganza's. You also know that they carried guns at the Chelsea. These two are not clergy."

O'Dwyer stared at his cluttered desktop, then gazed n a long time out his south-facing window through which the October sunshine streamed onto his flower garden. "But I cannot prove that they murdered Joseph Albi, and I am holding them without bail on a capital charge. Their attorneys will ask a judge to accept bail, and I will have to show cause why it should be denied."

"Percival owns a one-way ticket back to England. He's a flight risk" Trevor proposed. Shaking his head, O'Dwyer thought that without a capital charge the court would grant bail to Percival. "The man has serious British credentials and important friends in Washington."

This rejection required Trevor to request a personal favor. "Percival threatened me with death when he came out of the Bureau's lockup. My fiancée and I are safe only if he and Caprioli are in jail. In time evidence may surface that permits you to retain the murder charge, or you can drop it later." It was a bluff. Trevor did not know what evidence might surface.

"You're asking me to retain a murder charge now in hope that evidence might appear later? That's unethical. You charge people when you have sufficient evidence—or you don't charge them."

"Mr. O'Dwyer, prosecutors have some discretion. Please exercise it, and consider the dire consequences for us if Percival and Caprioli get out of jail. But, most of all, don't you believe they did murder Albi?" Out of legal tricks, Trevor pled the simple truth.

O'Dwyer grimaced, scratched the back of his head, examined his fingernails, then slowly replied, "If I didn't believe that, I wouldn't prosecute. I'll ask the court to retain the murder charge for two weeks against my promise to provide more evidence. If it turns up, the court will retain the murder charge. Otherwise, they will be released in two weeks You're an investigator. Find me some evidence." Trevor promised to do so, and thanked the prosecutor for this decision. That settled, O'Dwyer returned unerringly to the question of motive. The gloomy silence of two days earlier returned. Neither could propose a solution.

At last, again confronting necessity, the fabled mother of invention, Trevor recollected his conversation with Agent Lightner. "Why did Percival hand me two thousand dollars in front of the Chelsea? Obviously he wanted to buy something. What he wanted is his motive."

O'Dwyer puckered his mouth, drummed his fingers on the table, then replied, "The two thousand dollars is people's exhibit A."

Trevor slapped his left hand on the chair arm in excitement, and then leaned forward as if communicating a confidence. "Agent Lightner asked Percival what he was buying."

"What did he answer?" O'Dwyer inquired dryly.

"A fictional story about the *Lusitania*. Yes, Percival told Lightner that I had a fictional story about the *Lusitania* and he wanted to buy the publication rights. Percival feared that otherwise I might sell a pro-German story to the flickers."

"Percival said that?"

"Yes. He needed some reason for having given me two thousand dollars. No doubt he invented this lie on the spur of the moment, but now he's stuck with it."

O'Dwyer leaned back, pensive, and took another sip of cold tea. It puckered his lips. "It's nonsense," he snickered, "but thank you Jesus, it does bring the *Lusitania* into the courtroom." O'Dwyer's face brightened at the prospect, then clouded as an old objection darkened his outlook. "But what exactly was their motive in the hijacking?"

"Robbery. When I refused to sell my silence, he resorted to robbery. The first time, he kidnapped me in the taxi. The second time he pressed two thousand dollars on me, hoping I'd take his offer, but he carried a gun in case the money failed."

O'Dwyer look puzzled. "So it was a business negotiation gone sour? The seamy side of the entertainment business?"

"That's exactly what Lightner called it. Lightner also said the Bureau has no interest in any fiction I wrote about the *Lusitania*."

O'Dwyer stroked his clean-shaven chin, rolled his eyes, then pointed a stubby ink-stained forefinger at Trevor. "That's so absurd that it might work. Since Percival said that he wanted to buy your fiction, we can refer to Joe Albi from whom you derived artistic inspiration. Percival wanted to buy, you refused to sell; he threatened violence on two occasions. Mr. Howells, you should have been an attorney."

"I wanted to become one," said Trevor miserably, "but we were poor. I had to work at fifteen. I'm self-educated." This autobiographical admission opened a path to friendship for the two men.

"Hell, I never finished school either," confessed O'Dwyer. As it was six o'clock in the evening, the end of a trying day, he invited Trevor to continue their conversation over dinner at a nearby bistro. As luck would have it, Tammany Hall's chieftain, Charles Francis Murphy, was dining there that night, and O'Dwyer waved to him across the crowded dining room. Murphy waved back, stubbed out his fat cigar, tucked a linen napkin into his wing collar, and turned to a fourteen-ounce steak. "That's Charles Murphy. He runs New York," said O'Dwyer through his teeth, still smiling and waving. "And it's well for you that he does."

"Why's that?" Trevor asked in all innocence.

"Trevor, Wall Street hopes the U.S. will enter the war on Britain's side. Otherwise their loans to Britain don't get repaid. Do you think you'd have a chance against Captain Percival if bankers appointed the district attorney instead of Mr. Charles Francis Murphy there? In that case, I assure you, John O'Dwyer, formerly of County Mayo, would not be talking to you now."

"County Mayo, is that where you're from?" Trevor asked, hoping that his question might strengthen their friendship. It proved a shrewd guess. O'Dwyer loved to talk about himself. One invitation was enough.

"I left County Mayo at age eighteen. It was a sad day, but my parents were cottagers, may God reward them. They had nothing to offer their children. I arrived in New York City with two dollars in my pocket. I soon obtained employment as a bicycle messenger for the police department on the recommendation of County Mayo friends. They were associates of the Tammany Hall organization that has sponsored the careers of so many distinguished political leaders. People in politics require many friends, you know."

"Yes, they sure do," said Trevor, privately thinking that many of those "distinguished political leaders" had found their way into the penitentiary.

"Later I worked as a policeman while studying law at night. I was admitted to the bar, and obtained employment in the city's legal department. I specialized in the law of sanitation, a filthy business." His little joke earned a chuckle. "Years later, thanks to Charles Murphy, a grand man, I was appointed assistant DA, the job I now have, and, if Murphy backs me, I hope to receive the Democratic nomination for district attorney in 1916." O'Dwyer puffed his lower lip, gestured toward Murphy with his fork, then stabbed his steak. Trevor nodded back, signaling that he was ready to believe the best about Charles Francis Murphy. This encouraged O'Dwyer, still chewing, to continue his monologue. "Growing up in County Mayo, a fellow learns how Ireland's troubles became his own. Did you know that England did nothing to relieve the Irish during the Great Famine?"

"I heard that, but honestly I never thought much about it. I had my own stomach to fill."

"Well, that's why so many Irish came to America. But we got something for our trouble—political power. Here in New York City we have a little corner of the world that Irish people run. The Irish don't run Ireland, England does, but, damn it, the Irish run New York City, and we remind my darling King George of that fact whenever the sweet bastard forgets it." Smiling, O'Dwyer took a swig of Guinness, and roguishly continued, "And the man's very forgetful. Tell me, why is King George so concerned about the rights of Belgium but forgets the rights of Ireland? Do you think a punch in the snoot would improve his memory?"

"It might. I don't understand King George either. I'm of Welsh descent. We're Celtic too." This response satisfied O'Dwyer about Trevor's sincere lack of admiration for the English monarchy. Reassured, he clapped Trevor on the shoulder, and then redirected the conversation to the prosecution's case against Captain Percival. O'Dwyer confided that the kidnapping case had "legs enough" to prosecute. "We don't need Albi's murder to put Percival in prison, because we can build on what he told the federal boys," said O'Dwyer with satisfaction. "Percival's cock-and-bull story will keep you out of Atlanta and put him and Caprioli in Sing Sing." O'Dwyer sighed, then made a confession of political innocence. "But I do hate telling outright lies in a court of law."

"John, I wouldn't fib if the Bureau had not forbidden the truth," Trevor replied, hoping to soothe O'Dwyer's legal conscience. Their conversation then turned to Percival's business experience. The Cunard Line had told the Bureau that Guy Percival undertook independent business. Trevor thought that claim another transparent lie.

"Sure, he's no businessman," O'Dwyer agreed. "He was all his life in the artillery, and served ten years in South Africa bombing the Boers."

"An artillery captain! I assumed he was a naval captain." Trevor balled his left hand into a fist and struck his right hand palm, excited to extend O'Dwyer's observation. His left elbow on the table, he shook his open palm as if shaking out a fresh idea. "But it makes sense. Purchasing agent for Cunard provided a perfect cover for an ex-artillery officer whose job was to procure cannon shells and explosives. I bet Percival himself ordered the guncotton loaded aboard the *Lusitania*."

"And how about Percival's convenient arrangement with Caprioli?"

O'Dwyer paused dramatically as if testing Trevor's insight, and when a reply did not come promptly, he charged ahead. "Caprioli opened Percival's access to Kelly. When Joe Albi fenced the stolen explosives through Kelly, the news went straight to Caprioli and from him to Percival."

Trevor was impressed at the speed with which the district attorney drew the connections, and swiftly drew one of his own. "In a way, Albi's theft was good news for England," Trevor ventured. When O'Dwyer looked puzzled, he explained. "The *Lusitania* went to the bottom with all that ammunition onboard. Whatever the stevedore stole was all that remained of the original shipment, and the British were short of ammunition, so Percival offered to buy back what Albi had stolen, probably hoping he'd stolen all of it."

"I am not sure they ever wanted to *buy* it," O'Dwyer objected, still ahead of Trevor. "If Albi stayed alive, there always remained a possibility that the newspapers would get hold of the story. Percival may have intended to kill Albi from the start."

"Albi underestimated his risk," Trevor shuddered. "That's a mistake insurance investigators never make—well, hardly ever." He raised his Guinness, adding cheerfully, "To fools rushing in!" O'Dwyer clinked his glass, and they turned silently to their dessert, apple pie à la mode. The dessert did not sweeten the bitter truths they had exchanged.

Later that evening, gleefully free of the tensions that had troubled them for weeks, Lotte and Trevor first celebrated in bed. Then they opened a celebratory bottle of domestic Riesling. "It's just as well you missed dinner tonight," said Lotte. "If Detective Fulton knew you ate *Sauerbraten, Rotkraut,* and *Kartoffelpüree,* and washed it down with a Riesling, he'd know for sure you're a spy."

"Just eating German food is bad," Trevor joked, "but when the chef is a spy, it's the Wurst." It was a poor joke, but laughter came as easily that night as when they first fell in love. What a relief the laughter was after weeks of tension-provoking anxiety. So, both in excellent humor, they finished the wine, and, sitting back, Lotte idly wondered what had become of Percival's money. "I asked for six thousand. He gave me two.

Lightner has the money."

"The scoundrel cheated you, Trevor." Her champion should not be a simpleton. "And where is the two thousand now?"

"Lotte, it's a prosecution exhibit. I get it once the trial's over. Oh, my gosh." Trevor froze. "I forgot about Francine. No one's told her yet that Percival and Caprioli are in jail."

"I already did," said Lotte. "That is why you have not had a return visit from Filipo and Albert. Francine is delighted, but she needs her money right away."

"I'll withdraw it from the Chemical Bank tomorrow. A pity we could not get the whole twenty thousand for her. At least the murderers will do time." This cheerful thought enabled them to finish the wine. Then they fell asleep in each other's arms.

The judge set the trial date for Wednesday, December 8, seven weeks in the future. With Percival and Caprioli in jail, life resumed its normal routines for Lotte and Trevor. They got up and went to work daily, riding the same subway cars and entering the Flatiron Building at the same time. Then they left the Flatiron together in the evenings, unmindful of the curious eyes that noticed. At work, Trevor frequently visited Lotte's desk, and they exchanged loving glances even while retaining external formalities. Catherine Donohue watched, guessed the truth, and told the switchboard operators. Lotte and Trevor quickly became office gossip. One afternoon, Trevor saw Winthrop J. Tolson approach, his small face squeezed into a fist, malevolence in his pale eyes. Tolson resembled a distinguished bird of prey with a swooping thin nose, turtle mouth, thick brows, port-wine cheeks, floss of white hair, and small, contemptuous eyes peering out from under a silk top hat. Trevor braced himself.

"Mr. Howells, your relationship with Miss Schlegel has become public gossip."

"I did *not* know that," Trevor declared, feigning incredulity.

"Well, now you do. Gossip interferes with efficiency. It's intolerable. I must know whether there is any truth in it."

"I assume you mean a romantic relationship." Trevor was stalling in hope of finding a way around Tolson's inquiry.

"Yes, of course. Company rules do not permit romantic relationships between employees. Metro Life is neither a lonely-hearts club nor a dance hall. I thought you understood that policy, and supported it."

Trevor gulped. "Of course I do, sir."

"Well?"

"Mr. Tolson, I do not have a romantic relationship with that woman, but we are friendly, and others might wrongly suppose that we do." Tolson paused, frowned, studied Trevor's face, and slowly replied.

"Is that the truth?"

"Yes, sir." Trevor brazenly lied.

"Mr. Howells, I accept your reassurance. Let me warn you, however, that your innocent exchanges with Miss Schlegel must not arouse further gossip. You should amend your conduct, and advise Miss Schlegel to do the same. If the gossip dies away, I will disregard this report."

"Thank you, sir. But at the risk of impertinence, may I point out that friendly relationships among staff *improve* efficiency?" As Tolson's nose and chin seemed ready to collide, Trevor did not finish his objection; rather, to his happy surprise, Tolson, regaining self-mastery, took the objection as an opportunity to expound his philosophy of management.

"Yes, Mr. Howells, well spoke. Friendship promotes efficiency, but romance reduces it. If a man's mooning over the poppet at the next desk, he does no work and he prevents the poppet from working too. Then others gossip about them instead of working. In the end, no one works, and I will see the results in the balance sheet." Trevor gulped, nodded, and extruded his lower lip in mute recognition of Tolson's wisdom. That acknowledged, Tolson continued. "I know everyone's value to the company, including yours. Howells, you saved Metro one hundred thousand dollars last year."

"One hundred *fifty* thousand dollars. I trust you are satisfied with my work, Mr. Tolson."

"Yes, Mr. Howells ... except for these annoying rumors. Listen, I don't love playing the emperor of Japan." Trevor blanched, but the savage old man continued. "Of course I know that's what they call me, but if the fools had read political economy, they would understand that Metropolitan Life is a small cog in a great mill."

"What great mill is that?" Trevor asked, out of his depth and puzzled.

"Why, our insurance industry. If I do not prohibit romance, the men chase the women, the women chase the men, no one works, other companies get our customers, and Metropolitan goes broke. Then we're all beggars. Can you now understand what political economy dictates about office romances?"

"Uh, yes, sir, I get it."

"Good. Take the lesson to heart and you might get somewhere in business." Then, resuming hauteur of command, his normal facial attire, the company's owner stalked majestically away.

"I shall. Thanks for your explanation, sir," Trevor stammered after him. The lies had saved his job.

Riding to work alone the next morning, Lotte having taken an earlier train to forestall gossip, Trevor became aware that a large, neatly bearded cleric with rimless wire spectacles had taken a seat next to him. The man wore a Baptist preacher's black hat and clerical collar and carried a Holy Bible with large gold lettering on its cover, but instead of reading it, he now glared disapprovingly at Trevor. Clergyman or not, staring at another passenger violated subway etiquette. Annoyed, Trevor looked up from his *Times* in impatience, and, looking carefully at the rude cleric, suddenly perceived Ben Williams behind the Bible, beard, and spectacles. The abrupt mental transformation reminded Trevor of an optical illusion such as the psychologists from time to time published in the popular science magazines.

"Hello," said Williams, seeing that Trevor had recognized him. "Thanks for warning me about the Chelsea Hotel. Your message reached me barely in time. I was walking out the door when my landlady handed it to me."

"I owed you that," Trevor replied, furtively looking around the subway car. "I don't think I'm being followed, but it's possible," he joked.

"Me neither," whispered Williams, who was not joking. "I heard that Percival and Caprioli will be tried for kidnapping and auto theft because the federal cops won't release the documents. Is that right?"

"Yes, that's true. I can't even mention Albi's documents in court. But how did you know?"

"My friends know things. These friends would like to see Percival tried for murder. They think an English captain's murder conviction might blow the lid off the *Lusitania* cover-up."

"Your friends are German spies, aren't they?"

Williams ignored his question. "My friends have great resources, and they'll stop at nothing to prevent the United States from entering the European war. Isn't that something you favor?"

"I prefer friends who don't sabotage American ships."

"In war, you take what friends you can get," Williams shrugged.

"It doesn't matter. Whoever they are, your friends won't get their wish. O'Dwyer will drop the murder charge in five days unless new evidence turns up."

"He wants new evidence?"

"Yes, preferably eyewitnesses to the murder."

"Suppose we produce a witness?" Williams asked. Trevor sucked his teeth in surprise. "Maybe someone saw Roy and Percival drive up to the Cunard pier just prior to Albi's fall."

"That won't work. A defense witness claims that Percival and Caprioli were in Hoboken on the night that Albi died."

"Their witness is lying, right?"

"Yes, but we can't prove it. He's a Cunard employee named Francis MacMurray, and claims to have discussed a purchasing deal with Percival that evening."

"And Percival went to Hoboken on company business? In a rental limousine?"

"He has a receipt from Caprioli."

"If someone reached him, MacMurray might remember that the meeting took place earlier. If he won't, our witness would contradict him, in which case O'Dwyer will allege perjury. If O'Dwyer confronts MacMurray with an eyewitness who calls him a liar, well, that will make it easier to shake his testimony. So I need you to talk to Francine Albi."

"About what?"

"I want you to remind her that convicting Percival of murder would bring her the life insurance money. Ask her to cooperate with me. She doesn't know me, but she trusts you. Tell her right away. Time is short."

Trevor repliedthat he had never suborned witness tampering.

"Don't be a chump, Howells. Liars loaded the system against us. Hell, Wilson lies. Cunard lies. Percival lies. MacMurray lies. Lightner lies. The British lie. The Germans lie. In war everyone lies."

"You ask me to encourage Francine to cooperate in witness tampering?"

"That's our business, hers and mine. You're not involved. If she helps me, Percival gets the electric chair, and Francine Albi gets the money. It's all up to you now. Percival wins and Francine loses; or Percival loses, and Francine wins. You choose. You won't see me again."

"Why not?"

"My friends have decided that they cannot keep the U.S. out of the European war, so they are shifting their priority from propaganda to sabotage. That's not my agenda. I signed on to prevent the U.S. from getting involved in an imperialist war. I don't give a tin hoot which imperialist army wins that war, but my friends do."

"What happens to you now?"

"I go west, reconnect with the movement, and sing Wobbly songs in mining towns until the cops nail me." Trevor objected that singing songs seemed a silly way to organize workers. Williams disagreed. "It's a trick we learned from the Salvation Army. Music builds a crowd, makes them feel good, and then you tell the truth that wakes up the working stiffs. Didn't you ever hear Joe Hill's catchy tunes?" Trevor had never heard of Joe Hill. "Well, watch what happens when I sing one." Thereupon, arising from his seat, Williams belted out Joe Hill's revision of *Sweet Bye and Bye,* a familiar Baptist hymn.

> Longhaired preachers come out every night
> Try to tell you what wrong and what's right.
> But when asked about something to eat,
> They will answer in voices so sweet:
> You will eat, bye and bye,
> In that glorious land way up high.
> Work and pray,
> Live on hay.
> You'll get pie in the sky when you die.

It really worked. Williams had a strong baritone voice, audible above the subway's screeching, and the passengers looked up in surprise at the familiar melody. Williams had gained their attention. The verse concluded, instead of proceeding to a sermon, Williams bowed to his fellow passengers, waved his Bible aloft, then sat down. Another crazy revivalist, they thought, and they looked down at their reading again. Williams glanced out the window as the train ground to a station stop. "Oops, it's my stop. Bye-bye. Tell Francine right away, and good luck." Williams disappeared into the busy 14th Street subway station.

Riding uptown to the 23rd Street station, Trevor meditated on Williams's request. He was asked to promote witness tampering. It wasn't the risk that distressed him; the risks were someone else's. It was fouling a law court with lies. He still wanted to become an attorney, and despite the contorted legal theory he had cooked up with O'Dwyer, still wanted to believe that courtrooms were sanctuaries of truth. Trevor did not like, but could not reject, the ugly truths that Williams had uttered about the legal system in wartime, so it shocked him to realize that he agreed with the bearded fugitive that witness tampering was the only way to force the justice system to produce justice. In the past he would not have agreed. Now he did. "*To every thing there is a season.*" *Peace is the season for truth. War is the season for lies.* He could now tolerate witness tampering, and he would pass Williams's message along to Francine Albi that very day.

Tombs Prison (left) and N.Y. Criminal Courts Building
with "bridge of sighs" between them, 1905.

CHAPTER 14

THE OFFICIAL THEORY

TWO DAYS LATER, Francine Albi brought John O'Dwyer a new witness: Filipo Albi, who had "not wanted to get involved," but who, after much soul searching, and on the advice of his confessor, decided to spill his story. Filipo declared that he had been with his brother when Joe interviewed Guy Percival on Barrow Street. According to Filipo, Joe claimed to have found explosives onboard the *Lusitania.* Percival told Joe Albi that he wanted to protect the Cunard Line from liability, and offered him $1,000 in exchange for his silence. Joe agreed to sell but raised the price to $20,000, which Percival agreed to pay. Later, Joe Albi told his brother in confidence that he had no such evidence. It was all "a bluff," but, as Percival did not know this, Joe thought he stood a chance to make some "serious dough." That was all Filipo Albi knew. He was able to pick Percival out of a police lineup, but could not identify Rocco Caprioli.

The very next day, Francine Albi brought O'Dwyer another new witness, who had been working on the *Alneria* on the night Joe Albi died there. The new witness, Franco Gianni, had heard about the case in waterfront taverns, and offered his testimony in the expectation that it might prove important. Gianni had seen a Chevrolet touring car park in front of Pier 54 around ten at night on the same day that Joseph Albi died there. It was the same model that Caprioli drove. The driver and a passenger got out. The passenger was tall, wore a tweed sack jacket and an ascot cap, and spoke in a British accent, advising the driver to accompany him. The two men entered Pier 54. Gianni picked Percival out of a police lineup, identifying him as the passenger he had seen that day, but could not identify Rocco Caprioli.

The testimony of Frank Gianni and Filipo Albi enabled the prosecution to retain the murder charge against Percival, whose appeal for bail was again denied. O'Dwyer thanked God, but Trevor knew this gift was not from the deity. As anticipated, Gianni's testimony focused O'Dwyer's suspicion on Francis MacMurray, the defense's star witness. Gianni had seen Percival at the fatal pier at the same time and on the same day that MacMurray had placed him across the Hudson River in Hoboken. O'Dwyer dispatched a detective to interview MacMurray the next day, and to warn him of the existence of an eyewitness whose testimony contradicted his own. Trevor asked to accompany him, and received permission on condition that he asked no questions of the witness, but only prompted the detective, if requested.

Francis MacMurray lived in a substantial two-story house on Hudson Street, near the Hoboken Ferry Terminal. Detective Daniel Malone and Trevor visited the house, arriving at 5:30 in the evening. MacMurray opened the door. An elderly man with snow-white hair, he wore crisply ironed linen pants, a crocodile-skin belt, and a striped cotton shirt without a collar. He looked worried when Detective Malone introduced himself and "Dr. Howells," but nonetheless invited them in. A retired employee of the Cunard Line, with thirty-five years' experience as a purchasing agent, MacMurray now worked for Cunard in freelance sales; that is, he routinely got the company's purchase requirements and scouted for low-cost providers. When he found a winner, he got a percentage of the savings. He also advertised the Cunard Line to exporters, and earned a commission for any sales he made to new customers. Once seated in the opulent parlor, furnished in palms, marble, and mahogany, MacMurray consulted his gold pocket watch, then advised the visitors that he had only fifteen minutes. O'Dwyer had charged Malone with challenging the witness in the hope of shaking his testimony. It was not going to be a friendly interview.

"Did you know that a stevedore saw Guy Charles Percival in front of Pier 54 at ten o'clock on the night Joseph Albi died?"

"How would I know? I mind my own business."

"Sure, you do," replied detective Malone. "But didn't you tell the defense attorneys that Guy Percival and Rocco Caprioli were here at eight thirty on that very day? Could you have made a mistake about the time or date?"

"I don't think so. Let me explain. Hoboken is the American headquarters of the Hamburg Amerika Line. This was Cunard's major competitor before the war. Vendors would come to my house, but I had to be cautious because, you see, some of the business I scouted, the Hamburg Amerika Line would otherwise have obtained. I snatched business right out of their hungry jaws. A lot of Germans in this town work for the Hamburg Line. They resented my competition, and would sometimes fake attractive offers on behalf of nonexistent vendors. I would order goods that never arrived, which embarrassed me and distressed Cunard."

"Interesting, but how do you know that Percival and Caprioli were here on June fifteenth at nine in the evening?"

"I'm getting to that. I learned to keep a record of all my business discussions and to check identities. As I recall, Percival and I discussed bulk cheese." Detective Malone asked to see MacMurray's journal. In response MacMurray opened a desk, and withdrew a ledger that, on page 32, showed a "DISCUSSED CHEESE PERCIVAL" notation on 15 June 1915.

"What about the time of day?" Detective Malone persisted.

"Well, Percival always came around after working hours."

"So how do you know it was around nine in the evening, not earlier?"

"He always came around nine, and I remember that conversation because Percival was accompanied by a driver. He usually came alone." Examining the ledger closely, with the use of a huge magnifying lens, Detective Malone declared that he might have found a fault.

"Look here: 'Percival' has been entered in the ledger after the words 'discussed cheese.' That's why the name's so cramped and small. And I think a different pen nib has been used. Wouldn't you agree, Dr. Howells?" After inspecting the entry with the lens, and taking a great deal of time, "Dr. Howells" confirmed that it looked that way to him as well. The conversation made Francis MacMurray uncomfortable. He glanced furtively from one to the other of his visitors.

"I notice also," continued Malone, that other ledger entries, excepting only Percival's, show a return address and telephone."

"Percival was already known to me, so I just noted his name without inserting an address. Maybe I decided to make a note of the name later after writing the words 'discussed cheese.' I don't remember. The point is I fully trusted Percival. Now, if you will excuse me, I have another appointment."

"You have an appointment in court too. You're not under oath now, Mr. MacMurray, but you will be when you offer testimony. A man can get ten years for lying under oath. A handwriting expert will examine your ledger before your testimony and determine its authenticity using a microscope." This was pure bluff, but it frightened MacMurray.

"Sure, I know," said MacMurray uneasily.

Trevor whispered into Malone's ear. "What kinds of cheese do you usually buy for Cunard?"

"Brie is very popular onboard, and so is Gouda."

"In that case, why did you buy bulk cheese?"

"The Gouda and Brie are for the passengers, but an overseas customer wanted bulk cheese for delivery abroad."

"Who was the seller of this bulk cheese?"

"I buy from multiple wholesalers."

"How much cheese would you normally acquire for a passage?"

"Enough to feed the passengers over a seven-day cruise. About one thousand pounds."

Again Trevor whispered in Malone's ear. "Was that cheese refrigerated?" asked Malone.

"Of course it was," MacMurray said.

"Then why did the *Lusitania* carry two hundred seventeen thousand pounds of cheese on her fatal voyage?"

"There was a wholesale buyer abroad."

"Who was that buyer?"

"That information is a proprietary secret of the Cunard Line, as are the names of my suppliers. We don't want competition for cheese contracts."

"Why was the cheese not refrigerated?"

"Stowage is not my responsibility."

"Were explosives carried aboard in cheese cartons?"

The question considerably agitated MacMurray, who denied it.

"Did you ever scout munitions manufacturers that supplied the Royal Navy?"

"Of course. The U.S. supplies Britain with a great deal of ammunition, but it's illegal to load explosives aboard a passenger liner. That's why there were none aboard the *Lusitania,* if that's what you're getting at. I know there are baseless rumors to the contrary."

"Thanks very much, Mr. MacMurray. When you are under oath, you will be required to tell the court who was the wholesale buyer of that two hundred seventeen thousand pounds of bulk cheese, and who was the supplier, proprietary secret or not. Refusal will bring you a contempt of court conviction and jail time. Good day to you."

With Malone's report in hand, O'Dwyer felt renewed confidence about his ability to shake Percival's alibi. "MacMurray knows what cargo was onboard the *Lusitania.* He knows now that we have a witness who contradicts him. He fudged his ledger book, and he's lying about Caprioli and Percival," exulted O'Dwyer. "I will tear him to pieces on the witness stand," he promised, "but it won't be for want of expert defense counsel. Guy Percival has signed Angus P. Murdock, the best defense attorney in New York. Murdock is renewing Percival's request for bail." It was the defense's third attempt. Later that day Angus Murdock offered $200,000 in surety to the court, a vast sum; however, as no bail could be accepted in murder cases, the defense's motion was again denied.

"Where is Percival getting all that money?" Lotte asked Trevor that October evening.

"He says it comes out of his pocket."

"An assistant purchasing agent has got two hundred thousand dollars?" Lotte cocked a skeptical eyebrow.

"He's a younger son of an aristocratic family. He says that he has abundant means. O'Dwyer suspects that Cunard is paying his attorney fees under the table."

"What if that slick lawyer gets Percival off?"

"I will hire bodyguards with Percival's money! They can take over as knights errant. I'm out of the chivalry business."

Two days before the case came to trial, the Cunard Line notified the attorneys for defense and prosecution that Francis MacMurray had failed to respond to work assignments. Cunard had ascertained that MacMurray was no longer at home, but he had not advised the company of any travel plans. Cunard had no knowledge of his current whereabouts, and neither did his neighbors nor his adult children. MacMurray's house stood empty and his bank accounts were untouched. As MacMurray's testimony had placed Percival and Caprioli in Hoboken at the time of Albi's death, his disappearance hugely damaged the case for the defense, which requested and received a continuance of forty-five days in which to locate MacMurray or plan a case without his testimony. O'Dwyer told the judge in chambers that MacMurray had fled in order to avoid perjury on the witness stand, but privately O'Dwyer wondered why, in that case, MacMurray had removed no funds from his bank account. Trevor and Lotte guessed that MacMurray had been garroted and his body dumped into a New Jersey canal.

No one ever heard from Francis MacMurray again. During the six weeks in which the defense repaired its damaged case, O'Dwyer and Trevor, now friends, met frequently, and learned to move comfortably between what they called "the official theory," intended for the courtroom, and the simple truth they privately shared. Absurd as it seemed to Trevor and Lotte, the official theory fit all the facts that the prosecution would submit in evidence, and, given the prosecution's new witnesses, the theory might convict the defendant of all the felonies he was accused of, including the murder of Joseph Albi.

Nonetheless, unknown to Trevor, and despite their frequent discussions, O'Dwyer gradually became uncomfortable with the official theory. As an officer of the court, he could not in conscience prosecute someone for murder under a legal theory he himself knew to be false, even though personally confident that the defendant was guilty. It posed a moral dilemma for him. A sensible and decent man, as well as a conscientious prosecutor, O'Dwyer mulled his reservations for weeks, brought them to the attention of his confessor, and then finally broached them to Trevor a week before the long-deferred trial was to open.

"I don't want to present a bogus legal theory in court."

"I share your discomfort," Trevor replied, not yet realizing the gravity of O'Dwyer's defection, "but we are forbidden to tell the truth. Either we fib or Albi's murderers get off." Trevor expected O'Dwyer to accept this line, but this time he did not.

"*We do not have to fib!* If we play this case by the law, O'Dwyer replied, "you declare true facts in court, and if necessary go to prison for having done so. That's the price you pay to convict Captain Percival. Approaching the court with a cock-and-bull story, we pervert the legal process.

"John, does our white lie pervert justice," Trevor snorted, "or only the law? In this case, the law obstructs justice."

"No, what obstructs justice is your reluctance to do time in Atlanta. Sorry, but that's *your* moral dilemma. I swore to uphold the law. That's *my* moral dilemma."

"Rules before right?"

"Yes, and laws before justice. This is why you must tell the court what

Albi stole from the *Lusitania,* what his affidavits said, and what happened to them. I will bring the notary, Ferretti, to the stand in support. He will lend some credibility to your claim."

Trevor regarded him aghast, but O'Dwyer continued, "Just tell the truth, and let the chips fall where they may."

"The Bureau will deny that they seized any documents. They will bring out Lotte's letter to her uncle. Lotte and I will go to prison for espionage and perjury, and Percival will go free. He's a murderer, but Lotte and I will be in prison."

"That would probably happen, but—"

Face drawn and eyes agitated, Trevor interrupted, "And where was the law when the Bureau confiscated Albi's documents, refused me a receipt, and threatened to jail me if I squawked?" he demanded with furious indignation.

"No need to yell. Yes, the Bureau violated your rights, but the law has a remedy. You must sue the federal government and demand restitution of your documents. Maybe you've heard the legal maxim *Dura lex, sed lex*?"

"I don't know Latin, John, but the message is 'tough on me.' I can sue the Bureau of Investigation from a federal prison cell, demanding that they return documents they deny they took and whose existence I can't prove," snorted Trevor in derision.

"Trevor, if you want Percival convicted, you and your girlfriend have to do time."

"I was hoping the law could do more."

"Regrettably not. But you should also understand my political situation. The Bureau of Investigation contacted Governor Whitman. They requested that my boss, Ed Swann, withdraw all charges against Caprioli and Percival on grounds of national security. The Bureau believes that German agents murdered Francis MacMurray in order to frame Percival and Caprioli for Albi's murder. It's possible. I mean, where the hell is MacMurray?"

"Of course it's possible," scoffed Trevor, "but it's also possible that, facing a perjury conviction, MacMurray went to Tahiti and will live out his days under a coconut tree."

"Don't be stupid, Trevor. MacMurray's murder is a genuine possibility. The Bureau of Investigation is also concerned that, even if the prosecution makes no factual claim regarding the *Lusitania*'s secret cargo, as I have pledged not to do—"

"You pledged?"

"Yes, Ed Swann required it. What's the difference? You wanted to avoid that topic."

It was true, and Trevor made no reply. O'Dwyer continued, "The Bureau complained that the trial of a British army captain for the murder of a stevedore would attract international attention even if the captain was exonerated. As is, rumors are circulating all over the world about the *Lusitania*'s secret cargo of explosives. A trial's publicity would embarrass American diplomacy. Whitman and Swann are under federal pressure to suppress this case, and I am feeling their pressure. This trial is a hot potato. I know it's a disappointment, and I am sorry to have to pass this news along."

"A disappointment? Hell, no, John. It's a disaster," Trevor stammered. Then, thinking fast, he found a legal objection: "If New York State withdraws a murder prosecution at the behest of the federal government, doesn't that violate Joseph Albi's right to equal protection under the Fourteenth Amendment? I mean if you're murdered by foreigners whom the federal government wants to protect, state laws don't protect you, and your Constitutional right to life is violated."

"You really should have been an attorney, Trevor. I don't know the answer. Ask the Supreme Court," replied John O'Dwyer.

CHAPTER 15

THE TRIAL

FORTUNATELY, JOHN O'DWYER was not only a conscientious prosecutor but also an ambitious politician. In the winter of 1916, Ireland rang with nationalist agitation against British rule. Irish voters in New York City heard the clamor. Prosecution of a captain in the British army was popular in the Irish political clubs to which O'Dwyer owed his hope of someday becoming mayor. Additionally, Tammany's sachem, Charles Francis Murphy, had spoken favorably of O'Dwyer's prosecution of Captain Percival, pointing out, "Here in New York City, unlike Ireland, British officers must obey the laws against murder." The line won enthusiastic applause in Irish political clubs, and Charles Murphy took note. His favorable mention indirectly endorsed O'Dwyer's nomination as Democratic candidate for district attorney in 1916. Withdrawing the prosecution of Percival because of political pressure would have been unpopular with Tammany's election-day army of ward heelers, manhole inspectors, patronage appointees, bookmakers, municipal contractors, garbage collectors, crooked cops, and gamblers.

Although Governor Whitman had asked Ed Swann to dismiss charges against Percival and Caprioli, Whitman was a Republican and Swann a Democrat. Given the enthusiastic support that he expected his own political base to accord this prosecution, Charles Murphy decided to ignore pressure from the Republican governor. Just days before the trial began, Murphy's recommendation was delivered to Swann who then delivered it to John O'Dwyer. The trial would proceed.

The late-breaking news did not reach Trevor and Lotte. On the opening morning of the trial, January 19, 1916, after several sleepless nights, the couple took seats in the courtroom gallery. Watching the bailiff put the flags in place, Trevor gloomily remarked to Lotte that O'Dwyer would throw them both to the wolves that very day. Lotte squeezed his hand in tacit agreement, and then glanced apprehensively across the courtroom where Agent Lightner sat behind the defense table, occasionally passing notes to the defense counsel. Finally John O'Dwyer entered the courtroom and proceeded toward the prosecution table. As he reached Trevor's seat, O'Dwyer leaned over and whispered that he had determined to proceed to trial with the "official theory."

"Hallelujah! But why?" Trevor asked as wild relief overcame him.

"Justice requires us to try Percival for murder, and Governor Whitman can jump in the lake. But Murphy, out of deference to President Wilson, prefers that we use the official story."

Trevor wondered why Tammany Hall deferred to President Wilson, their political opponent, but he said nothing. Instead, he whispered the welcome news to Lotte and to Francine Albi. Francine had feared that her husband's murderers would go free that very day, in which case, she knew, Filipo and Albert would volunteer to exact a blood vengeance. Lotte had worried that the truth from the witness stand would send her and Trevor to prison, but when O'Dwyer took his seat they all knew that a trial would take place with the official theory emanating from the prosecution table.

Ten minutes later, Guy Charles Percival took a seat next to his celebrity attorney, Angus P. Murdock, who wore a gray homburg, a tailor-made three-piece blue suit, spats, and a white boutonniere. O'Dwyer made do with a plain blue serge suit, black shoes, and white shirt without gold stickpin. Percival and Caprioli had requested and received separate trials. "Jail pale," Percival wore his trademark tweeds, sat tall, and looked unemotionally around the room. He nodded to Agent Lightner, who returned the acknowledgment. If he noticed all the enemies seated in patient attendance, he showed no sign or any recognition of the resentment blazing in many eyes and the hatred in some.

A jury of twelve men and two alternates had been impaneled. Four jurors were of Irish descent or Irish immigrants; three were Italian immigrants; six were native white Protestants; and one was a Russian-born Jew. The defense had challenged two men of German descent during the voir dire examination. O'Dwyer had memorized the jurors' seating chart, and knew the name, occupation, and ethnic background of every juror and the two alternates. Seated at the prosecution table, an assistant was instructed to watch the jurors in the course of testimony and signal their favorable or unfavorable responses to whatever O'Dwyer was saying.

On the bench sat Howard J. McCarthy, indebted to Tammany Hall for his job, but competent, fair, and honest by New York standards. Once the bailiff had called the courtroom to order, Judge McCarthy outlined the special circumstances under which the trial would proceed. Although heard in a state court, he declared, the case had national-security implications. Therefore he had decided, after consultation with the U.S. Attorney General, to order a closed trial. Citing *Totten v. United States,* 92 U.S. 105 (1876) and sequel, Judge McCarthy explained that, in the interest of national security, courts had authority to set aside the Sixth Amendment guarantee of a public trial. In a closed trial, only jurors, police, the defendant, witnesses, principals, and attorneys could be in the courtroom. Moreover, no one was permitted to explain to outsiders, especially to news reporters, the nature of the proceedings or the evidence presented. This prohibition applied to jurors and principals as well as to court personnel. It extended into the indefinite future. The court would release a verdict to the public, but the trial transcript would not be made public, and neither would any other news of the trial. Judge McCarthy declared that any breach of these guidelines would bring fine and imprisonment.

As this decision was a possible source of reversible error, the judge asked both counselors whether they concurred. The defense immediately declared no objection; however, curiously enough, concurrence was not advantageous for the prosecution, the usual beneficiary of closed trials. From Tammany Hall's point of view, trial publicity would bring neutralist and Irish voters to the Democratic ticket in 1916, but, as he later explained, O'Dwyer dared not object to closure. Defying the president, the governor, and the mayor was trouble enough, so after some hesitation he accepted a closed trial.

Judge McCarthy then asked the jurors if everyone understood the restrictions. The jurors' heads tilted back, and there was an audible gasp, the simultaneous product of several throats, but none demurred. "You must not discuss this case with anyone during or after the trial on pain of prosecution." He polled the jurors by number, obtaining from each a statement that he had heard, understood, and intended to comply with the closure restrictions. The bailiff then cleared the courtroom of all persons not authorized to be present, including Lotte.

The first prosecution witness was Francine Albi, who wore a wide-brimmed black hat without additional ornament, a black veil, and a decorous floor-length dress with a loose-fitting black jacket that concealed her bosom. She had also tied her hair in a simple bun. Francine's rosy cheeks and characteristically bemused smile could not be made to disappear, but O'Dwyer's coaching enabled her to portray a distraught woman. O'Dwyer called her "widow Albi" on every possible occasion. His questioning revealed the desperate financial position in which her husband's death had left her "and her four orphaned children," whom he asked her to name and describe individually. As she did so, offering details of each child's angelic disposition, adorable habits, and worn-out shoes, and breaking down in tears at one point, her weeping face in her handkerchief, head cradled in elbow, Francine's recital evoked sympathy from all the jurors, some of whom daubed their eyes.

Then Francine testified that she had seen Percival and her late husband together on the day of their first meeting on Barrow Street. Trevor knew that was a lie; nonetheless, Francine correctly identified Percival in the courtroom, pointing an accusing finger and declaring, "That's the man who murdered my husband," an accusation the judge instructed the jury to disregard. Trevor knew that Francine had not been present when Percival first interviewed Joseph Albi on Barrow Street. He surmised that Williams had planted Francine's lie, a surmise that she later confirmed in private. He did not divulge her perjury to O'Dwyer, and neither did she.

On cross-examination by Angus Murdock, who expressed the defendant's immense sympathy for the widow and her children, Francine acknowledged that she had not actually heard anything Percival and Joseph Albi said. She also acknowledged that her late husband had "hoped to sell his story" for financial gain to the defendant. Murdock asked Francine what proof her husband had of his claims, and learned that he had only his affidavit. Francine did not mention the shipping labels. The defense attorney then thanked and courteously dismissed her, offering a helping hand to steady her weeping descent from the witness stand.

Filipo Albi testified to having heard every word that passed between his brother and Percival on Barrow Street. Here was another lie that Trevor attributed to Williams's coaching. According to Filipo, Percival had declared that he wanted Joseph Albi's documents in order to protect the Cunard Line from financial responsibility for the disaster. When Joseph had declared in outrage that Cunard should "pay the families what they owe," Percival sneered that this was "foolish and unrealistic."

As Francine Albi had also sworn that her brother had been present that morning on Barrow Street, Angus Murdock did not contest Filipo's claim. He did, however, compel Filipo to acknowledge that Percival was "under no obligation to disclose" any patriotic motive to Joseph Albi while negotiating, and in fact had a financial incentive to hide it. Also, the Mersey Commission in Liverpool subsequently exonerated the Cunard Line of any financial responsibility for the *Lusitania* disaster, so Percival's cynical comment proved correct: It had been unrealistic of Joseph Albi to expect that a British court would compel the Cunard

Line to assume financial liability for the disaster. Irish jury members snickered, their skepticism confirmed.

The third prosecution witness of the day, Frank Gianni, testified that he had seen Percival arrive at Pier 54 shortly before Joseph Albi died there. O'Dwyer asked Gianni to look around the courtroom and identify the man he had seen.

"The witness has identified the defendant, Guy Charles Percival," said O'Dwyer triumphantly, but the jury did not stir. Their indifference was a matter of private concern to O'Dwyer because Gianni was the prosecution's star witness.

On cross-examination, Angus Murdock did not dispute Gianni's presence at Pier 54 on the crucial day or question Gianni's eyesight. Had he done so, Francine later indicated to Trevor, he might have shaken his testimony because Gianni often wore spectacles. Murdock only obliged the witness to confirm that he had seen two men exit a limousine and approach the pier. He had witnessed no crime. He also compelled the witness to agree that his testimony did not contradict the defense's claim that Joseph Albi was alive when Percival left him.

The final prosecution witness was Frank Buono, who testified that he had accompanied Joe Albi to the offices of the notary public and had witnessed two documents that Albi claimed bore on the *Lusitania*'s secret cargo of war materiel; however, as Frank Buono could not read, he could not tell the court anything about their content. Albi had talked about an Englishman who wanted to buy the documents. O'Dwyer did not inquire of Frank Buono how Albi had come by the information he proposed to sell. Murdock excused Frank Buono without cross-examination.

On the second day of trial, the taxi driver, Elmer Boganza, and Trevor Howells both testified that Percival and Caprioli had hijacked the taxicab at gunpoint. Trevor also testified that he had surrendered the Albi affidavit to Percival under duress, and had been beaten and threatened with death after doing so. Asked the content of Albi's affidavit, Trevor replied that it concerned a secret cargo of munitions that Albi claimed to have stolen from the *Lusitania.* Trevor did not mention the shipping labels. The defense attorney dismissed Elmer Boganza without cross-examination, but Trevor did not escape it.

"So, Mr. Howells," Murdock asked, "why did you accept the defendant's offer of one thousand dollars for this material in Mr. Boganza's taxicab?"

"I did not accept. I declined it. Then the defendant threatened to kill me. I turned the affidavit over to him under extreme duress."

"Then why did you ask the defendant to inflict bruises upon your body?"

"I did not ask for that beating."

"Where was your socialist friend?"

"The socialist was a not a friend. He was taking me to a buyer whom he identified as the Socialist Party. They offered five thousand dollars for Albi's affidavit. As to the whereabouts of the socialist, well, I assume he was still lying in the gutter where Mr. Caprioli left him after slugging him with a bat." Here the judge cautioned the witness to limit his testimony to known facts.

"So you proposed to sell those Albi documents to Carl Houchins, a bank robber wanted in Montana?"

"Emphatically no." Trevor had experience on the witness stand. "I did not then know that the socialist's name was Carl Houchins. He called himself Ben Williams."

"However, you knew this radical socialist intended to pass the documents along to the German government?

"I knew no such thing. Houchins told me that he was purchasing the documents on behalf of the Socialist Party. I still do not know that Houchins worked for the Germans, and neither, I submit, do you, Mr. Murdock."

"I am asking the questions here, Mr. Howells. You proposed to sell these documents to the highest bidder, Houchins. You knew that Albi's documents raised fraudulent claims?"

"No. I knew only that his claims could not be proven. I reckoned their validity was the buyer's lookout."

"Cheat the gullible, eh? You do find the fast money, Mr. Howells. But let's address those documents. Were you not aware that Albi's documents tended to exculpate the German government for the crime of the *Lusitania,* and also contradicted public statements made by Secretary of State Lansing?"

"I knew that, yes."

"Do you now or did you then know of any proof of the validity of Joseph Albi's so-called eyewitness testimony regarding the *Lusitania*'s secret cargo of guncotton?" This was the question Trevor had dreaded, the one to which a truthful answer would send him to prison. Trevor stalled. Sitting in the audience section, just behind the defense table, Agent Lightner sat up straighter.

"What testimony would that be?" This was the moment of truth.

"Testimony that Albi discovered military explosive disguised as cheese in crates he had stolen from the *Lusitania* before she left New York on her fatal voyage. Do you know of any proof of these claims anywhere?"

"There's the supplementary copy of the *Lusitania*'s manifest, of which President Wilson has a copy."

"How do you know its contents support Albi's claims?"

"I don't know, but you asked if any proof exists. And, I do know—" Judge McCarthy directed the witness to answer the question without amplification.

"How do you know the president has the supplementary manifest?"

"Agent Lightner of the U.S. Bureau of Investigation told me."

"Might Agent Lightner be mistaken?" Trevor replied that anyone could be mistaken about anything.

"So you don't know for sure whether the document exists and whether the president has it, or having it has read it, nor do you know whether it proves or does not prove the existence of secret explosives aboard the *Lusitania.*" Trevor acknowledged that he did not *know* any of that. "So this document, Mr. Howells, if it exists at all, which you cannot assert in full confidence, might support or might not support the claims the late Joseph Albi made, and you always knew all of that. Isn't that summary correct?" Please answer yes or no."

"Yes," Trevor replied weakly. Murdock smiled in triumph, and then resumed.

"In sum, Mr. Howells, you knew that the memoir you offered for sale might be pure bunk, but you planned to sell it anyway. Yes or no?"

"Yes."

"We have a word for someone who peddles lies."

"An attorney?" interjected Trevor, provoking the jury's laughter.

"A swindler," rejoined Murdock, who nonetheless changed directions. "Do you know the meaning of treason, Mr. Howells?" Without awaiting an answer, Murdock continued. "No? Then let me explain. Treason is betraying your country, and doing it for money is the most despicable of reasons. As you—" Trevor took umbrage, interrupting Murdock.

"Where's your question? The United States is neutral in Europe's war, and President Wilson takes credit for keeping us out. Why shouldn't I get paid for helping him?" Judge McCarthy ordered Trevor to answer Murdock's questions without volunteering opinions. Nonetheless, the jury tittered. It was a telling rebuttal. Trevor's experience in the witness chair had surprised Murdock, who had expected a patsy, but the crafty lawyer got in a final dig before the judge declared the trial in recess until the next morning.

"If you'd sell the national interest for two thousand dollars, Mr. Howells, how many pieces of silver might you earn selling tickets to the funerals of all the *Lusitania*'s victims on the nation's silver screens?"

"Getting the truth out to the people is the national interest."

"Just a moment ago you acknowledged that you did not know the truth, so how can you maintain that you proposed to bring the truth before the public? Didn't you rather intend to encourage reckless speculation about an issue of national security in hope of financial gain?" These were rhetorical questions. Murdock gave Trevor no time to answer. "No further questions at this time, Your Honor."

After court adjourned for the day, Trevor and Francine rushed to O'Dwyer, who was packing his attaché case at the prosecution table.

"Thank goodness you promoted the official theory," said Trevor, "but I wish you had told us earlier. We haven't slept for a week."

"Trevor, I did not get Swann's permission to proceed until yesterday."

"That was close," said Trevor, glancing at Francine. "But why did you revert to the official theory?" He studiously did not call it the "official lie."

"I considered this issue from many angles, consulted others, and then made the decision in the interest of justice. I will seek conviction of Percival for murder and kidnapping, and I will not utter a falsehood in court or permit anyone else to do so, but I am not obliged to introduce everything I know. We'll forget the shipping labels. In fact," O'Dwyer chortled, "I am taking a leaf from Murdock. You did not know that Albi's documents were accurate. Even if you had the affidavit and shipping labels in your hand you wouldn't know for sure that they proved anything."

"I would not have compelling proof, but—"

"The prosecution will proceed on that basis, as will the defense. You did not know whether Albi's claims were true. You acquired politically explosive documents of dubious accuracy, and you proposed to sell them to interested parties who also knew their accuracy was dubious. You look like a shabby, money-grubbing tout, but that's not illegal, and the story might convict Percival."

"It's a relief to hear that you can convict him." Shabby or not, Trevor felt his shoulders and neck muscles relent and loosen. He managed a wan smile. "I can sleep again."

"Don't relax. We're losing the case." O'Dwyer paused, frowned, then continued. "Today's testimony went badly." O'Dwyer cocked his head as though testing how much of the day's proceedings his backward student had understood. "This round goes to the defense. I thought the defense would deny any knowledge of Albi. Then our witnesses could prove Percival met him on Barrow Street. I thought the defense would deny that Percival was at Pier 54 just before the murder. Then our witness would testify that he saw him there, but Murdock did not contest our witnesses, and the jury just bought it. I think the disappearance of

MacMurray actually worked to the advantage of the defense. Murdock has even accepted that Percival tried to buy documents on several occasions; you refused, wanting more money, and now he's putting you on trial for treason and war profiteering."

"It's preposterous."

"The jury won't agree. You really did try to make money out of a story whose truth you did not know for certain. The shipping labels would have helped, but you could not mention them. Result: All you had was the supplementary manifest about which you know nothing conclusive. To the jury you look like a fast-buck huckster. As Murdock said, you were, 'Selling tickets' to *Lusitania* funerals." It's a good line," O'Dwyer added ruefully, "and it might save Percival." At this point, Francine Albi, who had listened without comment to their entire conversation, intervened with a question.

"Mr. O'Dwyer, are you saying that Percival will get off?"

'We cannot convict him of the serious crimes."

"You mean the murderer of my husband is going to walk?" Francine demanded, her lips a thin line and her eyes focused.

"It's very likely," replied John O'Dwyer, biting his lip. "We'll see what Monday brings."

Hearing this, Francine conferred briefly with Filipo Albi in Italian. They left the courtroom in a hurry and went straight to the news island on Christopher Street. Paul Kelly's street agent, Slate, was counting money for the news vendor, Blind John. "Hello, Mr. Slate," she said. "I'm Francine Albi, Joe's widow, and this is his brother Filipo."

"I know," said Slate, not looking up from his task.

"We need to see Paul Kelly." Still avoiding eye contact, Slate suggested that Francine consult the telephone directory. Reaching across the barrier, Francine took Slate's arm. "Mr. Slate, you and Joe were friends. Unless I talk to Paul Kelly, your friend's children will beg their bread."

At this intrusion, Slate stopped counting, put a pile of coins aside, and looked belligerently across a stack of newspapers at Francine and Filipo. "Sure, Joe and me were friends," he said, shaking off her arm, "and I'm sorry for his kids, but Joe knew the rules. He broke them. He was punished."

Again reaching across the newspapers, Francine now took Slate's right hand in both of hers. "Yes, Joe earned a terrible punishment, the worst. But why should his kids be punished? It's too much. Please approach Paul. Point out that Joe was a loyal friend for many years, and his kids deserve some consideration for that. Please tell him, Slate. Please, I beg you." And Francine Albi cried real tears.

Now she had his full attention. "Francine, you don't understand everything. I'm sorry to be the one who has to tell you," Slate replied, retrieving his captive right hand, but his tone was now sympathetic and sincere. "It's not just about Joe. It's about you. You are helping the cops prosecute Rocco Caprioli, who is a good friend of Paul's. For that you earned Paul's anger. Stay out of his sight is my recommendation." Turning to Filipo Albi, Slate added, "And that goes double for you." Francine had anticipated this difficulty, and, looking up with tear-filled eyes, she made a shocking claim.

"I can get Rocco off." Francine explained that, by persistent begging, she had obtained the prosecutors' agreement to dismiss all charges against Rocco Caprioli if he would turn state's evidence against Captain Percival. They had only reluctantly agreed. Paul needed to hear about this. Francine knew that her so-called news posed a calculated risk. She hoped that Slate did not already know that the prosecutors had made this offer much earlier, and that Rocco Caprioli had several times rejected it. She was lucky. Slate did not already know. As a result, it seemed to Slate that Francine had obtained a very advantageous offer from prosecutors reluctant to make it. Twisting his index finger in his right cheek, a gesture that signaled emotional satisfaction, Slate could see "no reason" why Rocco should not "rat out the Englishman." This option made excellent sense to him, and he thought Paul might agree. In the end, Slate agreed to ask Kelly to grant Francine an interview. Thanking Slate profusely, she asked that it take place right away.

Early Monday morning, still depressed from O'Dwyer's pessimistic assessment on Friday, Lotte was summoned to Mr. Winthrop J. Tolson's corner office. Seated at his massive mahogany desk, the emperor pointed her wordlessly to a stool, then, glaring, he asked point-blank whether she was sharing an apartment with Trevor Howells. Long suppressed, Lotte's dislike of her boss could no longer be concealed. She sassed him back.

"What business is that of yours, Mr. Tolson?" she asked, hands folded demurely in her lap. Winthrop J. Tolson could scarcely believe that a twenty-year-old female employee had questioned his right to know her private life.

"Did I hear you correctly?" he sputtered. Assured that he had, Tolson tapped his pen on the desktop smartly, and looking past his long nose declared that he took her "impudent response" for a yes. Then he waited for her retraction. None came. Head high, Lotte looked blankly back, neither affirming nor denying his conclusion. Tolson picked up his desk telephone and ostentatiously summoned Trevor Howells. They waited wordlessly for him to arrive.

When Trevor entered his office, Winthrop J. Tolson did not rise. Still seated on the stool, hands still demurely folded, Lotte flashed Trevor a look that told the tale.

"Howells, I heard more rumors about you and Miss Schlegel. Now Miss Schlegel has confessed that you and she are cohabiting. Do you deny it?" Glancing at Lotte, Trevor read confession time from her eyes.

"No, sir, I don't deny it."

"You assured me that your relationship with Miss Schlegel was professional. You lied!"

"Yes, I lied to protect this lady's honor. Although Miss Schlegel and I were already engaged to marry, we were living together prior to the marriage ceremony. We still are. As you know, sir, a gentleman never tells tales that would embarrass a lady, and I determined that lying to you was the only honorable choice." Tolson tapped his pencil on his desktop, his cunning, old-fashioned eyes shifting from one employee to the other.

"I see. Your mendacity protected a lady's honor. I detest liars, but I appreciate chivalry. Your engagement also makes an honest woman of Miss Schlegel, and that speaks well of you. I even congratulate you, Howells. Miss Schlegel is quite a beauty, and intelligent to boot, though she lacks discretion. But Metropolitan Life forbids romantic liaisons between employees on penalty of discharge." He turned to Lotte. "Metropolitan Life has no further need of your services, Miss Schlegel. Clean your desk, collect your pay from Victor, and Mrs. Browning will escort you from the building. As for you, Howells, your work has suffered of late. I trust that, now that you have a fiancée, your days of mooning around the office are over."

When Trevor returned to Lotte's Brooklyn apartment that evening, she had prepared no dinner, but she had prepared a tirade. "Why didn't you protest?" she howled. "We had a secret engagement, you lied about it to Tolson, and he fired me, just me. Was that fair?"

"No, it wasn't fair."

"Well, why didn't you protest?"

"Had I protested, I might have been fired too, and then we'd have no income. As is, you can give up this Brooklyn apartment and move in with me. We'll lose your pay, but we won't have to rent two apartments anymore. You can find another job."

"But I was fired for immorality," moaned Lotte. "Employers will request a reference."

"Your fiancé won't work for your next employer. As long as you're unmarried, your office skills will get you another job, and you would have lost your job at Metro as soon as we married."

'It's easy for you to say," Lotte wailed. "I was drummed out of the building like a whore. Everyone came into the corridor to watch. Everyone except you! You hid in your office and allowed Victor to humiliate me." Then, tossing her head, she added, "Or did you consider protest too risky?"

CHAPTER 16

A SCOUNDREL AND A SWINDLER

On the fourth day of the trial, Guy Percival was the final prosecution witness. O'Dwyer first undertook to prove that Percival had hoped to sell the pro-German fiction to American audiences rather than to suppress it out of patriotic zeal. However, Percival acknowledged that he had never "earned a tuppence in trade," but it did not matter as he was independently wealthy and could live wherever and do whatever he liked. Financial success was unimportant to him. The success of British arms was all-important. Indeed, British victory was the only thing in life that interested him now. He acknowledged that he had twice offered to purchase rights to Howells's manuscript—or possible manuscript—in order to prevent that scurrilous trash from reaching a mass audience and thus besmirching the justice of Great Britain's cause. He never intended to promote Howells's lie, but only, by acquiring the rights to it, to prevent its propagation. "The unscrupulous man sold me those rights twice, not once," declared Guy Charles Percival.

O'Dwyer then turned to Percival's military career in an attempt to impeach his character. Percival had resigned from the British Army in 1914 after twenty-four years' service. Why would the British Army retire a career officer just as war began in Europe?"

Percival replied, "At forty-two years of age I am now regrettably too old to be of service in the field."

"But are not many captains now serving in France who are fifty or older?" asked O'Dwyer?

"I suffer from lumbago. More important, I was offered vitally important war work in New York City as purchasing agent for the Cunard Line." There seemed no point in questioning Percival's health status, so O'Dwyer turned to the circumstances surrounding his resignation from the British Army. He established that Captain Percival had never married.

"At the time you retired from the military, was there a public scandal regarding your conduct toward an enlisted man?"

"Scandal, no, but some questions were raised."

"Didn't you personally flog a naked man for the crime of failing to polish your boots to the desired luster?

"Naked was not proven."

"Did you attend an all-boys public school in Britain, Captain Percival? That would be a private boarding school in our American terminology. And did this boarding school use a 'fagging system'?" Percival now began to understand the prosecutor's direction.

"Fagging simply means that the younger boys, the fags, were obliged to perform duties under the supervision of the older. You have that system at West Point."

"True, but not the childhood equivalent. That seems unwholesome over here. Now, how shall I put this, did the fagging system result in the widespread practice of what you British call buggery, which we here in America call sexual perversion?"

"No, of course not." Percival folded his arms and frowned. In response to a question, he knew nothing of rumors to the contrary. Nonetheless, a stirring in the jury box suggested that this rumor had reached several of them.

"Isn't it true, Captain Percival, that buggery would be cause for an officer's dismissal from the British forces?" Here Murdock objected that the prosecutor was seeking to indict his client for immorality strictly on the basis of circumstances. Judge McCarthy sustained that objection, ordered O'Dwyer to discontinue that line of questioning, and instructed the jury to disregard it. O'Dwyer later acknowledged to Trevor that the judge had been right. The unfair questioning had been a dirty trick, but it served O'Dwyer's purpose to demean and impugn Percival by whatever means available, including sexual innuendo. The jurors would not forget the insinuation no matter what the judge ordered. Having succeeded to his own satisfaction and the limit of his information, O'Dwyer turned to apparent inconsistencies between the defendant's prior statements to the police and his current claims.

"Now, Captain Percival, can you explain why Mr. Francis MacMurray said that you were in Hoboken at the hour that Joseph Albi died?"

"MacMurray thought so. Taking his word for it, so did I, but on closer reflection, I realized that this particular trip had been on the next day, not the day of Albi's death."

"Before MacMurray vanished, you stated that you had been with him on the day and at the time of Joseph Albi's death. Since MacMurray vanished, you have recalled that you did not visit him in Hoboken on that day. Can you explain why your recollection changed after MacMurray vanished?" O'Dwyer's sneer was almost audible, but Percival ignored it.

"I had relied upon MacMurray to establish the date, and when MacMurray vanished, I realized, as did Mr. Caprioli, that we needed to verify it. That led to detection of the error."

"Didn't you fake an alibi in Hoboken, and then change your story when your perjured witness vanished?" Standing erect, O'Dwyer reared back, shoulders squared, as if he had just delivered the *golpe de muerte* in the bullring of Madrid.

"That is an outrageous accusation for which you have no evidence." At the defendant's response, coolly delivered, O'Dwyer's shoulders sagged, as he knew it was quite true. He had no evidence, and was planting another cheap innuendo. Frustrated thus far, O'Dwyer next turned to the hijacking.

"So, Captain Percival, you and Rocco Caprioli, guns in hand, hijacked the taxicab, kidnapped Trevor Howells, and later beat Mr. Howells inside that same taxi. Isn't that correct?"

"No, it is not. We had guns in hand, yes, but that was by prearrangement with Mr. Howells, who'd insisted that we display weapons during the so-called kidnapping. He said that he needed to convince the Germans that he'd given us the Albi memoir under duress—otherwise they would kill him. He assured us that Mr. Boganza was in league with him. Apparently, he lied. I regret any discomfort to Mr. Boganza and damage to his taxicab, but I have no responsibility. Those damages were inflicted by terrorists in the pay of the German spy network in your country. Neither Mr. Caprioli nor I ever struck Mr. Howells, who administered to himself a series of superficially disfiguring blows intended to lend credibility to his kidnapping story."

"Your associate, Caprioli, is a convicted felon, who served time in the penitentiary, isn't that right?"

"You say so. I do not know it. I engaged his limousine service. I asked no biographical questions."

"Didn't Mr. Caprioli's connection with waterfront criminals enable your access to information about who was stealing from the Cunard Line?"

"Mr. Caprioli has no connection to waterfront criminals."

"Did you acquire your initial information about Albi's memoirs from the Pinkerton Detective Agency?" A strong question, Trevor thought, as it compelled Percival to account for how he had first heard of Albi, and the Pinkertons would be asked to corroborate. The witness paused too, reflected, and answered no. "Well, then, how did you acquire that information?" O'Dwyer finally looked confident.

"I purchase supplies for the Cunard Line. I stock those supplies in warehouses, and I protect those warehouses from thieves. One of the ways I do this is to access information about black-market sales."

"All right, Captain Percival, but in this case, exactly how did you learn about the guncotton that Joseph Albi had stolen from the *Lusitania*?"

"What I learned had nothing to do with stolen guncotton. It concerned a memoir that a mendacious stevedore had fabricated and was preparing to publicize."

"You did not buy one hundred sixty pounds of stolen guncotton on the black market prior to meeting Joseph Albi, and then ask him to sell you more?"

"Of course not."

"Captain Percival, I won't quibble. Who told you about Albi's memoir?"

"Rocco Caprioli. I then went to see Albi, and learned from him that he would destroy his scandalmongering memoir in exchange for one thousand dollars. There never was any guncotton on the ship, but as a stevedore who had loaded the *Lusitania,* Albi could plausibly claim that he had seen some onboard. The Germans have already planted rumors to that effect, and no one could prove it was a lie. Albi understood that he could make money by promoting his fraudulent claim."

"Captain, you declared before that Mr. Caprioli did not serve as your intermediary to the underworld, and now you have admitted the opposite." The jury stirred. His associate signaled "more." O'Dwyer glowered at the witness, arms akimbo once more. He did not intimidate Percival, whose face showed no emotion as he prepared his crisp reply.

"Your question was confused, Mr. O'Dwyer. You asked if Mr. Caprioli served in this capacity. I said no; however, in this case he did relay information about Albi. That's not the same as routinely serving me as an intermediary." O'Dwyer choked back his disappointment at this clever response.

"How then did you routinely acquire information about resale of stores stolen from Cunard ships?" Showing exasperation, which the jury registered as failure, O'Dwyer was unable to force a damaging confession from Guy Percival.

"The Cunard Line retains the Pinkerton Detective Agency. I also kept close contact with the supervisory staff on the dock. I simply let it be known to all and sundry that I was interested in purchasing stolen stores, no questions asked, and news of their availability then routinely flowed to me from multiple sources." Guy Percival sat back, and then confidently asked his own question: "Does that make sense to you, Mr. O'Dwyer?"

O'Dwyer ignored Percival's question, but the jury thought it made sense to them. Even the Irish jurors shifted nervously. O'Dwyer's assistant signaled, "discontinue" from the prosecution table.

So O'Dwyer turned to Percival's firearm, which was clearly illegal under New York State's Sullivan law. Guy Percival had no license to own a firearm, much less to carry a concealed weapon. Under cross-examination, Percival explained that, as a former artillery officer, he was accustomed to carry a sidearm. He always carried a weapon when onboard the Cunard liners, which were under British law. He had assumed that his weapon was legal in New York City, and regretted any violation of American law. This admission permitted O'Dwyer a sarcastic cross-examination, intended to arouse anti-British passion among the jurors.

"Did you think you were in Ireland where English soldiers shoot whomever they like?"

"I have never been stationed in Ireland."

"Possibly you have not heard that King George does not make the laws in the United States?"

"Your question is absurd. I regret this violation of your gun law. It was part of the charade that Mr. Howells demanded and to which I unwisely acquiesced. I plead guilty to this charge of wrongful possession of a firearm, and will make whatever restitution your law requires."

"A month in prison is possible."

"I will make restitution in that form if necessary, but I would prefer to pay a fine."

Murdock's redirect established that the prosecution's questions had failed to prove any charge against the defendant save unlawful possession of a firearm, "... a misdemeanor with a fine of one hundred dollars, and for which the defendant has fully apologized."

Murdock then concluded by drawing attention to Percival's Irish ancestry on his maternal grandmother's side, a lineage expected to prove the defendant's enduring friendship with the Emerald Isle. Murdock also praised Britain's "gallant Italian allies, who show the Austrian tyrants how bravely free men fight." There were Italian jurors too. If O'Dwyer could court the Irish jurors, Murdock could court the Italians.

When Murdock had completed this redirect, the prosecution rested, and Murdock opened the defense case. A skilled litigator, Angus Murdock had his targets lined up. With the exception of Francine Albi, whom he did not recall, he recalled all the prosecution witnesses in the order in which they had originally appeared. His purpose was to limit or demolish the damaging implications of their earlier testimony. Albi's brother, Filipo, was compelled to acknowledge that Percival's presence on Barrow Street was entirely compatible with the supposition that he acted out of British patriotism. Filipo admitted that he had no way of knowing whether Percival's reference to the financial interest of the Cunard Line was simply a bargaining ploy. Frank Gianni was also compelled to remember that the number-three hatch on board the *Alneria* had safety stanchions in place on A-deck, but that someone intent on suicide could climb over them and jump.

Next, under determined questioning, Frank Buono acknowledged that Albi had said that he was "bluffing" about divulging his information to the newspapers because he had no such information. Asked whether he personally had seen crates labeled "Cheese" that contained cordite, Buono said no. It was a lie, as Buono had participated in the cargo theft from the *Lusitania* and had helped open the crates, but he would not incriminate himself. Later he tearfully begged Francine's pardon for this betrayal, explaining that he feared a prison sentence. She forgave him, but their friendship was over. Finally, the taxi driver, Elmer Boganza, agreed that he did not know whether the hijacking was a charade invented by Trevor Howells for the purpose of fooling the Germans. Murdock then pointed out that, as the organizer of the charade, Howells was legally responsible for any damages to Elmer's taxi or his livelihood, and, upon his release, the defendant would enable Boganza to sue Trevor Howells for the full replacement cost of his cab.

Murdock then called Lotte Schlegel. Lotte had dressed demurely for the courtroom appearance, wearing a white pinafore over a black, floor-length turtleneck frock with lace collar, a floppy but unadorned hat, medium-heel Mary Jane pumps, and no jewelry. She had braided her hair to play the youthful ingénue. Nonetheless, as the glamorous blonde woman ascended the witness stand, the jurors' eyes were on her, and some mouths were agape. Murdock got right to the point.

"Miss Schlegel, how long have you lived outside wedlock with Mr. Trevor Howells?"

"We have been planning our marriage for a year, and are only waiting to assemble the money we need. He maintains his own apartment in Manhattan. I live in Brooklyn. We are not ashamed of our love."

"But in that case, why do you keep your cohabitation a secret from your employer?"

"We deemed it best to suppress news of our romance so we both could have employment."

"Doesn't Metropolitan Life prohibit romances between employees?" Lotte acknowledged that Metropolitan did so. "Then you lied to protect your employment, Miss Schlegel?

"No, sir. They never asked and we never told." Seeing that this line of questioning was exhausted, Murdock made a side comment regarding the thin line between deception and lying, and then turned to Lotte's promiscuity, which he deemed a far richer lode.

"Does Mr. Howells give you money or pay your rent?" Murdock delivered this question with a regretful sigh as if deeply sorry to open this cesspool.

"Mr. Howells and I share all expenses except for his rent in Manhattan, which he pays from his greater salary." This answer implied that Trevor Howells only paid half of Lotte's rent, and Murdock next compelled Lotte to acknowledge in some confusion that Trevor paid all of her rent. Then Murdock turned to another financial issue.

"In addition to your rent, do you also get money from Mr. Howells for your, uh, other services? Answer yes or no." After a pause, Lotte said no.

"He gives you no money?"

"I perform no services." Lotte was seething, but she retained her composure. It was a telling rejoinder, especially from one so young. Murdock perceived that her thoughtful resilience impressed the jury despite her immoral conduct, so he took a new direction, inquiring whether she had sent a telegram in the German language to a certain Oskar Schlegel in St. Louis. That confirmed, Murdock then inquired whether her letter had been passed along to the German consulate.

"I learned later that my uncle forwarded my letter to a consular official. I did not ask him to do so."

"Did this letter contain information that would enable the German Empire to shift the blame for the *Lusitania* disaster to Great Britain?"

"Yes. I wrote my uncle about the military explosives that Joseph Albi found aboard the *Lusitania.* Without asking me, he decided this information was sufficiently important to forward to the German embassy."

"Did you realize that your letter bordered on espionage?"

"It did not. This letter only corrected the lopsided preponderance of Allied propaganda in our country," here Lotte speeded her delivery, "and, yes, I think that's a very good change. We get all the Allied propaganda, but never hear the other side."

"Your parents are German born, and you are a German sympathizer, isn't that right?" Here Murdock touched Lotte's sorest frustration, and she blurted out her resentment.

"People assume that the German submarine sank the *Lusitania* out of pure malice. They don't realize that the British were secretly shipping war materiel. The British used those civilians as hostages. And the public hostility to Germany is outrageous. Why just last week my five-year-old niece was expelled from the St. Louis Public Library for speaking German. Don't you think that's preposterous, Mr. Murdock?"

"I ask the questions, Miss Schlegel. But I infer from your response that you do sympathize with Germany." Lotte did not reply as there was no question. "Now, let me draw it all together," Murdock continued. "The jury heard you promote pro-German ideas. Also, the man with whom you live in sin proposes to introduce pro-German ideas into the entertainment arena. Taken together, you two could be called dedicated supporters of Germany. Isn't that right?" Murdock folded his arms, cocked his head to the right, and leaned back slightly from the waist, awaiting her reply.

"I support Germany's right to a fair hearing, and so does Mr. Howells," Lotte snapped back.

"Good enough, Miss Schlegel. Would you agree that Mr. Howells's interest in this pro-German 'hearing' was not strictly commercial? Like you, Mr. Howells actively propagates pro-German ideas, right?"

"He would like to keep us out of Europe's war, yes."

At this response, Murdock beamed. "In that case, it's not at all true that his interest in the Albi claim was strictly commercial. Oh, he wanted to make money, but he also wanted to keep our country out of the Great War. Isn't that right? When Lotte stubbornly answered no, Murdock rebuked her. "Miss Schlegel, you cannot have it both ways. Either Howells did it for the money or for the political effect or some combination of the two. Now which is it?"

"Ask him," replied Lotte icily. "I assure you that Mr. Howells likes money, if that's your question." Her irony was wasted on Murdock and the jury, but Murdock turned the substance against her.

"And does his money endear him to you, Miss Schlegel?" This brutal question hit multiple sore spots. Lotte asked if Murdock was insinuating that she was a gold digger. She showed outrage. The men of the jury showed gleeful interest. "I would not have used those words, but many young women want to marry men with money. The reasons are obvious, and the line between entrapment and harlotry is often blurred, as it is in this case. That is quite enough testimony from you for now."

The defense next called Trevor Howells. Murdock easily forced Trevor to admit that, like Lotte, he too wanted to obtain a fair hearing for Germany in the court of public opinion, and that he hoped the Albi story would accomplish that goal as well as earn money. But, countered Trevor, to seek a fair hearing regarding the *Lusitania* did not amount to being pro-German. His political goal was to keep the United States out of the European war, and he thought that the pressures of war had prevented the whole truth from getting out.

"You know, Mr. Howells, given your great interest in fairness for Germany, I cannot understand why you took two thousand dollars from the defendant in exchange for abandoning your project."

"He handed me the envelope on the street. I did not make a deal with him."

"Your hand in the cookie jar, you plead innocence. I am amazed by your temerity. Now let me ask you this same question in a new way. You value fairness for Germany, and you wanted to propagate a pro-German story in the hope of financial gain, but at the first real opportunity to sell that story you took money from the defendant. Mr. Howells, you sold out fairness to Germany for money, didn't you?" Trevor reiterated his denial. "Then why did the defendant give you two thousand dollars in exchange for the contents of your briefcase?"

"The briefcase was bait for Carl Houchins. He did not show up, but Captain Percival did, and now claims that he thought my briefcase contained propaganda."

"You did nothing to make Captain Percival believe you proposed to sell pro-German propaganda to German agents?" Trevor denied having done so. Then Murdock turned to another issue. "Mr. Howells, you have testified that you had an abiding interest in fair play for Germany. In that case, wouldn't you and your German mistress . . . ."

"My fiancée," Trevor snapped.

"Wouldn't you and Miss Schlegel want to see Captain Percival indicted for crimes he did not commit just because he represents the dauntless battlefield enemy that now frustrates the German emperor's dream of world conquest?"

"I support fair play for Germany, but I would not perjure myself to indict a person who is pro-British."

"You trapped yourself, Mr. Howells." Murdock looked triumphantly around the courtroom, but the jurors looked perplexed. "I asked whether you had a *motive* to perjure yourself. The answer must be yes if you care about fair play for Germany. And you did have that political motive, didn't you?" Trevor sputtered that a theoretical motive was of no importance. Murdock did not relent. "Your girlfriend stated that she is pro-German. You just testified that you also care about fair play for Germany. You and Miss Schlegel are embroiled in a grossly immoral personal relationship, which you lied to conceal. Additionally, you and she both had a political motive to betray, entrap, and denounce with lies to the authorities the pro-British defendant Guy Charles Percival." Here Murdock pointed at the defendant. "I am sure the kaiser wishes you well in your endeavors. No further questions at this time, Your Honor."

Murdock's last witness of the day was Felix Lightner. Murdock asked Lightner to explain why the Bureau of Investigation had arrested Guy Charles Percival, and then released him forty hours later.

"We arrested Captain Percival because we wrongly thought he was Carl Houchins. Then, after holding him overnight, and clarifying his identify, we released Percival with an apology."

"Did Mr. Trevor Howells protest your decision?"

"Yes, he asked me to turn Percival and Caprioli over to the New York City police for prosecution. I declined on the grounds that there was inadequate evidence to do so."

Murdock beamed at this answer, then, turning toward the jury, continued, "And would you please explain why you were in contact with Mr. Howells?"

"Detective Fulton of the New York Police Department advised us that Trevor Howells helped this Carl Houchins. Their goal was to spread rumors that the *Lusitania* carried war materiel in her cargo hold. They would do this by publicizing the so-called memoirs of a stevedore who had loaded the ship in New York Harbor."

"Trevor Howells was collaborating with this revolutionary socialist in the employ of German spymasters?" Agent Lightner confirmed it, and was able to point out Trevor to the jury. "Agent Lightner, did you ever see the documents that Mr. Howells was hoping to sell?"

"I did. When we arrested Mr. Percival in front of the Chelsea Hotel, Mr. Howells carried a briefcase containing the documents he offered for sale. He had transferred that briefcase to the defendant, and carried in his right hand an envelope with two thousand dollars that the defendant handed him in payment."

"Please tell the court the nature of those secret documents."

"They were discarded papers from his wastebasket."

"And this junk is what Mr. Howells sold Guy Percival?"

"Apparently so." The courtroom hushed. Lightner continued. "Guy Percival paid good money for a load of junk, but stupidity's no crime." The jury roared, and even Judge McCarthy joined the laughter.

"Would it be fair to say, then, Agent Lightner, that Trevor Howells was literally peddling trash?" Lightner agreed, and the courtroom again disintegrated into uproarious laughter. It seemed to Trevor that the general hilarity would never end. When the laughter finally quieted, Murdock, still grinning, continued, "Agent Lightner, as an experienced police officer, why in your expert opinion would someone pay two thousand dollars for trash?"

"I would suppose that a swindler had convinced the purchaser that he was obtaining something of value."

Murdock thereupon elicited from Agent Lightner a firm declaration that in his opinion Trevor Howells was a swindler. Pointing to Trevor, Murdock obtained from the witness assurance that this man, and not the prisoner, was the scoundrel. The jury became very still.

"Thinking that, what advice did you give to Mr. Howells?"

"I advised him to return Captain Percival's money and to explain that it had all been a misunderstanding. Mr. Howells refused. Instead, he contacted Sergeant Reilly of the New York Police Department, a personal friend, and Reilly arranged the arrest and arraignment of Guy Charles Percival as well as his chauffeur, Rocco Caprioli."

"So in your estimation, Trevor Howells took the initiative to persecute Mr. Percival despite and against your contrary advice?"

"Not my opinion. That's what happened."

"Agent Lightner, why would a swindler undertake to obtain the rearrest of a man in whom the Bureau of Investigation could find no crime?"

"Howells is pro-German, so having cheated Captain Percival out of money, he next wanted to incriminate a strong supporter of the British cause. That rankled me because the Captain has been helpful to the United States government."

Murdock pointed to the defendant, accentuating the jury's dramatic impression. "Captain Guy Percival was helpful to the United States?"

"Yes, he helped us in matters of maritime security. German spies have planted incendiary time bombs on vessels in our harbors. These bombs exploded at sea, endangering the lives of the crewmen and compelling the ships to return to port. The financial loss has been great. Captain Percival helped us to prevent many such attacks, and the United States government is grateful."

"Thanks very much, Agent Lightner. Your witness, Mr. O'Dwyer."

Because of the lateness of the hour, Judge McCarthy intervened to delay the cross-examination of Agent Lightner until the next morning. Court was adjourned.

Lightner's testimony devastated the prosecution. The jury had listened in confident attention to a respected police officer declaring Trevor Howells a swindler and a scoundrel. Worried and disturbed, Francine, Filipo, and Trevor had an anxious conference with O'Dwyer before he could leave the courtroom.

"I have to tell you," said O'Dwyer, looking grim, that our evidence will not support a guilty verdict on the charges of murder, kidnapping, battery, and grand theft. It's their word against yours every time. Plus, Trevor, you really had a political motive to set him up; plus you apparently swindled him out of two thousand dollars; plus we have only circumstantial evidence, which can be interpreted as well their way as ours. Murdock has successfully portrayed you and Lotte as German sympathizers who would stop at nothing to hang Percival. He also depicts you both as grossly immoral in personal conduct. The outlook could hardly be worse."

Francine clutched O'Dwyer's arm. "But you believe Percival killed Joe, don't you?" she asked anxiously.

"Yes, Mrs. Albi. I personally believe that. I also believe that the Captain's mission was to suppress the evidence your husband had discovered aboard the *Lusitania.* I also believe he gets money from the British government. Unfortunately, I can't prove any of it. Brace yourselves. Percival will escape with a one-hundred-dollar fine for unlawful possession of a firearm." Trevor and Lotte exchanged agonized and despairing glances.

"What about Rocco Caprioli?" Francine asked, still grasping his arm.

"Our case is even weaker," O'Dwyer replied gently, as if reluctant to break bad news to a desperate woman clutching at straws. "Caprioli was Percival's chauffeur, and if we cannot convict Percival, we cannot convict his chauffeur."

"What about the gun charge?" Francine persisted.

"We can nail Caprioli on that one. As an ex-felon, he could get five years."

"Caprioli understands that?" Francine asked.

"You bet," O'Dwyer retorted. "When we began this prosecution, Davies and I offered him immediate release and immunity if he would implicate Captain Percival. He refused twice. It makes no sense to us, but he won't crack."

Hearing these words, Francine stared intently into O'Dwyer's face. "Rocco Caprioli will talk now. I know he will."

"Mrs. Albi, How can you know that?" said John O'Dwyer, pitying a desperate and bereaved widow.

"Paul Kelly told me. Just ask Rocco Caprioli again. Please, ask again."

CHAPTER 17

JUDGMENT

As the courtroom filled on Tuesday afternoon, preparatory to the prosecution's cross-examination of Agent Lightner, John O'Dwyer strode in with a confident air. He stopped midway to his seat and signaled thumbs-up to Francine, Filipo Albi, and Trevor. Then, to the entertainment of the jury, he jigged to his seat at the prosecution table, arms at his side, Irish style. His little dance implied that some favorable development was afoot, and Percival, noticing it, whispered to his counselor. Seated behind them, Agent Lightner looked puzzled and concerned. All rose as Judge McCarthy entered the chamber. As soon as the judge took his seat, O'Dwyer petitioned to approach the bench. Angus Murdock went up as well. O'Dwyer whispered something to the judge, who replied, and then turned to Murdock, whose expression revealed panic.

Back at his seat, O'Dwyer moved to waive cross-examination of Agent Lightner, and instead reopen the prosecution's case because a new witness had become available. The prosecution called Rocco J. Caprioli who, accompanied by a policeman, swaggered into the courtroom and plopped into the seat on the witness stand. His balding head lolled lazily back in ostentatious self-confidence. He stretched out his legs to take full advantage of all the space the witness box afforded, tugged at his shaggy moustache, and, having been sworn, glanced lazily around the courtroom as if enjoying mountain scenery. Percival glared at him, and Caprioli returned the hostile stare.

"Now, Mr. Caprioli, you were Captain Percival's chauffeur, were you not?"

"Yeah, for eleven months he hired out my limo."

"Please tell the court what you saw on Pier 54 on the day Joseph Albi died there."

"Percival and I went up to the loft of the *Alneria.* Albi was alone up there around eleven o'clock at night. Percival said he brought the two thousand dollars. Albi said another buyer was offering five thousand, so his price was now ten thousand. The Captain said, 'You drive a hard bargain, but I brought more money just in case.' Then he handed the money to Albi, who counted it. 'Now the documents,' Percival said, and Albi retrieved a clasp envelope that he had concealed under a tarpaulin. Percival looked inside, checking all the writing. It took about two minutes. Then he handed me the envelope and pulled his gun. He said, 'Give back the money.' Albi did, and said, 'Don't get sore. If money's so important, take the documents for nothing. I'm deaf and dumb. Ask Paul Kelly.' Percival said, 'I did ask him, now turn around.' When Albi turned, Percival slugged him with a bat and knocked him out cold. Percival and I moved the safety stanchions back from the hatch. They were heavy, but we moved them enough to squeeze past. Then Percival dragged Albi to the edge and kicked his body into the hold. We heard it hit with a thud below. We pushed the stanchions back. Then we left with the money and documents."

"Did anyone see you enter or leave?"

"Only the watchman."

"Do you see the man who murdered Joseph Albi in the courtroom?" asked O'Dwyer. Caprioli pointed to Percival.

Percival could contain himself no longer. "You filthy, lying wog, *you* slugged him, *you* dragged him to the edge, and *you* kicked him into the hold." The judge cautioned the defendant against another outbreak, and the bailiff grabbed his collar to settle him back in his hard wooden armchair.

"Now, let's discuss the hijacking of Elmer Boganza's taxi. Please tell the court how that worked."

"Percival told me he was faking a hijacking, and the cab driver was in on it. He pulled a gun, and the driver ran away. I drove the taxi to a deserted spot on the west side, and Percival beat up the passenger. I was surprised because he didn't say nothing about beating anyone when he hired my car."

"Do you see the taxi driver in the courtroom? If so, please point him out."

"It's that fat load over there," said Caprioli, pointing.

"And do you see the passenger whom Captain Percival beat?" asked O'Dwyer. After a brief pause, Caprioli pointed at Trevor Howells.

"He beat up that guy. Then he got some papers off him and threatened to shoot him, but a Chevrolet rolled up and three crazy guys started shooting at us. I got out of there as fast as I could, and the passenger crawled out of our taxi."

"You lying bastard," screamed Percival, jumping to his feet. Two bailiffs seized him and roughly returned him to his seat. Caprioli continued. "The next time I seen him was couple weeks later near the Chelsea Hotel around nine o'clock. I waited in the car. Percival gave him some money, and the next thing I knew, the federal cops landed on us."

"Did you have a revolver?"

"Yes, Percival handed me a gun and asked me to carry it in case the Irish came back." As the bailiff's hand weighed on his shoulder, Guy Percival made no attempt to get to his feet, but rage was now visible on what had once been his composed face.

"No further questions. Your witness, Mr. Murdock."

Murdock arose from his seat and slowly approached the witness stand, his face ashen. He asked Caprioli if he had been offered a reduced sentence in return for testifying against his former employer. Caprioli acknowledged that he had.

"Would you lie to save your own life, Mr. Caprioli?"

"Sure," replied Caprioli. His candor amused the jury. Murdock asked Caprioli about his prison record.

"I did three years for burglary."

"What penalty might you receive if, as a convicted felon, you carried a concealed firearm?" Caprioli did not know. "Then let me tell you. You might receive five years' imprisonment."

"Oh, my goodness!" Eyes wide, mouth agape, Caprioli mugged surprise, entertaining the jury again.

Undaunted, Murdock pressed on. "Didn't Brian Davies offer you exemption from prosecution in return for testimony against Captain Percival? And didn't you accept that offer out of fear of five years in prison?"

"Yeah, and I took his offer. That don't mean what I'm saying ain't the truth. I had no idea that my limo customer was planning a murder. I didn't know the hijacking was for real."

"That's what you say now, but only to save your wretched neck." It was a desperate parry, but Murdock could not undo the damage of Caprioli's testimony. Murdock requested and received a two-week continuance in view of the unexpected testimony. Court was adjourned, and policemen escorted Percival and Caprioli back to jail. Passing Percival, Caprioli spit in his face, called him "a goddamned fairy," and tried to butt him with his head, but the bailiff restrained him. Percival had recovered his stiff upper lip. He stood erect, silent, and ignored the taunt.

Listening in the gallery, Francine, Filipo Albi, and Trevor were in shock at the courtroom drama they had witnessed. Court in recess, they joyfully swarmed around O'Dwyer, who explained that after Francine's assurance Friday, he had alerted Brian Davies, who had immediately approached Caprioli's attorney, Vincent Carranzano. In exchange for Caprioli's testimony against Percival, Davies again offered to drop all charges against Caprioli, except possession of a firearm, and to request a suspended sentence on the firearms charge. Carranzano agreed to discuss it with his client, and an hour later he called Davies to accept the plea bargain.

O'Dwyer turned to Francine in amazement. "You were right. Caprioli was ready to deal. What happened?"

"We reached Kelly."

"You met Paul Kelly?" asked O'Dwyer, who had never met the celebrated racketeer.

"Yes, we went through Slate on the news island. I knew that Slate talked to Kelly, and that Slate and Joe had been friends."

"Francine, why didn't you mention Slate earlier?" Trevor interjected with some heat. "I might have exploited this lead."

"I have to agree, Mrs. Albi," O'Dwyer volunteered, also somewhat indignant. "You endangered the prosecution. With this information my prosecution could have proceeded more directly, saving us all a lot of anguish."

Moving to the front, Filipo Albi began to speak in Francine's defense, but she signaled him to silence with a slight rotation of her open right hand from the wrist, and, taking charge of the quarrel, cast oil on troubled waters. "Slate was Joe's friend. That mattered. But he don't know you. Also, Filipo and I were desperate or we wouldn't have risked it."

"Risked what?" Trevor asked in innocent incomprehension.

"Risked Paul Kelly. From Paul's point of view, Joe got the punishment he deserved," interjected Filipo. "But we helped the cops prosecute Paul's friend Caprioli. That irritated Paul. Didn't you notice that none of your witnesses could identify Caprioli in the lineup? They could only identify Percival."

Francine picked up Filipo's narrative. "By siding with the cops, we defied Paul. When I heard that Percival would get off, I had to risk Paul's anger. At first, Slate would not help. I reminded him that he and Joe was friends, and I begged him to help Joe's kids. Finally, he agreed to approach Paul on my behalf. Slate reminded him that Joe had worked with Paul's family for many years, and he persuaded Paul that Joe's widow and children deserved a clemency hearing. Kelly agreed to see us on Saturday evening."

"Good heavens, what happened there?" O'Dwyer asked, incredulous at Francine's exposure of the hidden underpinnings of waterfront racketeering.

"We met Paul in the Club Room on Seventh Avenue. That's his

nightclub. They took us into the back office. Paul was dressed to the hilt like always. He said right away that Joe got what he deserved. He asked whether I agreed. I said yes. I had to accept it. Then I kissed Paul's hand and went down on my knees and begged for mercy for Joe's kids. Paul listened, then explained that he had a serious business relationship with the English. That relationship would suffer if Caprioli testified against Percival. Paul was sorry, but Caprioli had to do time for the welfare of the family. I begged again with tears in my eyes. Joe paid for his mistake in full. Why punish his children?

"Paul hesitated, whispered to Slate, called in some new advisors, and they whispered some more together. Finally, Paul turned back to us. He announced that his friends agreed that Joe had been punished enough. In view of Joe's years of loyal service, his kids and wife deserved clemency, so Paul would let Caprioli rat out the Englishman." Her somber mood suddenly lifting, Francine laughed wickedly. "You just had to ask him the right way, and I did!"

"Caprioli needed permission to testify against Percival?" The prospect astonished O'Dwyer.

"Soldiers take falls. Hell, the Englishman is taking one too," said Filipo, who turned tenderly toward Francine, then continued, "That nightclub was full of guys who loved Joe. They spoke up. Francine didn't understand how many friends Joe had. Now she knows how much he was respected." Trevor and O'Dwyer looked at each other in amazement. Francine daubed her eyes.

"My hat's off to you, Francine, and to you too, Filipo," said O'Dwyer, ceremonially tipping his straw boater. "I would never have thought of this."

"You don't understand *omertà,*" Filipo declared, "That's the Sicilian law of silence."

"*Omertà,* is it? Lieutenant Petrosino used that word back in '09, but I never considered that some Sicilian custom would be carried into Manhattan in the twentieth century—and by an Irishman."

"You fell for it," snickered Filipo. "Kelly's Sicilian, not Irish."

"A Sicilian named Kelly? Sure there were no Sicilians named Kelly in Ireland when I left. Times have changed more than I realized."

"His real name is Paolo Vaccarelli, but he calls himself Paul Kelly so that Irish coppers will like him better."

"Well, I'll be doggoned," gasped O'Dwyer, looking at Trevor for validation of his astonishment. "Did you know that?" Trevor acknowledged with a grimace of chagrin that he had not known that Paul Kelly was an assumed name.

"It's embarrassing," said Trevor. "I should have known."

At this point, Filipo and Francine had a brief conversation in Italian. Filipo asked her a question, Francine answered, "*sì,*" and Filipo switched back to English. "We didn't want to ask for clemency unless it was absolutely necessary," he said. "Paul was angry at us."

"But when our case looked lost you decided to approach him anyway. Is that right?" O'Dwyer asked, evidently enjoying the insight the conversation gave him into a foreign civilization.

"Yeah, that's it," conceded Filipo, with a shrug.

"Well, you saved the day, Filipo."

"I made the decision, and I did the talking, but we went to Paul together," corrected Francine with some hint of pride.

Two weeks later, court reconvened. The night watchman, Michael O'Connell, testified that Captain Percival and his driver entered Pier 54 around ten o'clock on the night of Joseph Albi's death. As the Captain was a Cunard official, he had authorization to come and go on the pier whenever he pleased. His arrivals and departures were not logged. The police took the log, but no one inquired about unlogged entries. Hearing that, Murdock changed Percival's plea from not guilty to not guilty by reason of insanity, and requested another two-week continuance in which to arrange a defense on these grounds.

On February 22 the court reconvened. In his opening statement, Angus Murdock requested leniency on the grounds that the defendant had been overcome by passionate concern for the welfare of his beleaguered country. He had suffered temporary insanity during which he could no longer distinguish right from wrong. Percival sat through this plea without comment. Testifying for the defense, Dr. John Thornton, an alienist affiliated with Presbyterian Hospital, declared that he had found the defendant calm, in possession of his faculties, but "unaware of the legitimate boundary of violence in civilian life."

"Do you mean, Doctor, that Captain Percival was unable to tell right from wrong at the time he murdered Joseph Albi?" asked Murdock.

"Yes. Captain Percival thought any action morally justified that accrued to the military advantage of Great Britain."

"Isn't that what any British soldier would think, Dr. Thornton?"

"No, sir. Operating in a war zone, soldiers kill enemies in uniform, but spare civilians. Captain Percival expresses no remorse for murdering Joseph Albi, and even remarked that he would do it again. This choice would be impermissible even in Belgium. But New York State is not a war zone, Joseph Albi was a civilian, and Captain Percival is no longer on active duty."

"What conclusion do you draw, Doctor? Does Guy Charles Percival qualify as criminally insane?"

"That's a legal determination, Mr. Murdock, but understanding the M'Naghton rule, I would say yes, Captain Percival qualifies as criminally insane. He did not know he was doing wrong at the time that he murdered Joseph Albi."

Rising for the cross-examination, O'Dwyer dismissed Dr. Thornton, but called Guy Charles Percival back to the witness stand.

"Captain Percival, let me put this hypothetical before you. Suppose a British soldier could murder a foreign civilian, living in a foreign country, and thereby obtain British victory in the current war in France. Would it be right or wrong to do so?"

"Of course it would be right. Ending the war would save millions of lives. It would also be right because the fate of civilization depends upon British victory. This war is barbarism versus civilization, and civilization must triumph."

"So it was right to murder Joseph Albi to prevent him from raising damaging questions about Britain's cause?"

"War is about duty, not rights." Percival was not past caring what happened to him.

"Well, would it have been wrong not to kill Joseph Albi?"

"It would have been dereliction of a soldier's duty."

"Doing one's duty is right, and not-doing one's duty is wrong?"

"When civilization's fate is at stake, yes, that seems correct. Wouldn't you agree, Mr. O'Dwyer?"

"My opinions are immaterial, Captain. Now, please tell the court whether your judgment is unique. That is, regarding other officers now serving in the British forces, how many would answer these questions as you did?" A few, many, most, or all?"

"I hope that all would answer yes. I am confident that nearly all would do so. There are always some softies."

"Captain Percival, you think it right to approve this hypothetical murder, and wrong to disapprove, and you think most British officers would agree, and that those who do not agree ought to. Are these not moral judgments?"

"No, they are based on duty, not morality."

"That is a quibble, Captain. You applied and still apply right here for all to see a shared moral standard based on duty." Sensing the direction of this cross-examination, Percival declared this inference speculative, but O'Dwyer ignored his reply. "Can it be said that you do not understand the difference between right and wrong? Or is it not rather the case that you understand that difference very well, but you apply a moral standard that is in conflict with the laws of the State of New York?"

"You're the attorney."

"Very well, how does this sound? You do not qualify as insane under the M'Naghton rule because you distinguish right and wrong now, and could do so at the time that you murdered Joseph Albi. However, your concept of right conduct transgresses the law of New York State. Therefore, Captain, haven't you earned the penalty that the laws of the state of New York prescribe for first-degree murder?"

Murdock objected that the prosecution was leading the witness, and the judge supported his objection. O'Dwyer thereupon discontinued cross-examination. Both sides offered summations and the jury went into deliberation. After two hours, the jury rejected the insanity defense and found Guy Percival guilty of all charges, including the premeditated murder of Joseph Albi.

Twenty days later, at the sentencing hearing, which Francine, Filipo Albi, and Trevor attended, prison guards brought Percival into the courtroom. Asked to rise, he faced Judge McCarthy, who declared, "Guy Charles Percival, you have been found guilty of premeditated murder, kidnapping with bodily harm, grand theft, and illegal possession of a firearm, and amply merit the death penalty, which the state of New York prescribes for these crimes. May God have mercy on your soul."

Now wearing a prison-issue striped uniform instead of his elegant tweeds, Percival heard the judge sentence him to die in the electric chair at Sing Sing Prison on July 29, 1916. The prisoner had nothing to say and was returned to his cell.

Agent Lightner was present in the courtroom for the sentencing. Looking composed but glum, he acknowledged Trevor with a nod, but left without comment. His preparations had worked. Neither American nor foreign newspapers reported the case, the verdict, or the sentence. The public learned nothing of what had transpired inside the courtroom or outside.

The night of the sentencing hearing, Francine and her brother, Albert Castagno, and Filipo Albi joined Lotte and Trevor for an impromptu *celebrazione* in Lotte's Brooklyn apartment. There were not seats enough, so Filipo and Albert sat tailor-style on the floor underneath the window out of which they had earlier threatened to throw Trevor. O'Dwyer was invited, but excused himself because it was St. Patrick's Day and he had many speaking obligations. It was as well since there was not seating for another person. It was an international dinner. Francine brought ravioli and cannoli. She also baked small pies that they called pizzas. Lotte provided Braunschweiger, rye bread, dill pickles, and white wine. Albert brought a quart of gin. Filipo had stolen twenty pounds of Cunard's finest French Brie. The cheese, sausage, and pizza pies provided bountiful hors d'oeuvres amid endless jokes and congratulations.

They all had reason for gaiety, but none more than Francine. With Guy Percival convicted of her husband's murder, the coroners would change their suicide verdict, and Francine would receive the full insurance benefit from Metropolitan Life. Joe's body would be exhumed from the unconsecrated section of the cemetery and reburied in sanctified ground. "Now he can rest in peace," said Francine, feeling herself at peace for the first time in months. Trevor did not tell her that his employer was furious about his role in changing the coroner's verdict. It might have spoiled the party.

Francine thanked Trevor again and again. Now she could quit the hat factory and take proper care of her children. "If not for you, I would never of seen a dime; my kids would of been neglected, and they would of gone wrong. You saved us. I love, love this guy. You took a beating for us. You might have been killed. We might of killed you ourselves. And you didn't ask for money. You're an angel, an angel from Heaven." Bending over him, Francine grabbed Trevor's burning ears and fiercely kissed both his cheeks. Grateful for such spirited and sincere recognition, Trevor was uncomfortably aware of the graceful curve of her neck and the petticoat that peeked out under her frock, and so was Lotte. Then, a thought striking her, Francine released Trevor and sat bolt upright. "Poor Joe, he wanted a better future for us. He wanted it so much that he risked his own life. The poor sap. I wish..."

"What do you wish, Francine?" Lotte asked gently.

"I wish I'd ragged him less about money. I made him feel like he failed his family, so he stole. He bought the life insurance to protect us." Francine brushed away tears. "Oh, why didn't I understand that instead of criticizing him for not earning more? I didn't appreciate a good man, and now he's gone." She sobbed into her hands. Francine's tearful remorse depressed everyone, but it soon became apparent that this was not the occasion for regret. This was a celebration.

Sensing the change of mood, or perhaps causing it, Lotte impulsively threw her arms around Trevor, partly out of enthusiasm for the community's recognition of her man, but also as a signal to herself that, defying death and the devil, Trevor had passed a strenuous test of courage and devotion. She felt her secret reservations about his character drop away. Lotte called Trevor "a modern knight" and offered a toast, fully confident now that this was the man she wanted to marry and whose children she wanted to bear.

"To Trevor," Lotte cried, "a brave crusader for widows, orphans, and for…" She paused, and then added, "justice." Glasses clinked around the room. When the wine was exhausted, they toasted Trevor in straight gin with lemon peel. "What I meant," Lotte tipsily explained after two more drinks, "is this: Although Trevor works for the skinflint, he's a genuine human being. A *Mensch,* we call it. And he's the only one in that whole company."

Trevor arose from his seat, gratefully acknowledging her accolade and the general applause. "Insurance fellows don't assume risks without thinking hard. Francine's story tugged at my heart, but to be honest, I volunteered for a pillow fight and then was drafted into the European war. Luckily, Percival didn't shoot me. Luckily, Filipo and Albert did not throw me out this window. Luckily, New York City police arrested Percival, and luckily, John O'Dwyer was the prosecutor. Luckily, Francine asked Paul Kelly for clemency, and luckily, he granted it. Well, that was not luck. That was Francine's shrewdness and courage. Thank you, Francine! My efforts would not have mattered without your insight and determination." They applauded Francine, who smiled in appreciation, and Trevor continued, "That's so many contingencies in a row that it's a miracle we succeeded—but we did! In the end, by God, we got the money for Francine and justice for her husband." He raised his glass, bowing to Lotte. "And without Lotte, I might have, no, I *would have* given up along the way. Add yet another lucky contingency. Luckily, Lotte made me take risks for justice. Well, that wasn't luck either. That was the spunky gal I love." And he knew it was the truth.

As evening wore into night, the toasts followed one another and the celebrants got pleasantly intoxicated, but decisions needed to be made. Possibly the only one who was still sober, Francine offered Trevor the original $2,000 that she had promised him that first day in his office. "It was no pillow fight. You earned it."

Trevor pointed out that the Bureau of Investigation would pay him $1,000 for offering to trap Houchins, and the court would turn over to him the $2,000 that Percival had paid for his wastepaper. That made $3,000, almost two years' salary. Francine could keep all of the $20,000 insurance benefit. Trevor would take none.

Renouncing Francine's money gave Trevor another opportunity modestly to disclaim the heroism that the others ascribed to him. He had taken Francine's case in hope of an easy fee, not "just because" he wanted to assist a widow and her children. "I have to eat too," he said, and the company's laughter acknowledged the point's validity. Their acknowledgment was not wasted on Lotte. Then, the hour being late, and having exhausted the gin, they disbanded. Francine, Frankie, Filipo, and Albert returned to Manhattan; and Lotte and Trevor retired to bed.

Three weeks later, the coroner's office notified Metropolitan Life that it had changed its verdict *in re Joseph Albi* from suicide to homicide. Metropolitan Life would have to pay Albi's beneficiary the full death benefit. Furious and suspicious, Winthrop J. Tolson summoned Trevor Howells to his office.

"Howells, I thought you got rid of this Albi woman."

"I did, but the police later arrested a foreigner. He was convicted of murdering the lady's husband, then faking a suicide to cover his tracks."

"They say that you assisted the police in this inquiry, and that you attended the trial. I hope none of that is true."

"Are these more rumors?" Trevor was stalling to see how much Tolson knew. This was the audit he had dreaded.

"You accompanied two policemen to the office some months ago, and handed them documents that Miss Schlegel withdrew from our safe. Is this correct?" Trevor acknowledged the fact. "And these documents enabled the police to make an arrest and convict the murderer of this Joseph Albi?"

"No, the documents were of no help to the police."

"The claimant paid you for assistance."

"No, I received no money from her."

"Nonetheless, you voluntarily assisted this claimant to make good her legal case against the interest of the company? You attended the trial, slighting your duties here, and gave testimony that convicted the defendant?"

"No, sir, my testimony did not convict the defendant."

"Damn it, sir, don't equivocate. Didn't you assist the claimant and attend the trial of the murderer testifying for the prosecution?" The cat was out of the bag, and Trevor decided to acknowledge it.

"Yes, I did that."

Tolson did not wait to hear more. "You're to be congratulated for assisting the authorities to convict a murderer. That was your civic duty." Trevor brightened. Here was unexpected praise.

"Thank you, sir. I thought so too."

"Unfortunately, that was someone else's job. You work for the Metropolitan Life Insurance Company, which has now to pay a huge death benefit. Metropolitan Life employs investigators to deflect claims, not to settle them to the company's disadvantage."

"I realize that, sir."

"You realize? Then did your incompetence arise from a bad memory or from sniveling sentimentality? Either way, you cost the company a great deal of money. I am canceling the two percent salary increase you received in January. Instead, Metro will cut your pay ten percent. Your pay rate will be restored in four years if your work merits it. In this way you partially compensate the company for this outrageous incompetence. That's only fair, don't you agree?"

It was one degradation too many. "Don't you think you've taken your skinflintism too far, Mr. Tolson?" Trevor replied with some heat.

Tolson took a step back, brought his nose and chin together, then recovering, permitted them to separate. "What did you just say?"

"I said don't you think you've taken your damnable skinflintism too far? It was a foul murder, and a widow was cheated of her death benefit by the contrivance of the victim's employer. Yes, I helped her to get justice. I am proud of it. I would do it again. You cannot ask your employees to check their consciences at the door."

Aghast, Winthrop J. Tolson raised his right palm in a gesture of finality, and then shook his index finger like an irritated schoolteacher. "I've had enough, Howells. Enough of your blunders, your maudlin sentimentality, your lies, your tawdry romance, and now your insolence. Metropolitan Life has no further need of your services. Clean your desk and collect your pay from Victor. Mr. Sims will escort you from the building. You will get no reference from me. Good day to you."

Lotte was delighted. She prepared a feast to honor the occasion. They would worry about money some other day. Happily, Trevor's loss of employment did not matter for long. The court returned to Trevor the $2,000 that Percival had handed him in front of the Chelsea Hotel. The case closed, the defendant could file a civil suit for restitution. It seemed unlikely as, awaiting execution in Sing Sing prison, Percival showed no interest in his money. That made a $3,000 net gain, approximately seventeen months' salary for Trevor. Additionally, Lotte's uncle, Oskar Schlegel, got Trevor a job as an investigator with an insurance company in St. Louis. Lotte looked forward to returning to her hometown and to the safety of its big German-American community. "Why assume unnecessary risks? They can't lynch me in Saint Louis."

"They can't lynch *us*," Trevor corrected.

A solemn duty kept them in New York City. Francine, Filipo, and Trevor were invited to witness the execution of Guy Charles Percival at Sing Sing Prison. Guards escorted the chained and manacled prisoner, accompanied by the Anglican chaplain, into the execution chamber at 8:45 on the morning of July 29, 1916. They strapped him into the electric chair, known as "old sparky," and attached the metal "thinking cap" to his skull, the back of which had been shaved to receive it. The officers also affixed a black mask that covered the prisoner's eyes and nose. At 8:55, the warden read the death warrant. At 8:59, the warden asked the prisoner for last words. "England expects every man to do his duty" was Percival's reply. At nine o'clock a hooded executioner introduced the first of three two-minute cycles of 2,000 volts of AC current into the electric chair, which buzzed and hummed. The thinking cap showered sparks that eerily resembled a halo. Percival bucked against the restraints and groaned. His mouth opened, blood spilled from his nostrils onto his shirt, his head jerked back, and then dropped onto his chest. He emptied his bowels.

Two minutes later, the executioner introduced the second jolt of 2,000 volts, which was also sustained for two minutes. The execution chamber now began to stink of feces and burning flesh. The stench nauseated Trevor. A prison guard fainted. Francine yelled, "Fry in hell, you murdering bastard." No one else spoke. The third and final jolt of 2,000 volts came two minutes later. At 9:12 a.m., a doctor pronounced Guy Charles Percival dead, and his corpse was removed on a gurney.

During Percival's trial and imprisonment, the government of the United Kingdom had shown no interest in him. Nothing had been done to assist or comfort him. He received no mail, visitors, or gifts, not even a toothbrush, but Percival had never asked the British consulate for any support or supplies, and he received with equanimity the news that the consulate denied all knowledge of his activities and any responsibility for his crime. He mailed no letters. News of his impending execution never reached Britain. As a result, any friends there knew nothing of his plight, and did not write or visit him during his months on death row. As news of his crime never reached the press either, the public learned nothing. Yet, Captain Guy Percival never complained of his trial, his treatment, or his sentence.

The execution completed, however, the government of the United Kingdom claimed the body of Guy Charles Percival, and shipped it to London in a coffin draped with the Union Jack. Percival was buried with military honors from St. Paul's Chapel in London. Six mourners attended his funeral. Two were members of Lloyd George's war cabinet, two were colonels in the artillery, one a general in the artillery, and one was Percival's older brother, Alfred. The London *Times* gave the burial a half-inch on the sixteenth page; *The New York Times* did the same. No other newspapers reported it. Amid the horrifying casualty reports from the Western Front, one man's death was unimportant.

Trevor, Filipo, and Francine returned from Ossining to New York by train. On the way, Francine told Trevor that she was "seeing" a widower. He owned a bakery on West Fourth Street, and had two adolescent children. He had proposed marriage, and she was considering it. Francine gave Trevor's hand a warm grasp as they parted.

Back in Brooklyn, Trevor took a long walk with Lotte through the Botanical Garden. They walked together in the early evening, and held hands, smelling the flowering lilacs, magnolias, and orchids of spring. Lotte wanted Trevor to unburden himself of the grisly experience, but he was reluctant to talk. At length, in response to her encouragement, he described the execution, not sparing the gruesome details. Lotte said reassuringly, "Percival murdered Albi, and he would have murdered you."

"And he paid with his life," said Trevor, grimly carrying her observation forward. "But, Captain Percival won the political game. If not for him, Houchins would have passed Albi's memoirs to the Germans, and the world's newspapers would have carried the story. Thanks to Percival, the world never learned about guncotton disguised as cheese aboard the *Lusitania*."

"But thanks to Percival I also learned something," returned Lotte, hoping to lighten his mood. "I learned that my fiancé's not a knight errant but 'a swindler and a scoundrel.'"

Her wry jest did not change Trevor's mood. Turning to Lotte, he ventured his own bitter inquiry. "Wasn't Guy Percival also a knight errant?" Lotte sighed agreement, then acknowledged that Sir Percival had been one of King Arthur's favorite knights. Knighthood had proved more complicated than she once understood.

"But Guy Percival was a wicked knight. They always wore black," Lotte continued, then added ruefully, "but if knights come in two flavors, good and evil, what's the point of knighthood?"

Hopeful that Lotte might finally divest the maddening knight fantasy that had almost cost his life, Trevor deemed a charitable silence the best response, but after a good-natured delay, he followed up with a second, equally wry observation. "Your wicked knight might have taken his money and returned to London a winner. Going after revenge, he took one wicked risk too many."

"Yes, he took an unnecessary risk, and that was a fatal mistake," Lotte replied defensively. "But he had courage, even if he was a murderer."

"And you admire courage, even in a wicked knight, don't you?"

After a thoughtful pause, Lotte disagreed. "I did, yes. No more. Now I acknowledge it, but I don't admire it."

"By George, we finally agree about that knighthood rubbish." Rubbish was not a friendly word, but Trevor's choice expressed the relief he felt from Lotte's nuanced enthusiasm for raw courage. It would make his life easier, and he hoped the change would be permanent. Lotte, however, posed a question of her own. Putting her hand on his shoulder and looking into his eyes she asked, "Trevor, if you were cautious all the time, then you wouldn't have helped Francine. You'd still work for the skinflint emperor, and Francine would not have gotten her insurance benefit. Aren't you glad you weren't that cautious?" Having made a thoughtful concession of her own, Lotte wanted one from Trevor.

Trevor reflected, and then, to Lotte's surprise, agreed. "Yes, I see your point. Isn't that what you always hated about the emperor—supremely cautious but indifferent to justice?"

"Yes, that's right." Lotte gulped, surprised that Trevor had summarized her view so exactly, and then fully agreed with it.

"Amazing. We now agree on all that stuff," said Trevor, adding gaily, "A gal as smart as you should have the vote, and they should take it away from the skinflint!" Then Trevor turned to Lotte and gazed into her eyes with an earnestness he had never before achieved. "You bring out the best in me, Lotte."

"Yes," she agreed. "We're better together than apart."

Early the next morning, July 30, 1916, as they lay sleeping in Lotte's Brooklyn flat, tremendous window-rattling explosions awakened them. They rushed to the window and saw the sky alight in the east. Huge blasts continued for thirty minutes. The flames burned for hours, illuminating the night sky amid the clanging of distant fire engines. Neighbors poured into the streets to watch the explosions and flames. They milled about in night clothing, exchanging rumors. The morning's newspapers reported that tons of war munitions stored on Black Tom Island had exploded in New York Harbor. Produced in American factories, these munitions were awaiting shipment by sea to Great Britain. The newspapers assured the public that the massive explosions, which even damaged the Statue of Liberty, had resulted from carelessness, not from German sabotage. There was "no cause for alarm." However, when Agent Lightner handed Trevor the $1,000 the Bureau owed him later the next day, he remarked that the Bureau of Investigation believed that German saboteurs had caused the destruction. "That Franz von Rintelen planned it. Your girlfriend's uncle is lucky that I am your friend."

Nine months later, on April 17, 1917, denouncing Germany's resumption of unrestricted submarine warfare and her "spies and criminal intrigues," President Woodrow Wilson asked Congress to declare war on Germany.

EPILOGUE

THE HISTORICAL CONTROVERSY over the *Lusitania* long centered on the second explosion aboard the ship. This explosion sank the giant liner in eighteen minutes, whereas RMS *Titanic,* a ship of approximately the same size, had taken two and a half hours to sink. A German torpedo caused the first blast, but what caused the second, which occurred about one minute later? The British Admiralty maintained that a German submarine, the U-20, fired a second torpedo. The submarine's log, however, recorded that the U-20 fired only one torpedo. On the basis of this evidence, the German government claimed that the second explosion was caused by guncotton illegally and secretly stowed in the ship's cargo holds. Guncotton was the principal explosive in British artillery shells, and the British imported most of theirs from the United States. The day the *Lusitania* was sunk, the British Army's supply of guncotton was critically low. A week after the *Lusitania* went to the bottom, the London *Times* blamed the failure of the British Army's offensive on Aubers Ridge on a shortage of artillery shells. This damning accusation compelled Herbert Asquith to organize a new government.

The sinking of the *Lusitania* cost the lives of 1,195 crew and passengers, of whom 128 were Americans. Almost all the victims were civilians, and many were children. The Entente declared the Imperial German Navy's attack on a civilian transport ship a heinous crime under international law. They were unquestionably right about that—it was a heinous crime, but whose heinous crime was it? In the British view, which President Wilson accepted, the Germans bore exclusive responsibility because they attacked the ship without warning. Thanks partially to

British domination of the American newspapers, the Entente's view met no effective challenge in the United States. If, however, the second explosion resulted from ignition of the ship's secret cargo of munitions, then the vessel had been a legitimate military target for the submarine. What is more, as Wilson's secretary of state, William J. Bryan, pointed out, the British would have knowingly permitted civilian passengers to sail into a war zone aboard a military target, rendering them in effect hostages. In that case, the British would bear co-responsibility for the heinous crime along with the Germans.

Victory or defeat for the Entente, and war or peace for the United States, hung on the successful assignment of responsibility for the crime. If the Germans were entirely responsible, then the sinking of the *Lusitania* could be added to their other war crimes, which included the violation of Belgian neutrality, abuse of French and Belgian civilians, naval bombardment of English coastal towns, execution of nurse Edith Clavell, the razing of Louvain, unrestricted submarine warfare, the introduction of poison gas on the battlefield, raping nuns and nurses, and bayoneting and roasting babies. The Great War could then be summarized as "civilization vs. barbarism." Confronting that summary, the American public could readily justify joining the Entente powers in a just war.

If, however, the British had permitted civilian passengers to enter a war zone aboard a target vessel, daring the Germans to attack it, then the choice facing the American public was more complex. Even if all the other war crimes alleged against the Germans were true, the crown jewel of German war crimes, the martyred *Lusitania,* would have become a British/German co-crime. The American public might then conclude that the *Lusitania* displayed the depravity to which desperate war makers on both sides had finally stooped, a pacifist and antiwar message very close to what Secretary of State Bryan had delivered. If the Great War amounted to one gang of war criminals fighting another, then why would Americans want to join the fray?

The point here is not that changes in American opinion about the *Lusitania* would have prevented the United States from entering the Great

War. The point is that the American public's attribution of all responsibility for the *Lusitania* crime upon Germany rendered it *more likely* that the U.S. would enter the war rather than remain neutral. Understanding this, the belligerent powers had reason to contest the information about the *Lusitania* that the American public actually received, and a larcenous stevedore's testimony might have moved the *Lusitania* issue from the pro-war side of the ledger to the neutrality side.

When it came to explaining the sinking, it seemed to the American public in 1915–1917 as if the only choices were either a second torpedo or secret explosives aboard the ship. Had it been entirely certain that there was no second torpedo, as is known now, the German version of the sinking would have appeared correct, and the political implication would have been continued neutrality. In effect, the "second torpedo" propaganda line prevented the American public from reaching that conclusion. We know that the second torpedo was a fabrication; however, we also understand now that the *Lusitania* stored her coal along the ship's length and under her waterline. It is possible that the second and fatal explosion was coal dust ignited by the single German torpedo, not concealed munitions. In that case, we have the option of supposing it possible that coal dust sank the ship rather than hidden explosives, but Americans chose between war and peace in 1917 on the basis of information to which they then had access. Strictly speaking, on the basis of what was then known, the *Lusitania* crime should have moved the American public toward continued neutrality rather than toward war, yet the *Lusitania* always appears in history books as a big reason that Americans chose war.

Even authorities who dispute the existence of secret explosives aboard the vessel, as some do, acknowledge that, in the aftermath of the sinking, official cover-ups took place on both sides of the Atlantic. British and American authorities behaved as if they feared that unwelcome facts about the *Lusitania* might come before the public without a cover-up. Their guilty conduct does not prove that her cargo blew up the *Lusitania,* but it does suggest that the authorities wanted to avoid any imputation that it had done so lest that imputation damage the moral advantage of the Entente's cause. It also suggests that British and American authorities had no persuasive alternative to offer the public if the second torpedo explanation was rejected.

The issue today is no longer whether secret explosives sank the ship, but what kind of explosive and how much of it the *Lusitania* carried. We now know that the civilian ocean liner was carrying more war materiel than was acknowledged at the time. It was already known in 1915 that the *Lusitania* carried 4 million rifle cartridges in her cargo hold. These had been manufactured to British Army specifications. Additionally, it was already known that the *Lusitania* carried anti-personnel artillery fuses and artillery shells, fully packed with projectiles, but said to lack explosive charges.

What was not available in 1915–17 was the supplementary ship's manifest that was radioed ashore from the *Lusitania* at sea. President Wilson had the only copy of this manifest, and he never made it public. Instead, he deposited it in a sealed envelope on which he had written, "To be opened only by the President of the United States." Decades later, Wilson's copy turned up in the Franklin D. Roosevelt Library. Roosevelt had been assistant secretary of the navy when the *Lusitania* was torpedoed. A recent lawsuit under the Freedom of Information Act finally enabled researchers to obtain access to this document, whose contents, concealed for a century, anyone may now view at *www.lusitania.net* or *www.rmslusitania.info/controversies/contraband*. The supplementary manifest shows that the *Lusitania* carried 4 million rifle cartridges, 1,248 cases of *live* shrapnel shells (four to a case), and eighteen cases of artillery fuses. Made in the USA, these artillery shells were *fully loaded* with explosive and ready to fire from British cannons. Additionally, there was 120 tons of unrefrigerated cheese addressed to the Royal Navy Weapons Testing Facility, Essex. Asked about these suspicious crates of cheese, the controller of the Port of New York, Dudley Malone, replied that no one could guarantee what was in any of the crates without actually opening them, and no one had done so. The world will never learn what was in those crates.

BIBLIOGRAPHY

NONFICTION

ALLEN, OLIVER E. *The Tiger: The Rise and Fall of Tammany Hall.* Reading, MA: Addison-Wesley, 1993.

ASBURY, HERBERT. *The Gangs of New York.* New York: Alfred Knopf, 1927. An account of organized crime in New York City before the Five Families.

ALLEN, KEITH. "Lusitania Controversy." www.gwpda.org/naval/lusika00.htm, 1999. Accessed 24 Feb. 2014.
Keith Allen, a U.S. Navy historian, attacks Colin Simpson and, through him, the conspiracy theories that have surrounded the *Lusitania* sinking for ninety years.

BAILEY, THOMAS A. 1935. "The Sinking of the *Lusitania.*" *The American Historical Review* 41 (1): 54–73.

BAILEY, THOMAS A. and RYAN, PAUL B. *The Lusitania Disaster: An Episode in Modern Warfare and Diplomacy.* New York: Free Press, 1975.

REX, ROBERT D. with SPENCER DUNMORE. *Exploring the Lusitania: Probing the Mysteries of the Sinking that Changed History.* New York and Toronto: Warner Books and Madison Press, 1995.

BARONE, MICHAEL. *Shaping Our Nation: How Surges of Immigration Transformed America and its Politics.* New York: Crown Forum, 2013.

BEESLY, PATRICK. *Room 40: British Naval Intelligence 1914–18.* New York: Harcourt Brace Jovanovich, 1982.
Beesly argues that Winston Churchill handed the *Lusitania* to the Germans in order to create a war crime that would bring the United States into the conflict.

BELL, DANIEL. "The Racket-Ridden Longshoremen." Pp. 175–209 in *The End of Ideology.* New York: Collier Books, 1988.

BLUM, HOWARD. *Dark Invasion: 1915: Germany's Secret War and the Hunt for the First Terrorist Cell in America.* New York: HarperCollins, 2014.

BUTLER, DAVID. *Lusitania.* New York: Random House, 1982.

CAREY, CHARLES W. *Eugene V. Debs: Outspoken Labor Leader and Socialist.* Berkeley Heights, NJ: Ensloe, 2003.

CHURCHILL, WINSTON S. *The World Crisis.* New York: Charles Scribner's Sons, 1931.
Churchill was First Lord of the Admiralty, 1911–1915. He advanced a two-torpedo explanation of why the *Lusitania* sank so rapidly. "This crowning outrage of the U-boat war resounded through the world. The United States … was convulsed with indignation, and in all parts of the great Republic the signal for armed intervention was awaited by the strongest elements of the American people." 451

COOPER, JOHN MILTON. *Woodrow Wilson: A Biography.* New York: Alfred Knopf, 2009.

CREEL, GEORGE. *How We Advertised America.* New York: Arno Press, 1972 [1920].
George Creel was in charge of the Committee on Public Information that directed the US government's theretofore unparalleled effort to control public opinion.

DEBS, EUGENE VICTOR. "The Canton Ohio Speech." Pp. 113–146 in *Writings of Eugene V. Debs.* St. Petersburg FL: Red and Black, 2009.

ENGELBRECHT, H. C. and F. C. HANIGHEN. *Merchants of Death: A Study of the International Armament Industry.* New York: Dodd, Mead & Company, 1934.

FERRARA, ERIC. 2011. *Manhattan Mafia Guide.* Charleston SC: History Press.

FERRELL, ROBERT H. *Woodrow Wilson and World War, 1917–1921.* New York: Harper & Row, 1985.

HAYWOOD, WILLIAM. "The General Strike." Pp. 61–79 in *Writings of Big Bill Haywood.* St. Petersburg, Fla.: Red and Black, 2011.
This was the IWW program.

[H]OEHLING, A. A., and MARY HOEHLING. *The Last Voyage of the Lusitania.* [Ne]w York: Henry Holt, 1956.

HOUT, MICHAEL, and JOSHUA R. GOLDSTEIN. "How 4.5 Million Irish Immigrants Became 40 Million Irish Americans." *American Sociological Review* 59: 64–82, 1994.

JENKS, JEREMIAH W., and W. JETT LAUCK. *The Immigration Problem*. 3rd ed. New York: Funk & Wagnalls, 1922.

KOBLER, JOHN. *Capone: The Life and World of Al Capone*. New York: G.P. Putnam's Sons, 1971.
Young Al Capone was a member of Paul Kelly's gang.

LAURIAT, CHARLES E. *The Lusitania's Last Voyage*. Boston: Houghton Mifflin, 1915.
A survivor tells his story of the disaster. Lauriat denies that the *Lusitania* carried explosives, and endorses a second-torpedo explanation.

LEBRUN, GEORGE P. *It's Time to Tell*. New York: William Morrow, 1962.
A history of The New York City Coroner's Office.

LIPPMANN, WALTER. *Public Opinion*. Filiquarian Publishing Co., [1921] 2007.
This classic of political science analyzes the U.S. government's control of public opinion during the First World War.

O'SULLIVAN, PATRICK. 1998, *The Lusitania: Unraveling the Mysteries*. New York: Sheridan House.
O'Sullivan concludes that exploding steam pipes sank the *Lusitania.*

PRESTON, DIANA. *Willful Murder: The Sinking of the Lusitania*. London: Doubleday, 2002.
Preston concludes that the German torpedo ignited coal dust whose explosion sank the ship, but acknowledges that there was a huge cover-up.

RAMSAY, DAVID. *Lusitania: Saga and Myth*. London: Chatham, 2001.

RENSHAW, PATRICK. *The Wobblies*. Garden City, NY: Doubleday & Company, 1967.

SIMPSON, COLIN. *Lusitania*. Boston, Mass: Little Brown, 1972.
This book still offers the best rendition of the main conspiracy theories that swirl around the *Lusitania.*

STROM, SHARON HARMAN. *Beyond the Typewriter.* Urbana, Ill: University of Illinois, 1992.
A socio-historical study of women clerical workers between 1910 and 1930.

THE LUSITANIA ONLINE: www.lusitania.net. Accessed 19 May 2014.
An American website that compiles indispensable *Lusitania* information, especially information about the ship's deadly cargo.

THE LUSITANIA RESOURCE: www.rmslusitania.info, 2013.
Accessed 20 Feb. 2014.
This British website offers much valuable and current *Lusitania* lore, links, and information.

WEINER, TIM. *Enemies: A History of the FBI.* New York: Random House, 2012.

WHITE, ANNE TERRY. *Eugene Debs.* New York: Lawrence Hill, 1974.

ZIEGER, ROBERT H. *America's Great War: World War 1 and the American Experience.* Boulder, Co.: Rowman and Littlefield, 2000.

FICTION

ALLEN, CONRAD. *Murder on the Lusitania.* New York: St. Martin's Press, 1999.
In 1907, a detective solves a drawing-room-style murder mystery on *Lusitania*'s maiden voyage.

COLLINS, MAX ALLAN. *The Lusitania Murders.* Las Vegas: Thomas & Mercer, 2002.
A female detective teams up with a reporter traveling incognito to catch jewel thieves aboard the doomed ship.

GILBERT, MICHAEL. *Into Battle.* New York: Carroll & Graf, 1997.
British Intelligence defeats German spies who planted incendiary time bombs on merchant ships in order to aggravate the cordite shortage.

ABOUT THE AUTHOR

IVAN LIGHT GREW up in New York City, received a bachelor's degree in history from Harvard College, then a doctorate in sociology from the University of California, Berkeley. He was for many years a member of the faculty at the University of California, Los Angeles, publishing books and articles on immigration, immigration history, the ethnic economy, social and cultural capital, entrepreneurship, world urbanization, and the history of organized crime. His publication record and many individual publications are viewable at his university website <www.sociology.ucla.edu/faculty/ivan-light>.

Deadly Secret of the Lusitania is his first book of fiction. The novel's website, www.deadlysecretofthelusitania.com, offers more information about the *Lusitania,* American politics of the period, and the author.

The *Lusitania*.